UNDER FIRE

Balloons and gift bags are everywhere. A few kids are running around screaming. Everyone is regaling each other with stories of childbirth and poopy diapers.

This is not the kind of party my favorite bar normally has and I'm not sure how to feel about it.

I guess I shouldn't complain. It's the middle of the day and I'm having a free beer with my friends, eating some free food, and the baby this shower is for isn't mine. Knock on wood for that one.

Still, it's a little trippy watching some of our friends *oooh* and *aaahhh* over random baby shit. Speaking of...

"Why the hell is Heath Germaine so excited over tiny socks?"

My teammate and good buddy Liam and I watch as Heath, a huge cornerback for the San Antonio Steer holds up the socks like they're part of the circle of life.

Liam chuckles. "You know how he is with other people's kids. He's just excited."

"It's weird," I counter.

"We're celebrating his best friend's baby."

"Celebrating is a stretch. I'm just here for the free food," I admit.

Liam gives me a pointed look, which doesn't scare me at all. He should know better than to expect anything other than the truth from me. "Did you at least bring a gift, or did you just go full asshole."

I hold my hand to my chest and fake offense. "I'll have you know, they're opening my gift right now."

As soon as he pulls it out of the bag, Jaxon Hart, the baby daddy, looks over to me and yells, "Thank you! We needed this!" He holds up the weird pillow shaped like a *C*.

"What is that anyway?" Liam asks as I tip my beer bottle at Jaxon in response.

"No idea. It was on the list and the first thing I saw that wasn't something to do with nipple chafing or leakage. I don't need to know anything about all that."

"Good call."

"What did you bring, anyway?"

He shrugs. "I made the food. The rest of it was up to Ellery."

"She still having regular margarita parties with the ladies?"

It's no secret Liam's significant other fell in with a group of old girlfriends who like to be together regularly. If one of them is here, they're all likely to show up and cause more of a raucous than we do. And we're pro athletes chock full of testosterone. Those women are like a girl gang, except with devoted boyfriends who pick their drunk asses up and cart them home frequently. If nothing else, it's entertaining to watch.

"I no longer have to use my GPS to find Heath's house, if that answers your question."

"Does the security guard at the neighborhood checkpoint just wave you through now, too?"

"Yep," he says and takes another swig of his beer.

I shake my head with a huff. "Why don't we do that? All

converge on Heath's mansion of a house and drink until our girls have to come get us?"

"Two reasons," Liam says without skipping a beat. "One, there is not enough booze in the world to get us as shit-faced as they get. And two, even if we could get that smashed, we're too big for them to carry us out to the car. They'd leave us lying face down on the outdoor patio and that would hurt like a bitch the next morning."

Solid points. Plus I don't have a significant other to leave me laying in a pool of my own vomit, so I guess that blows my idea out of the water.

Another round of *awwwws* come from the crowd as Annika shows off a blanket. A *blanket*. I don't understand any of this and I'm starting to get bored, so I wait until Liam is getting ready to swallow before making my next move.

"When are you and Ellery popping out one of those kid things?"

Liam begins to choke on his beer which might be the highlight of this whole thing. Or at least a close second behind the amazing barbecue.

"That is not a conversation I'm having with you." He coughs a couple more times and pounds his chest with his fist.

"Why not? I'm your bestie. We share everything."

"First, don't ever call me your bestie. That's weird. Second, *when* we start talking about kids, I'll be discussing it with Ellery before bringing it up with you."

"Ooooh! So the idea is on the table."

"For the future. Why wouldn't it be? I'm going to be with her forever. Isn't that what everyone wants when they find their one and only?"

"Nope," I say popping the *P* for emphasis. "Don't have them. Don't need them. I've got too much hockey to play and too much tail to chase."

"You do realize you'll have to retire eventually and both those things will dry up."

I could pretend he's wrong, but for the last year, Liam thought he was going to be forced into retirement because of an injury. He's not, but he's also never going to be a starter again. Hell, he may never play another professional game unless something drastic happens.

"Part of the fun of life is pretending things are perfect," I announce. "My social media is proof of that."

Liam snorts a laugh. "Okay then."

"I am a highly revered hockey player in the great city of San Antonio, Texas. I will never retire. I will never settle down. And not even your piss poor reality check will change that. I will die on this hill."

My phone rings. Glancing down, I see it's my agent calling.

"Speaking of," I wave my phone at my friend who gave up on arguing with me long ago. "This is probably about that endorsement deal he's been working on. I'm gonna buy a travel smoker with the first payment from them."

"Oh god, no, Tucker. You'll set your hair on fire."

Maybe. But I don't have time to argue my point, I have a deal to secure.

"Morty, my man. How much money are they offering?"

"I hear you've heard the news," my long-time agent Morty responds with a strange tone of surprise in his voice.

"The news about this endorsement? Of course. We've been working on it for weeks. Does my check have a lot of zeros after it?"

Liam rolls his eyes at my arrogance.

"Uh... nope. That's not why I'm calling."

"It's not?" Well now I'm curious. And suddenly there's a sinking feeling in my gut.

He sighs deeply and that sinking feeling bottoms out. "Are you alone?"

"No, I'm standing right here with Tremblay."

"Okay listen. I don't know how to tell you this so I'm just going to blurt it out."

"What's happening, Morty. You're scaring me."

"You're being traded."

My feet begin moving toward the exit before I tell them to. I need to be alone for this conversation. "Traded? What the fuck do you mean I've been traded?"

"Tampa wants you and San Antonio has to cut some financial fat. You may as well start house hunting. They're being generous and giving you two weeks to get there."

Well fuck.

I guess whatever hill I die on, it won't be here in San Antonio.

CHAPTER TWO

TUCKER

6 months later

Florida can suck it.

I've been here more than five months and I haven't found one good thing about this place yet.

The mosquitos are the size of vultures only they don't wait until you're dead to attack. The same fucking alligator likes to interrupt my afternoon commute every day and no one has figured out how to relocate him. Some dude got naked on the roof of the local Publix and peed all over the parking lot mere minutes before I got there to do my shopping. And it rains ninety-five percent of the time.

Maybe ninety-five percent is a slight exaggeration. It's not like I had any problems being here before, but those were quick trips for games and maybe a night out. Somehow living in Tampa makes it feel different. The humidity in this part of the state is unreal. I should be used to it. It's not like San Antonio is dry, but something about it raining so much keeps this place damp as hell. Even my hair frizzes and no one has ever mistaken me for having so much as a wave in this mop.

Okay fine. Maybe Florida isn't that bad. I just miss the easy camaraderie of my pals from the Slingers. The team here isn't bad. They're at least welcoming. And I have enjoyed the regular outings my new teammates have set up.

The Florida Glaze is made up of a good group of guys. Mostly everyone is single, being that it's a pretty young team, so no one except our captain Patrick ditches our bonding time to go home to a wife or girlfriend. Unlike that fucker Liam Tremblay at the Slingers who became somewhat of a buzz kill once he got himself a steady girlfriend.

Speaking of, I should probably call him and see if he can try making a smoked turkey on his new YouTube channel. He's got some good recipes on there, but I could use a little help with my new smoker.

Slamming my car door, I make my way to the entrance of the most opulent building I've seen in this part of Tampa so far. Not that I should be surprised. Caine hotels aren't known for being shabby and there's no shortage of women who are looking to have a good time with no strings attached.

I'm greeted by a valet who holds the door open for me.

"Honeysuckle Bar and Grill?" I ask as I step inside the air-conditioned entry.

He points across the huge lobby. "All the way past check-in and take a right."

"Thanks so much."

I start to feel a little more in my element the closer I get to my destination. I could use a night out with my new buddies to take the edge off my game. We're starting to work together well on the ice, but it's taking some time to gel. That's part of why I never say no when someone suggests a night out. The more we know each other off the ice, the better we'll communicate on it. We've only got a couple weeks until preseason starts so we're almost out of time.

Entering the small venue, I take a quick look around and almost immediately find who I'm searching for. It's not hard to spot the huge guys taking up almost the entire back of the room. The poor business dudes sitting at the bar who came here looking for a hook-up appear awfully dejected knowing all the ladies are ogling the wall of men in the back instead.

What can I say— hockey players are always going to snag the attention of a pretty woman over some schmuck in a discount suit.

"Hey! You made it!" my teammate Maksim Ivanov greets, arms wide like he's going to come in for a hug. If a table full of beer and half-eaten appetizers wasn't in his way, he probably would. When it comes to food, Maks doesn't let anything get in his way. Our left defenseman has lived in the States since he was a little kid, but still claims the parts of Russian culture he thinks make the most impact. Like kissing your teammates on the mouth in celebration or interrupting every meal with a toast.

Frankly, I think he likes pushing buttons and gets a kick out of the shock value. I humor him because... well mostly for the same reason he does it. The reaction we get when I don't act like his behaviors are weird cracks me up.

"Of course, I made it." We clasp hands for a second because that's as close as we're going to get to each other with all these people around us. "You think I would miss a night out? This is a... decent place to start."

My guess is it has amazing bar food which is why he's having us start here instead of in some roped off VIP area in a dark night club.

"Of course, it is! Nothing but the best for us!" Maks turns and gives flirty eyes to a blonde on his left. She's draped on him like a second skin and he loves it. "Nothing but the best for all of us," he practically purrs.

I can see they're about to take the eye-fucking to the next level and take that as my cue to get out of dodge.

"What are you drinking, Ivanov? Looks like you need a refill."

Only the thought of free booze can pull Maks away from the

possibility of immediate sex, even if it's just a temporary distraction.

"Vodka. Beluga Gold if they have it."

I shake my head. Of course, he'd choose the most expensive brand when I'm picking up the tab.

I push through the crowd and head toward the bar and lift my hand to catch the attention of the bartender at the far end of the bar. It takes a second for her to notice me, which gives me just enough time to take her in. She's... wow.

Not a lot of women are as tall as their male counterparts, which may be why she stands out so much. I like tall women. With my six-foot four frame, I usually tower over everyone to the point where I feel like I'm a giant. But with her, I can already tell how well we'd fit together.

It's not just that, though. It's the confidence she has as she moves behind the bar. Almost like a dancer, with the graceful way she carries herself. I can almost imagine what it would be like to slide up behind her and move to some sultry music.

Wait.

Have I met her before? The beginning of a memory starts to form in the back of my brain, but I can't quite grasp it before. She looks my direction, a smile on her face. A smile that just about knocks me off feet.

A smile that immediately falls and morphs to a look that can only be described as a sneer.

That was weird.

I glance around, wondering if she is actually looking at someone behind me, but no. It's me that's causing her sourpuss reaction.

I settle in and wait for her to move to my end of the bar and take my order.

And wait.

And wait.

It's obvious I am being ignored so I lean forward, my elbows on the bar and I flag her down again. She huffs, clearly irritated by me but I have no idea what I've done. I just got here. Maybe she's annoyed with Maks and saw me talking to him. Wouldn't be the first time. The man doesn't always make a good first impression, although he does grow on you over time. Like a fungus.

She finally approaches, her dark hair pulled back in a sporty ponytail, her black and white uniform crisp and clean. Despite the less than welcoming look on her face, she is beautiful and someone I would remember if we had met. Still, there's something about her that feels familiar.

The thought that we've met before has me pausing. Surely, I'm mistaken. The look on her face isn't at all the friendly expression I would expect from someone I know unless I'm on the ice. Hell, it's not what I would expect from someone working in the service industry who relies on tips.

"What do you want?"

I'm taken aback by her aggressive tone, but I play it off. Maybe she's having a frustrating night or I look familiar too and remind her of someone she hates.

"Um... do you have Beluga Gold?"

One of her eyebrows rise. "Big spender, aren't you?"

"It's for my buddy over there. I just want a beer. What do you have on tap?"

She rolls her eyes. "Beer." Before I can ask for a list, she walks away. I watch as she pulls the tap, filling the cold glass with an amber liquid. I hope that's for me, it's what I would have chosen if given the opportunity.

Leaning against the bar while I wait, I turn around to see Maks's tongue practically down the throat of the woman he was making googly eyes with just moments ago. I chuckle to myself. I should have known it wouldn't take him long. If her wandering hands are any indication, I may end up shooting this vodka by myself when they take off and get a room.

I hear the slam of a glass hitting the mahogany bar behind me right before the feeling of liquid covers my elbow. Sure enough, half my beer has spilled over the rim.

As the pissy bartender grabs a shot glass and begins filling it with Maks's liquid gold, I wipe myself off and pull out my wallet. She doesn't make any eye contact with me, just treats me like a pest.

I'm so confused but feel like I need to get to the bottom of this. "Um... Miss?"

She finally looks up, clearly still annoyed but at least I'm getting a response.

"Have I done something to make you mad?"

Her nostrils flare and her eyes narrow. "Really? You're seriously asking me that?"

The longer this goes on, the more my head spins. "Really." Then it hits me. I smack my face in disbelief that I didn't put it together before. "Oh boy. You've served me before. At that other place." I snap my fingers together, trying to remember the name of it. "That sports bar over on Elm. Listen, I'm so sorry if I didn't tip you enough. My friend Maks there," I gesture over my shoulder at Don Juan himself, "he dragged me out of there that night before I could add anything to the tip jar. But I'll make it up to you tonight. I promise."

If it's possible, the look of anger on her face gets even more severe. She huffs a humorless laugh before finally looking me dead in the eye. "Fuck off, Tucker."

I'm not sure which surprises me more — that she knows my name, or that she throws a twenty-dollar shot in my face before storming off.

No matter how many calming breaths I take, it's not bringing my heart rate down. Nor is it bringing my breathing under control. Nope. I'm still furious. Raging actually.

I was finally okay with the fact that I was never supposed to see Tucker Hayes again. Finally resolving myself to that fate and just rolling with it.

But no. Of all the bars in Tampa, this is the one he shows up in. Of all the places for him to party and scout out his flavor of the night, it's at this bar. Where I work. Making decent money for the first time in a while.

The worst part of it all—he's still just as hot as he ever was. My body picked up on it immediately even if my emotions stayed solidly in the fury category. That's the part I'm choosing to concentrate on, which is how he ended up smelling like vodka.

I stop my pacing and drop my head back against the wall as I realize what I've done. *Oh god, I hope I didn't just lose my job over this. He's not worth it even if he does have that fine-ass V in his pants.*

The door flies open and my boss comes barreling in. And he's pissed.

"What the fuck was that, Lacy?" He gestures toward the front and I know he didn't just hear about it; he saw it all happen. That's even worse.

"I'm sorry, Miguel. I...I know him from before and he's not a great guy. I just...snapped," I try to explain, knowing it's not going to get me anywhere.

"I don't care if he's an ex-boyfriend or a complete asshole. Hell, I don't care if he just got out of prison. You serve him with a smile and move the fuck along. Do you know who he is? That's Tucker Hayes and with him is Maksim Ivanov. And Becker Bell and Nicholas Williams and who knows how many others. Professional athletes, Lacy. High profile athletes who have the ability to get us both fired or at the very least, tell others not to come here. Imagine what would happen if they told their friends that's how our bartenders treat customers."

"I know, I know." All my bravado from earlier is gone as I realize the gravity of what I've done. Panic starts to take over. I have to fix this. "I'm so sorry. I'll go out there an apologize to him and whatever his tab is you can take it out of my paycheck."

I cringe knowing I can't afford that, but what choice to I have?

Miguel looks at me like I've lost my mind. "You think I'm letting you anywhere near the bar after that let alone speak to the man?"

My gut sinks, fearing the worst.

"Please, Miguel. How can I fix this? You know I need this job and I'm good at it. What can I do?"

He crosses his arms and looks away as he considers my plea. I hold my breath as I await his verdict.

"I won't fire you for this because you're right. You're a good employee, tonight's incident aside."

"Oh thank you, Miguel!" I hold myself back from hugging him, knowing he wouldn't appreciate that.

"Don't thank me just yet. I'm going to have to write you up for this and you are done for the night.""

My elation plummets. "But…"

"No buts. You screwed up and he's still here. Maybe we'll get lucky and he'll never come back. But for tonight, you're gone."

I sigh in disappointment but know he's right. I can't very well go out there and try to serve the people who saw me lose my shit. That's not good business.

Leaving means I'm going to have to survive on Ramen for the next week or so, but it's my own damn fault I'm in this situation.

"I understand and I really am sorry, Miguel. Thanks again for not firing me."

He nods once. "Just so we're clear, I will fire you if it happens again."

I turn toward the door but it opens before I can reach for the handle. The last person I expect to see walks through.

"Tucker?"

Miguel is obviously as puzzled as me to see the man in question standing in the doorway, but quickly schools his reaction and shifts into management mode. "Mr. Hayes. I'm so sorry for my employee's behavior. Ms. Hawkins is on her way home now and I assure you nothing like this will happen again. Whatever you and your party need the rest of the evening is on me."

Miguel gives me a pointed look and I begin moving around Tucker to leave. The sooner I'm away from him, the better.

"Actually, I came back here to apologize."

That stops me in my tracks.

"Apologize?" Miguel asks with all the same confusion I feel.

Does Tucker finally remember he knows me? Has he put two and two together? I'm not sure how to feel about this or that I can take one more thing tonight.

Tucker glances down at my name badge. "Lacy. That's your name?"

I puff out a breath and nod my head. Of course he doesn't remember my name. Doesn't matter that I've spent four years not able to forget his. Because unless it has to do with partying and hockey, everyone else is insignificant to the great Tucker Hayes.

"Lacy was right to call me out. My buddies and I, the last time we were out we completely forgot to tip her. It was an oversight but I used to wait tables in college and I know how shitty people can be with that, especially when it's a huge tab. I plan to make it up to her tonight."

"Well, I'm leaving so feel free to tip the rest of the staff well." The words come out angrier than I intend, but I can't help what I feel. He has some nerve coming back here to apologize for being a shitty tipper when that's the least of my worries when it comes to him.

Miguel looks completely baffled at this entire situation. "That's still not an excuse to throw a drink in your face, Mr. Hayes. So please accept our sincerest apology and your drinks are on the house tonight." Turning to me, he tacks on, "Lacy, you can leave."

I don't wait for another hint from my boss. I walk out of the room as fast as I can, saving Tucker the trouble of trying to figure out why "tip money" could make a lowly bartender like me so angry.

———

Ellie's feet plunk to the floor as she shifts her body to the sitting position on our ratty couch, not even bothering to hide her surprise when I walk in the door. Her guilty pleasure in the form of *The Bachelor* reruns is forgotten.

"What are you doing home so early?" she demands. "You're not fired are you?"

I plop down next to her, rubbing my eyes. "Not yet."

"That doesn't sound good."

"It wasn't," I admit.

"What happened? It's not like Miguel to make someone leave early."

"Two words—Tucker Hayes."

Her eyes widen with shock. It's probably exactly how I looked when I first saw him. "Nooooo."

"Yep. Showed up at the bar, all floppy hair and super cut physique, looking spiffy in an expensive suit. And didn't have any idea who I was."

That last part still stings.

"Oh that sucks. What did you do?"

"Threw a twenty-dollar shot in his face."

I chance a look at the woman who has been my best friend and most supportive person I know for almost three years. She's fighting a smile, which reminds me of why I love her so much.

"Well, that explains being sent home early."

"Yup." Sighing deeply, I lay my head back against the couch and turn to look at her. "I'm so sorry Ellie. I promise I'll still be able to pay my part of the rent this month. I might have to give it to you on the first instead of a couple days before."

"Stop." She grabs my hand. "We'll figure it out, okay? We always do."

I'm so grateful for how Ellie's always gone above and beyond for us. If it weren't for her, I'm honestly not sure where we'd be right now.

"Thanks."

Sitting up straight, she faces me, her expression all business. I could start talking about something. Anything to distract her but this conversation is going to happen regardless.

"So. How did he look? Still dripping with sex appeal?"

I shake my head and pinch the bridge of my nose. "More so. I didn't even know it was possible for him to fill out even more than he already was. And he still has the same hair that flops in his face. And the same smile that melted my panties right off last time we met." I huff. "God, I hate him for being so sexy."

"It's not his fault he won the genetic lottery." Ellie pulls a stray hair off her pants and drops it on the floor before looking up at me and I know what she's about to ask. "Did you tell him?"

"You mean when I threw the drink in his face or when he told Miguel it was his fault because he's a shitty tipper so I have a right to be angry."

"Oh no. That's why he thought you were pissed?"

I shrug.

Ellie pauses for a few seconds before asking the inevitable question. "What are you going to do now that he's back in town?"

I can honestly say I don't know. I wish I could call my mom and talk to her about it. Pick her brain and get her advice. She'd have some words of wisdom to help me out. But that ship sailed years ago. I'm on my own with this one. At least I have Ellie to help me sort through it all.

I don't get a chance to respond to her question before Sutton stumbles out of the bedroom rubbing her eyes, her blond curls a rat's nest on her head. She's clutching her stuffed puppy, as per usual. "Mommy?"

I pick her up and kiss the top of her head, snuggling her close.

"I don't know Ellie. I really don't. But I have a strong feeling life is about to change."

CHAPTER FOUR

TUCKER

I thought about her all day. Lacy, I mean. It feels like I should know her. There's a random thought that keeps niggling in the back of my brain telling me I'm missing something, something important, but I can't figure out what. It's been driving me crazy since she walked out of that back room and left the hotel bar, a dejected look on her face.

I have to make this right with her. Again, I'm not positive why, but I don't think I'll be able to let it go until I do.

"Hey, Tucker. You coming out with us again tonight?" Maks claps me on the bare shoulder, unconcerned that we're naked in the showers and he has no sense of personal space. That's part of what I like about him.

"Where are you guys headed?"

Maks' eyes light up. "A titty bar! Tiger's birthday is this weekend so we're celebrating early with a lap dance and maybe a motorboat or two."

"No motorboating, dude. That's how you got kicked out last time."

"I still think that chick set me up. She knew I wasn't supposed to touch her but how could I stop when they were just right there in my face?" He holds up his hands, overexaggerating the size of the dancer's boobs compared to his head.

"That's easy dude. When they say 'look, don't touch,' sit on your hands."

He lets out a gruff noise that's a cross between a growl and a bark. Fucking weirdo.

"Does that mean you're in or out, Hayes? We only have a short amount of time before we have to cut back on the partying."

"Like the regular season has ever stopped you before."

He ignores my quip. "In or out, Hayes?"

I open my mouth to tell him I'm in, but the look on Lacy's face runs through my thoughts again, stopping me. I really need to get that fixed before anything else. I can't afford to have any distractions in my game right now.

"I think I'm gonna pass, man. Got some stuff I need to take care of."

"Really? Like what?"

I'm not really sure, but there's no easy way to explain that. "Just stuff that's none of your business."

"Eh. I don't really care anyway. Just trying to sound like a caring friend.," Maks says with another clap on my naked shoulder. "You change your mind just text me."

"Will do."

"And don't forget to wash your ass crack."

He guffaws at his own joke on his way back to the locker room. Fucking Maksim. He's one hell of a hockey player with one strange sense of humor.

By the time I'm dressed and out the door, I decide to go straight to the hotel bar. Maybe she's not working tonight, but I'm hopeful she will be there. I'm even more hopeful she'll actually speak to me.

The hotel and the bar look different in the light of day. Or maybe it's that the party crowd just hasn't infiltrated yet. Regardless, I'm feeling lucky because there she is, behind the bar.

I stop for just a second to admire her from a distance. If circumstances were different, she'd be the kind of woman I would be hitting on. Her long dark hair is pulled back in a sporty ponytail just like the other night. Her uniform is once again crisp and sharp. But that's not what draws me to her. It's the quiet confidence. The way she moves around like she can anticipate what's coming before it happens. And let's not forget the easy smile she flashes to the few customers sitting at the counter.

She's intriguing in a way I can't explain. Even the other night, when I found her in the supply closet being sent home by her boss, as I got close enough to her and caught of whiff of her fruity and floral scent, my body instantly knew we have a connection.

I approach cautiously, not wanting to scare her off. As soon as she sees me, that easy smile falls.

"You shouldn't be here. I can't afford to get sent home again tonight." Lacy doesn't even look at me as she speaks. Just continues filling an icy pint from the tap.

"I'm here to talk, not here to make you angry. And I really don't want another shot in my face anyway."

In spite of my smile, the joke falls flat.

Putting the beer down in front of another customer, without spilling it all over them I might add, she finally turns to me, wiping her hands on a towel. "What do you want, Tucker?"

"To make it right."

"To make what right?"

I pause briefly before quietly admitting the truth. "I...don't know."

She throws her hands in the air, clearly annoyed. "Of course you don't know. I only tried to reach you for like a year."

Lacy tried to reach me? I haven't even lived here six months yet, so we met before that? I'm not understanding any of this. "Wait...what?"

She forcefully grabs a small bowl off the counter and begins filling it with pretzels. "Nothing. Forget I said anything. What can I get you to drink?"

"Forget the drink." Clearly that's not the most important part of this story What is she not telling me? "I'm serious. What am I missing, Lacy? What did I do? I'm trying to fix whatever I broke."

The pretzels scatter everywhere as she drops the bowl on the counter. She angrily pulls out her phone and swipes a few times, before turning it to show him.

"That's what you did."

It's a picture of a little girl. She's got wavy, dirty blonde hair and a big smile. She's holding a stuffed dog on one side and the hand of another child on the other, but the picture is zoomed in so I can't make out the other person.

My heart starts beating rapidly as the pieces of the puzzle begin to fall together as to why Lacy looks so familiar but not enough for me to place, and why she's so pissed about my lack of memory.

I'm guessing the girl is three or four years old.

Which means a little over four years ago...

My brain stalls out, knowing I'm about to have a bomb dropped on me, but still in too much disbelief to put it together on my own.

"Wha... What do you mean I did this?"

Lacy places the phone down in front of me and points at the picture. "That's your daughter. But you wouldn't recognize her, would you? Not since you and your agent or whoever froze me out. Way to go, Super Dad."

"Wait." I rub my forehead, trying to get my brain to stop spinning as I sort through all my memories wanting to remember how this could have happened. "She's mine?"

Lacy looks at me like I'm the most disgusting thing she's ever seen. Clearly, she's not understanding that I'm trying to wrap my brain around this. But another thought begins to percolate, this one beginning to bubble into something much fiercer than confusion. Part of me is mad. How did I not know before? How do I have a child that I know nothing about?

"No really. When did this happen? And why the fuck didn't you tell me?"

Lacy rears back, her eyes so wide they just about bug out of her head.

"Didn't tell you!" She glances around, realizing how loud she's being and lowers her volume to a low roar. "Are you fucking serious right now?"

"I had a right to know," I say through clenched teeth.

She leans in, refusing to back down. "Then maybe you should have better communication with your agent."

My jaw ticks. I have a bad feeling I know where this is going. "What are you saying?"

"I sent a dozen emails. When I found out I was pregnant, when I had her. All of them with the same response – 'Have my attorney forward any correspondence regarding this issue to whoever the fuck your attorney is'." She uses air quotes to emphasis her point.

"And did you?"

She stands up straight, giving a haughty laugh. "What the fuck kind of charmed world do you live in? I was a twenty-one-year-old college student. Have you ever tried getting a decent job when it's painfully obvious you'll be going on maternity leave in a few short months? How the hell was I supposed to hire an attorney?" She raises an eyebrow at me, knowing she's got a solid point and that the breakdown in communication wasn't on her end. It was on mine. "You know what? Fuck you, Tucker. We've survived this long without you. We don't need you now."

She walks away plastering a smile on her face as she approaches another customer.

"Sorry about that, Dan. What can I help you with?"

The older man glares at me before turning back to her. "Need me to take out the trash for you? I may be old, but I've still got some moves on me."

She pats him on the arm. "That's really nice of you, but I'm okay, I promise. Nothing I can't handle."

"Well you just say the word and I'll take care of it for you."

I ignore the rest of their conversation when I realize she forgot her phone. It's sitting in front of me with the picture of this child who is supposedly my daughter right in front of me.

I run my finger over the picture again. All shock aside, there's no doubt this is my child. She looks exactly like my mother when she was that age. Same wave to her hair, same small dimple on her cheek, same eye shape when she smiles.

Before I can stop myself, I forward the picture to my phone, having the sudden realization that it's the only thing I have of my daughter.

My *daughter*.

How could this happen? How could a child—my child—be brought into this world without me knowing? Why was the information not passed along to me years ago?

I'm not sure how it happened, but I'm about to find out. I'm beyond angry at this turn of events but not at Lacy. I was warned Morty my agent wasn't all that trustworthy, but I followed the dollar signs when I signed my first contract and here we are. Eating crow. And feeling a guilt that I've never felt before.

I have to get some air.

I flag Lacy down, showing her that the phone is still on the counter before dropping a twenty next to it and leaving. I have some phone calls to make and some people to fire.

CHAPTER FIVE

LACY

I am dead on my feet. It was a rough night, and not just emotionally. Some sort of conference is in town, and the attendees spent hours in the bar, keeping us on our toes. It was great for tips, and I really need the money for my half of the rent after being sent home the other day. Plus, Sutton's shorts are looking a little too booty, so she needs a few things. Maybe the local big box chain will have a sale rack tomorrow. I'll take the kids shopping. It'll get them out of the apartment and give them something to do...

My thoughts all but disappear when I see Tucker leaning against the wall in the lobby just outside the bar entrance. As much as I hate to admit it, he looks good. Damn good. His floppy, dirty blond hair is just the right length to frame his handsome face. His grey t-shirt highlighting his muscular physique.

I can see why the me of a few years ago was attracted to him. Hell, I can see why the me of now is attracted to him, despite my reservations. He's beautiful.

But he's also the reason my life has been both blessed and cursed, so the physical attraction isn't enough for me anymore.

As if he senses me watching, Tucker looks up and pushes off with his foot as I approach.

When we finally meet in the middle, I cross my arms defensively. I'm not sure I want to hear what he has to say. "What are you doing here?"

"I was hoping we could talk."

"What else is there to say?"

"For starters, you can tell me her name." He shakes his head and for the first time, I think I see a hint of something other than the fun-loving party animal I remember Tucker to be. If I'm not mistaken, I might see a little bit of remorse. "I have a daughter and I don't even know her name, or when her birthday is. Do you know how jacked that is?"

"What makes you so sure she's yours? You haven't demanded a DNA test yet."

"She looks just like my mom."

I cock my head, assessing him, trying to figure out his game because in my experience there is *always* a game. But I can't pin down what it is. There are too many warring emotions on his face.

"Look, Lacy, if I had known—"

"What?" I interrupt. "You would have helped? Sent money? I got all the answer I needed when your agent blocked me from even discussing how you wanted to handle my pregnancy."

"I fired him."

"What? Who?"

"My agent. When I left earlier to get some air and wrap my brain around all this, I called him. Told him I didn't appreciate him keeping me from my daughter for so long and then canned his ass. Frankly, I should have fired him long ago."

I'm not sure what to think about this. All these years I thought Tucker made his agent do his dirty work and now I'm second guessing myself.

"I..." he runs his fingers through his hair. "Can we talk? For real? I have so many questions."

"I can't believe I'm even considering this," I mutter.

But I am. Somehow everything feels different now. Everything has changed. All the feelings I had over the years about Tucker, every time I wished that he'd drop dead or get his teeth knocked out or whatever, it all seems a little over the top when he's looking at me like this. Maybe it's because it's the same wide-eyed, hopeful expression my daughter gives when she wants something. And yet, I can see a hint of fear in his eyes, too. For the first time, it feels like I'm holding all the cards in this situation. It's not as fun as I imagined it would be. Dammit. "Fine. Come on."

I take him further into the huge lobby. It feels very open air with trees planted in various areas throughout the building. There's even a small stream running through it. Actually it's a fountain, but it looks like a stream. With how late it is, we're easily able to find a quiet spot.

Settling onto my chair, I just look at him, waiting for him to make the first move. He left me, left us when we needed him the most. The least he can do is be the one to start this conversation.

After a few moments of awkward silence, Tucker clears his throat. "What's her name?"

"Sutton."

"Sutton." He says it a few times, like he's rolling it around on his tongue, trying it on for size. "I love that. Sutton what?"

"Sutton Rose Hawkins."

His brows furrow. "She doesn't have my last name?"

"Why the fuck would she?"

"Sorry," he quickly backtracks. "You're right. You would have no reason to give her my name."

"No I wouldn't."

"And she's healthy?"

Interesting. He hasn't asked for proof of paternity yet and his second question is about her health. I don't trust him or his intentions, but he's at least asking the right questions. It's what's keeping me here. For now.

"She's perfect," I answer, feeling a small sense of pride that I'm doing something right. "Right on track with all her milestones. No unusual illnesses or diseases. Not even a cavity."

Tucker sighs in relief and runs his fingers through his hair. "That's good. Really good."

The awkward silence returns, but I just wait for him to think of more questions. I don't mind answering them, but I don't plan to volunteer any information either.

"How old is she?"

I bristle. The fucker doesn't even have a reference point for how long ago she was created. That sits the wrong way with me and judging by his expression, he knows it.

"I'm sorry, I know that's the wrong question to ask, but I don't..." He pinches the bridge of his nose. "I have tried a million times to place you. You are so familiar, but I can't remember the night we were together."

I glare at him, my anger rearing its ugly head again. There's so much venom in my voice even I can hear it. "Of course you can't. You've been off living a charmed life, sleeping with whoever you please while we were sleeping in my car."

His eyes widen and his shoulders fall. "You were sleeping in your car? Sutton too?"

Dammit.

I look away, pissed at myself for saying too much. I didn't mean to say that, to give him so much information. I don't trust Tucker with my story. Not even a little bit.

"You have a real place now, though, right?" he asks, almost sounding frantic. "You can come stay with me if you need to. Both of you—"

"Let me stop you right there," I interrupt. Leaning forward, I look him in the eye to make sure my point is made. "I pulled us up, both of us up, by my bootstraps with the help of a good friend. I'm no longer at the point where I need you or your money. I'm only having this conversation with you because you need to know before Sutton comes looking for you one day. I will never lie to you about her because this reaction, you being shocked to have a kid you didn't know about will likely ruin my relationship with her. I'm not willing to be turned into the bad guy in this situation. I'm not talking to you because I want something from you. Frankly, I'd prefer if you just walked away and never looked back. Because I don't trust you, Tucker Hayes. Not one bit. So if you have more questions for me about my daughter, fine. But if you're just going to try and jump in and save the day, you may as well leave now."

"I'm not trying to be a hero," Tucker snaps back. "I missed her entire life so far because someone else blocked me from finding out. I'm trying to do what's right here. For my daughter and for me."

I sit back and consider his words. I don't know if I believe him, that he didn't know. But if he's telling the truth, even I have to admit, that sucks. Sutton is the best part of my life. I can't imagine missing out on anything because of someone else's carelessness with important information.

Taking a deep breath, I school my temper and give him the benefit of the doubt. "She was born on August fourteenth, three years ago."

Tucker's eyes snap up to mine and I know I've got his full attention. I can also see the wheels turning in his brain as he tries to put the timeline together.

"We had a crabby nurse and the birth wasn't textbook perfect but she was. Sutton was textbook perfect. Seven pounds, thirteen ounces, nineteen inches long. Her APGAR scores were bang on, her hearing test normal. Everything was exactly as it should be."

Not willing to tell him about the hard parts, not yet at least, I skip to present day.

"We live with a friend of mine in a two-bedroom apartment. She has a three-year-old son so we're like a little family and the kids always have someone to play with." I smile as I think about how often we're asked if Sutton and Kody are twins. It's happened so many times, the kids always say yes before I can answer no.

"She knows all her colors and numbers and doesn't go anywhere without her puppy."

"She has a dog?" Tucker smiles just a little, seeming to enjoy every little morsel I'm giving him. As a mom, nothing makes me more excited than talking about my child, so I just keep talking.

"A stuffed dog," I clarify. "I found it at a thrift store for twenty-five cents. I don't even remember why I got it. Maybe as a joke or something. But she latched onto it and it's her favorite thing in the whole world. With the possible exception of Kody."

"Kody?"

"Her twin." I flash air quotes as reference. "I don't do everything right. I know that. But somehow, she's the most right thing I've ever done. She's perfect in her own little way. And you need to know that. That she's fine. We're fine. And if you choose to walk away from this, I'll be mad. But at least I'll have the peace of mind that you know what you're walking away from now. That you made a choice and didn't just avoid knowing the truth to try and avoid financial responsibility."

"I really didn't, Lacy. If I had known..." he runs his fingers through his hair again, the aggravation practically bleeding off him. "I'm so angry someone else took the choice away from me. That's something I'm going to have to deal with. But for now, I'd just like to meet her. If that's okay with you."

I wish I could say I'm surprised by his request, but somehow, I'm not. He came back to find me. He asked questions. He apologized. I don't trust him at all, but I have to at least give him a chance to try and make things right, even if it's just for closure's sake. Or maybe I'm just telling myself that because I'm tired of being angry.

"On one condition."

"Anything," he says quickly.

"You say nothing about being her father. Until I know you're sticking around for good, I'm not about to give her information that could potentially cause irreparable damage to her little heart."

He shakes his head. "I hate that. I hate that you would even think I plan to get out of this."

"You should. But this is the hand we've been dealt. Everything we do from here on out is about her. Me giving you a chance. You maintaining boundaries. Got it?"

I'm willing to set aside my pride for a lot of things, but I absolutely won't set it aside so much that Sutton ends up being the one hurt.

He takes a deep breath and nods, seeming to understand where I'm coming from in a way I didn't expect a few hours ago. "Got it."

"Will tomorrow evening work for you?" I offer.

"Dammit. It's the first game of the preseason tomorrow."

"And that's more important than meeting your daughter?"

He frowns. "Of course not, but I'm under contract so they can fire my ass if I don't show up. You wanna take a day off work instead?"

"You're right," I admit. "That was unfair of me. We can work around our schedules and do it a different day."

"No," he says quickly. "I don't want to wait any longer. I've already missed too much. How about lunch time? You guys have to eat, right? I can bring a special lunch over or something."

Once again, my pride wants me to say no. That he can meet us somewhere in public, somewhere the kids are distracted and won't give a shit about meeting him. But I have to put that demon aside. I told Tucker this is all about Sutton and her well-being, so I need to let him have a real chance. Plus, I'm tired. The idea of not having to make a grocery run in the morning and making lunch is more appealing than it should be.

"Fine. Bring Mexican food. The kids love cheese quesadillas and I'm emotional so I could go for some queso."

His shoulders relax and he smiles a real genuine grin for the first time tonight.

"I'll be there."

I have no doubt he will. And that makes me more nervous than it should.

CHAPTER SIX

TUCKER

With our first preseason game tonight, we just had a morning skate today. The powers that be want me to head out so I can eat, nap and be ready for tonight's game, but I need a few more minutes to myself.

I continue skating around in circles, absentmindedly, letting my thoughts wander however they want. The only place they're going is to Lacy. And Sutton. And the years of their lives I've missed. What was my daughter like as a baby? Did she cry a lot? Did she smile? Did she have that weird baby scent women are always going on about?

I'm still so pissed at Morty for not telling me about Lacy's emails. There's so much I could have done, so many ways I could have been involved if he had just asked me if there was a chance I accidentally made a kid. I have no doubt I would have remembered her if he'd only said Lacy's name so soon after our night together, because she is just dynamic.

She's beautiful, yes, but she's also a ball buster. She's like a mama bear who gets shit done, but if you get in her way and she feels threatened, you better watch out. I like that. It's a personality trait I'm wildly attracted to. I just wish I could remember if she was like that back then, too.

After several more minutes of hearing nothing but the sounds of my blades on the ice, maintenance finally has enough and gives me the evil eye. I know they have work to do to prepare for tonight's game so I leave them to it.

The locker room is thankfully quiet and almost empty by the time I begin stripping off my gear. The quiet is probably why I hear my phone ding with a text.

Grabbing it out of my locker, I see that it's Lacy giving me their address. I respond with a thumbs up, intending to start moving quickly so I can grab lunch and make it on time. But I accidentally scroll up and there it is, a picture of my daughter. Of Sutton. She's the most beautiful thing I've ever seen.

Our goalie, Nicholas Williams suddenly comes around the corner. "What are you doing here?"

I shouldn't be surprised to see him. He's either the first one gone or the last one out, depending on the day, but even for him it's unusually late.

"I was about to ask you the same thing."

He grabs some runners from his locker and sits next to me, sliding off the Crocs he wears around the locker room. "Nothing much. Getting a little extra work done on my hips and knees today."

"Your joints giving you trouble?" That could be bad news if our goalie is having flexibility issues before the season even starts.

"Nothing more than normal," he says. "Just trying to stay on top of the pending arthritis I'm sure to have in my old age."

I snicker. "As much as I try not to think about it, even I have to admit I'm not looking forward to all those athletic injuries coming back to haunt me in a few years."

"It won't be all bad. I'm already planning on an endorsement deal with some arthritis medication company in about forty years, so at least all the aches and pains will be worth some money."

"I'll be sure to take out some medical stock before then. I'm sure your pretty mug will make the value skyrocket."

"Ah. You're so good to me." Nick isn't just a damn good hockey player. He's also so good looking, like startlingly so even to a guy like me, that multiple modeling agencies have put in tentative offers to sign him once he's done with hockey. He calls it ridiculous and laughs it off, saying it would make him uncomfortable to "make love to a camera". He's probably right, but it can't hurt having a plan B for retirement. Although it sounds like he already has one.

Looking back down at my phone, I remind myself I need to get moving. I don't want to be late for my first meeting with Sutton. And yet, I find myself frozen to this seat.

"Cute kid," Nick says. "Who is she?"

"My daughter."

It's the first time I've said it out loud, and it only makes it more real.

I have a three-year-old daughter named Sutton Rose. That just knocks the wind right out of me.

"I didn't know you had a kid, man."

"Neither did I."

Nick freezes next to me, his vibe completely changing. I suspect I'm going to get a lot of that in the near future. "Uh... I feel like there's a story here. Care to elaborate?"

I sigh and click my phone off, needing to get this off my chest. I haven't told anyone about Sutton yet. Not even my mother.

Shit. I have to tell my mother.

One step at a time, Hayes. I'll call her on my way out of here. If nothing else, I need to let her tell me she told me so about Morty.

"I fired my agent last night."

"Wait, what does that have to do with having a kid?" Nick asks, and rightfully so. The story feels so convoluted, even to me. And I'm living it.

"Sutton's mom, Sutton is my daughter." He nods like he's following. "She emailed my agent like a dozen times when she was pregnant. Morty blew her off. Never even asked me if it could be true."

"Oh fuck," Nick breathes.

"Exactly. Lacy didn't have money for an attorney to sue me, so they ended up living in a car, and all this other stuff that I'm sure I don't even know about." I rub my hand over my face, still frustrated by the situation. "I missed the first three years of Sutton's life because Morty thought it would be better if I didn't know so it wouldn't mess up my game. How fucked up is that?"

"Holy shit." Nick's expression mirrors what I've been feeling for days. It's a mixture of disbelief and anger. Maybe a little fear swirling in there. Or maybe that part is just mine. "What are you going to do?"

"I don't know. I'm going to meet her today though." The thought brings a smile to my face.

"That's good. Good first step. You nervous?"

I laugh in response because that's the understatement of the year. "More nervous than stepping on the ice for a playoff game."

"Also good." He claps me on the shoulder and stands.

"Why?"

"It means you care. Not everyone does when they find out there's a child out there that they made."

"I don't get how some guys have that reaction, you know? All I had to do was see her picture and it felt like my chest was ripped wide open. I have no idea how I'm going to feel once I actually see her for the first time."

Nick shoves his keys in the pocket of his athletic pants and drops his Crocs in his locker. "It'll be good. Just take it slow. I know how you are. You go in all guns ablazin' and don't hold back. Just remember that yes, you missed three years, but you have dozens more to go. Don't force anything."

I nod because that's good advice. He's right. I do tend to go full steam ahead when I want something. But this isn't a some-thing. This is a someone. I don't want to scare her and I really don't want to piss off her mom. Lacy's a fighter and I'm sure that would include fighting me if necessary.

———

I am unimpressed.

The building they live in is old and looks dilapidated. There is dirt and weeds where grass should be. The gate around the prop-erty is completely useless and the sidewalk is buckling. And that's just on the outside.

Inside, it smells faintly of urine and the carpet has holes worn in it, it's that old.

This is not where my daughter should live. Hell, it's not where anyone should live. I want to pack all their shit and move them out now, but one step at a time. First I need to get through this meeting without throwing up.

I knock on the door and wait. My back feels sweaty and I have to flap my arms to try and cool my pits. *I'm so fucking nervous.* I'm about to meet my daughter. My *daughter* for the first time. This is unreal.

The door finally opens and Lacy has a tight smile on her lips. I'm sure she's just as nervous as I am, except for different reasons.

Looking down at the bags in my hands, she tilts her head to the side.

"What's all this?"

"You said to bring lunch." Did I misunderstand that part?

"How many people are you planning on feeding?"

"I eat a lot."

She purses her lips at me and I cave.

"Fine. I wasn't sure if the kids would be in the mood for quesadillas, so I got a few options. I figured it wouldn't hurt to have leftovers."

Lacy waves me in and I briefly take in my surroundings before my eyes land on the most beautiful thing I've ever seen.

My daughter.

Her wavy, dirty-blond hair is down around her shoulder, part of it pulled back so I can see her face. The curls around her face make her look angelic. She looks at me with eyes that she definitely inherited from her mother. They're dark and full of curiosity about the man standing in her living room.

All the breath leaves my lungs and I know the truth before any science lab can confirm it. This is my daughter, my child.

"Tucker?" Lacy says gently.

I blink my eyes a few times and clear the emotion trying to clog my throat.

"Sorry. Uh... where do you want me to put these?"

I glance up at the mother of my child who is smiling at me knowingly, tears in her own eyes. Although, I'm not sure if they're from relief or fear. I guess either is possible.

"Let's put them on the counter over here."

We walk into the very small and dingy kitchen with a counter overlooking the living room. I place most of the bags on top and begin unloading all the food.

"I know you said they liked cheese quesadillas, but they also had a kid's meal with chicken nuggets, and they had macaroni and cheese, and these mini corn dog bite things so I got two of each."

"Why two?"

"Didn't you say there are two kids?"

"Wait, you got some for Kody, too?"

"Well yeah. How shitty would it be to feed one kid and not the other? Plus, you said they call themselves twins so I didn't want him to feel left out."

Lacy gets a strange look on her face that I can't quite decipher. Whatever it is, she's definitely still scrutinizing me. "That was really nice of you, Tucker."

"I'm generally a nice guy, Lacy," I try to joke but I'm still a little too nervous to find myself funny. I dig in the bags a little more to distract myself from my jitters. "And here's your queso."

"Holy shit, you got me a large?"

"With extra chips."

I pull out a gallon sized Ziplock bag filled with tortilla chips, making her laugh. I don't think I've heard that sounds from her before but it makes my heart swell knowing I did that. She's beautiful when she's not smiling but when she does, she about knocks me over with how gorgeous she is.

For a split second, I feel a memory trying to reveal itself. I can't make out anything, but I know how I feel. It's like a glow in my chest, a sense of belonging. When Lacy takes the bag out of my hand and pulls it open, the memory quickly fades back into oblivion.

"So much food... this is a little over the top, don't you think?" She pops a chip in her mouth.

I shrug, not sure how to even explain how I feel about all this. Nothing seems like too much right now. On the contrary, it all seems like it's not nearly enough.

"You've spent the last three years, actually more than four years if you take your pregnancy into the equation, taking care of my daughter while I was living in a self-absorbed, oblivious world. Extra food is the least I can do."

This time it's Lacy who clears her throat. Something about the movement tries to trigger another memory I can't quite grasp. Dammit. I really want to remember her from before.

"Well, it's still a little early for lunch and they're obviously curious about you."

We look over to see two sets of eyes peering over the back of the couch.

Lacy giggles. "We don't have many visitors, as you can tell. You want to meet them?"

I take another deep breath and roll my shoulders. "Yeah," I croak out.

"Hey." Lacy nudges me, forcing my attention on her. "It's going to be okay. I'm just going to introduce you as my friend and we'll see how it unfolds, okay? We've got lots of time."

"That's what Nick said."

"What?"

"Nothing. Just, a teammate I ran into today. Told him what was happening and he reminded me we've got years ahead of us to sort this out."

"He's right. Give her time to get to know you. To adjust. She'll be okay."

"It's not her I'm worried about," I mumble to myself. Not quietly enough apparently.

"You'll be fine, too." Lacy pats me on the arm, the shot of warmth like a salve to my racing emotions. "Just try not to barf on my carpet. It's stained enough as it is."

"No promises," I joke.

In just a few steps, I'm standing in front of my daughter for the very first time. Looming over her is more like it. I knew kids were small but it feels like I'm a giant next to her. Once Lacy moves them out of the way so I can sit on the couch, I feel a little better. Maybe it's because we're able to make eye contact easier. I have no idea what to say, or how to even start.

Thankfully, Lacy seems to know exactly what to do and takes the lead. "Kiddos, this is my good friend Tucker Hayes. He brought us lunch. Can you say hi?"

"Hi," the boy, Kody, if I'm remembering correctly, says shyly.

Sutton, on the other hand, doesn't say anything. Just looks at me curiously.

"You know how we watch hockey on TV sometimes?" Lacy asks them, grabbing my attention.

"You watch hockey?" Now I'm curious.

Lacy shrugs. "It was the only connection to you we had."

I feel like I've been sucker punched. This woman who was so

furious at my absence still made sure my daughter knew at least part of me.

She turns back to the kids, maybe to give me a reprieve, maybe because she left them hanging. Either way, it gives me a second to pull myself together.

"Tucker plays hockey."

"On TV?" A wide-eyed Kody looks like his mind is blown. Sutton is still just observing me.

Lacy laughs. "Yes. Tucker plays hockey on TV."

That's all Kody needs to hear before one of his toys distracts him, but Sutton is still watching me.

"Sutton, baby," Lacy says gently. "What are you thinking about?"

My daughter holds out a ratty, stuffed wiener dog. "See my puppy?"

The sound of her voice makes me smile. It's the first time I've heard her speak and I don't know how to process it. Not only that, she asked me a question and is waiting for an answer. It's such a small thing, but it feels huge in my world.

"That is a very cute puppy." It doesn't seem like I've said enough, like I should have some words of wisdom or something profound to tell her. Some way to let her know how much I love her, even though I just met her.

But for her, it's apparently the right answer. "Ruff, ruff." Sutton starts bouncing the dog up and down, moving closer to me until she's standing right between my knees, jumping the dog up my legs and chest until it gives me a fake kiss.

Who knew a pretend kiss from a three-year-old's ratty stuffed animal would be the best kiss of my life?

"Sutton," Lacy says. "Why don't you back up and give Tucker some room?"

"It's okay," I interject quickly, wishing I could get her closer, hug her, smooth down her hair, and feel her baby arms around me.

But I remind myself to slow down. This is the first time we're meeting. We have time. I don't want to scare her off.

"I actually brought you something, Sutton."

Ohmygod, I just said her name. And not just to myself so I can hear what it sounds like.

Her eyes light up and I feel like I'm on top of the world.

Yep. Thirty seconds and I'm already wrapped around her little finger. I'm in so much trouble. In the best way, of course. My mother warned me that would happen. Right after she yelled at me for being an idiot and hiring Morty against her advice. Then she demanded I text her a picture of her granddaughter, which I did immediately.

"Me, too?" Kody comes bounding over, not willing to miss out on present time. It makes me laugh.

"You, too," I say with a smile. Reaching down next to the couch, I grab the bag Lacy didn't notice when I first came in.

Knowing they're exactly the same, I put my hand into the bag and pull out two boxes, giving one to each of them.

"Tucker," Lacy breathes. "You didn't have to do this."

"I wanted to. I've got a lot of Christmases and birthdays to make up for."

"Three. There were three."

"Which makes six major events, plus Easter and Valentine's Day. Flag Day..."

"Okay, okay." She cuts me off with a laugh. "I get it. Your guilt is eating you alive."

"Not guilt exactly. More disappointment than anything."

Lacy furrows her brow as she looks at me, observing me with the same expression Sutton had just moments ago. "You really are sad you didn't know, aren't you?"

"I don't think I could ever explain to you how much. I didn't even realize this part of my heart was missing until you showed me that picture."

A squeal from one of the kids makes us table our side conversation.

"Mama! Look! Legos!!" Sutton yells.

"Oh boy..." Lacy deadpans. "Legos."

"What? What did I do wrong?"

The kids seem excited. Isn't that what was supposed to happen?

"It was a great idea..."

My heart sinks. "Oh crap. I've already failed at parenting."

"No, no!" Lacy says quickly. "They'll grow into them. They're just still too small for their age. Choking hazard."

I throw my hands over my face. "Ohmygod, I almost killed them already."

Lacy tries to pull my hands away but I'm stronger than she is. "No you didn't. I'll just put them away for now. They'll be surprised for the second time when I pull them out of the closet. When they're like six."

"Oh man. Why didn't anyone tell me three is too young for Legos?"

"I mean, it says right there on the box they're for ages eight and up."

I pick up one of the boxes that's already been dropped on the floor, the kids too busy staring at the picture on the present Kody is still holding. Sure enough, right there in bright letters it says, "Ages 8+".

"I have no idea how I can see everything on the ice from a distance, and I missed this glaring warning sign right in front of my face."

"It happens. And the idea was really nice. Just know, for their age, there are bigger blocks that fit their hands. You just have to find the right aisle for them."

"I'll be sure to ask for help next time. But..." I pull more stuff out of the bag, glad I have a backup plan. "That wasn't the only present. Hey guys, why don't you give Lacy the Legos so you can open this box, too."

Lacy groans as she takes the death toys from the kids. "Seriously, Tucker. You don't need to spoil them. They're going to like you even without gifts."

"Yeah, well, they'll like me better with them."

Sutton and Kody rip open the white boxes and pull out matching jerseys, the official brand from our pro shop.

"Me and Kody is twins again!" Sutton yells and they begin jumping up and down, possibly more excited about matching than what they'll be wearing.

Lacy takes the jersey out of Sutton's hands and pulls it over her tiny body. Then she sees the name on the back.

"Jerseys with your name and number? Really?"

I shrug. "I got them something useful. They can wear them on game nights and be twins again."

"Well thank you. That was really thoughtful. We'll make them our official hockey wearing shirts."

"You need one too, Mama! Then we can be three twins!"

"And my mommy, too," Kody interjects. "Four twins!"

"Oh goodie. Quadruplets," Lacy says sarcastically.

That gives me an idea of what to bring next time.

"Don't worry kids. I got you covered." They each jump up for a high five while Lacy slaps a palm over her face.

"You're never going to stop spoiling them, are you?"

I shake my head. "Not ever. Be prepared. I plan to give her the world."

Because nothing is too good for my daughter. And no one will ever be able to convince me otherwise.

CHAPTER SEVEN

LACY

My heart pounds as I take in the scene, trying to squelch my flight mode so I can fight instead. I'm the only adult here which means it's all up to me.

The screams are piercing my ear drums. I want to join the kids and stand on the safety of the couch, but I can't. I have a mission. Thank God they're out of the way, though. It's so much harder to defend us when they cling to me.

I lift the shoe over my head...

But before I can smack it down killing the little terrorist, the door opens, distracting us all.

Ellie takes in the scene slowly, cocking an eyebrow in question. "What the hell is going on?"

"It's a bug, Mama!" Kody yells and runs for his mother. Probably a smart idea. She's much calmer in these kinds of situations than I am.

She picks Kody up and nuzzles into his neck. "A tiny bug is causing all this commotion? I can hear you from down the hall. I'm surprised the police haven't been called yet."

"Everyone minds their business in this building, you know that. Plus, that isn't a tiny bug. That's the world's largest roach.

Look." I point to an empty spot on the floor. "Dammit. Where did he go?"

Kody wriggles down and Sutton jumps off the couch. They start looking around for the disgusting germ-carrying insect who already made his getaway.

"Of course they're not terrified now," I grumble as I toss myself on the now vacant couch. "But did they help when we were all in danger? No. They ran for high ground and left me to do it. Stinkers."

"It's nice that they trust you to handle all the adult stuff around here." Ellie sits next to me and starts pulling her shoes off. "Wouldn't want you getting too comfortable while they raised themselves."

"If you'd only been home on time you could have done the killing for me. You know I'm not good at this kind of thing. And you distracted me."

She curls her feet up under her as we watch the kids roll around on the floor. Somehow bug hunting turned into *Wrestlemania*.

"Poor roach was just trying to make a living."

"When did you become all one with the earth, including cockroaches?"

She shrugs. "The kids used to try and carry food with them all over the place, remember? I got used to seeing little antennae peeking out sometimes. As long as they don't fly, I'm good with them quietly going back where they came from."

"You say that now. Wait until he shows his disgusting little face after I leave for work. Then you'll be the one having to deal with it and there's no place to catch and release."

"It's the price we pay to live large." Ellie gestures around like the room like a game show host showing off the crack on the wall.

"Ugh. I wish we could afford a place that had extermination. Or maybe just afford extermination. Christmas is only a few months away. That would be a great gift."

"One step at a time, babe. We'll get there. Remember before we got hired at the bar and only had enough money for a one bedroom and you crashed on my couch? You were just grateful for hot water then."

"I've gotten spoiled over the years, I suppose," I say with a sigh.

"Speaking of spoiled, how did it go with Tucker."

"I see you noticed the jerseys the kids are wearing."

"I did, but I didn't want to say anything until I knew what kind of mood they put you in."

I haven't had much time to think about Tucker's visit yet.

That's not actually true. I've been distracting myself from thinking about it because I'm a little surprised by how I feel. It didn't go like I expected. I thought he'd come in, pat them on the head, talk to me and play on his phone while eating, and then leave. But that's not what happened at all.

He really engaged with the kids, both of them. He was interested in what they had to say and humored them by playing with puzzles. It was unexpected and exciting. A little two exciting. I could feel myself warming up to his charms like I did all those years ago because there is nothing sexier than a man who loves his children. Who wants to get to know them. It was exhilarating to watch how easily he took to them and how much he seemed to enjoy himself.

As much as I hate to admit it, it was a total turn on. Nice to know my lady bits aren't broken, but terrifying at the same time. I don't want to have any kind of attraction to Tucker, but my body and my heart seem to have other ideas, even just sitting here thinking about it. I hate it.

After all these years of despising him, it's also kind of a hard pill to swallow. I don't really want to admit that, even to myself, but Ellie sees right through me anyway so there's no point in attempting to lie.

"Surprisingly, the entire visit went well. And I begrudgingly admit I approve of him bringing some gifts."

"Really?" She looks as shocked as I feel.

"Really. It's weird, but I think he's telling the truth, that he didn't know. He seems really sad that he missed out on so much and was making a real attempt to get to know her. Well, them."

For as much as Ellie pretends, she doesn't seem all that surprised. "He did fire his agent the night he found out about Sutton. That has to count for something right there."

"He says he fired his agent," I shoot back. "I haven't gotten confirmation of that information yet."

Ellie pulls at her ponytail holder and shakes out her almost black hair. "And how do you plan on confirming it? Emailing his agent again? You really want to open up that can of worms after all the interactions you had with him before?"

"Nah. I bet the email address doesn't even work now that Morty, or whatever his name is, is unemployed."

"Sounds like you really do believe Tucker."

"Maybe. Maybe I just don't *want* to believe him so it's taking me a minute." I turn to look at her. "Is that weird?"

She bobbles her head side-to-side, which means I'm not about to get a real yes-or-no answer. "I think you made a lot of assumptions for a lot of years and it's going to take some time to sort through those feelings. Like, he isn't the one who broke your trust, but that doesn't mean it wasn't broken by someone else, not unlike your whole family disowning you."

She's not wrong about that. Going from a strong family unit with lots of siblings and everyone in each other's business, to out on the streets because you're unmarried and pregnant would do a number on anyone.

"I don't think it's unreasonable for him to have to earn your trust anyway," Ellie continues. "You may know of him, Lacy, but you don't really *know* him. Well, beyond a certain appendage."

I shove her, making her laugh.

"It does kind of sting that he doesn't remember me," I admit.

"I couldn't forget him, and Lord knows I tried. It sucks that this night that changed my life monumentally means virtually nothing to him."

"Maybe. But the night he'll never forget is when you threw that drink in his face. That was the night his life changed."

I snicker. "I hope I never forget that part either. The shock on his face was priceless. It was almost, almost worth it to be sent home early."

"Speaking of which, I'm late because there was an accident on the way home so you need to leave if you're going to make it to work on time."

One of the good things about working opposite shifts at the same place is having the exact same commute so I always know when the roads are blocked.

I groan and slowly pull myself up from the couch. I'm exhausted now after the living room battle where I saved the world. Or at least our apartment.

Stretching my arms above me, I reach over and point to the kitchen. "There are tons of leftovers in the fridge if you're hungry."

Ellie gasps and jumps up from the couch, racing to the fridge with much more pep in her step than I feel. "From what?"

"Tucker overdid it with lunch." I lean down to my daughter. "Give me a hug, baby. I've got to go to work."

Her little arms wrap around my legs in a giant hug. Kody takes it as his cue and wraps his arms around my neck. I will never take these snuggles for granted. Not ever.

"Oooooh, I love all the love from you guys," I coo. "Now give me a kiss."

They both comply before turning back to their toy cars. I guess they've moved on to a racing game now. I swear, nothing holds their attention for long. Ahhh, the life of a three-year-old.

"Alright, I'm out," I shout to my roommate.

Ellie just waves, her face already stuffed with leftovers.

"Look at you living large with a cold quesadilla in your mouth," I chide.

She flips me the bird before swallowing. "Tell Tucker to bring Thai next time. That shit's expensive and I'm hormonal."

I shake my head and make my way out the door, careful to lock it behind me.

We may not be living large, but at least we've got each other.

CHAPTER EIGHT

TUCKER

I love it when I kick ass on the ice. Although tonight doesn't hold nearly as much luster as it normally does. Sure, the Glaze wiped the floor with the Slingers, winning with a score of five-to-two, but it wasn't even a fair fight. For some reason, none of San Antonio's starting lineup were even there.

I'm not complaining. Winning the first preseason game is always a good indicator of what's to come. And as a bonus, I get to hang out with one of my best buddies tonight. Which is also weird because Liam Tremblay is on track for retirement due to his age and a shoulder injury. He usually doesn't even suit up, so for him to be on the first line during preseason is some strange shit.

I honk as I drive up. Liam shoves his phone in his pocket, and ambles toward my brand new Porsche Cayenne. I may be a dad now, but that doesn't mean I can't do it in style.

Liam whistles as he folds his big body inside. "Nice ride. When did you get this?"

"Couple days ago. Decided I needed something a little bigger that comes with a better safety rating."

"So you went with a Porsche? That's pricy, man. You got the decked-out model too, didn't you?"

He runs his hand over the center console, as I pull out of the parking lot. The longer he does it, the more uncomfortable I start to feel. "You want me to leave you two alone so you can give the car a few more lover's caresses?"

Liam playfully shoves me. "Shut up, man. I've been thinking about upgrading lately so I've got cars on my mind."

"You planning on getting rid of that old ass truck? Never thought I'd see the day."

"Yeah, well, it's great to help people move but harder to transport ready-made food."

"Sounds like this chef thing is starting to take off."

Liam isn't just a good cook; he's fucking phenomenal. Everything he makes is like eating at a five-star restaurant. Now that retirement is looming, he's starting to make YouTube cooking videos designed for the athlete that needs more than the three small bites you'd get at an actual Michelin-rated establishment. If he's looking to transport food, though, sounds like it's turning into something more than he expected.

"Nah. I'm still working on the videos and stuff but every once in a while I help Paul out at the bar when he has an event," Liam explains. "It would be nice not to have to make more than one trip."

Damn. I miss that bar. It was my favorite place to be off the ice when I lived there.

Liam rolls his arm reminding me how unusual it is for me to be seeing him tonight.

"How's that shoulder hanging?"

He shakes his head but answers honestly. "Fucking hurts, man."

"Well yeah. You haven't been checked like that in what, a year?"

"About that. Since before surgery."

"I tried to keep everyone off you," I say with a shake of my head. "I warned them you were post-surgery and not a starter but you know how Maksim is."

"A fucking hothead?"

I laugh because he's right. "I was going to say aggressive on the ice, but we'll go with hothead. Also, not to be insensitive—"

"Which you've never worried about before."

"—but what the fuck, man?" I ask, dying to know what has him suiting up. "No offense to you, but how did you even end up on the ice? I had to check the line-up twice when I saw your name because I didn't believe it was you."

Liam starts laughing and I know something major has gone down. "Dude, the most god-awful stomach bug has been working its way through the team."

"Aw." I purse my lips in a fake pout. "A little upset tummy has those losers staying home?"

"No man. It's bad." Liam snorts a little. Damn. This must be good. "It's wiped out half the team so far, but It started with Gomez. He started feeling bad during practice. He ran off the ice to barf in a trash can."

I laugh at that fucker having to hurl during drills. It was bound to happen at some point. He probably has a hangover at practice more times than not.

"You laugh now, but it gets so much worse. He was heaving so hard, he started shitting himself." Liam guffaws, and I laugh even harder at the visual image. "When he finally stopped throwing up, he went straight into the showers, fully clothed to clean himself of his own filth. The janitorial staff was so pissed."

"Ohmygod, that's classic."

"But then..." Liam is laughing so hard, he has to stop to breathe before continuing. "Then, he started throwing up in the shower and the same thing happened. So he laid there butt naked on the tile floor with the water running over him while he barfed and shit everywhere for like half an hour. The locker room smelled so bad. They were still trying to get rid of the stink when we left."

We're both laughing so hard now I can barely see the road. Liam wipes tears from his eyes. This is the funniest shit I've heard in a long time. Once we finally get ourselves under control again, I still have questions.

"Is he still laying in the shower or did he finally get better? Don't stop now, man. Tell me more."

"Eventually Coach Diaz had pity on him and took him home. But I'm pretty sure he barfed in Coach's truck—" And the laughter starts up again "... So we're waiting for Coach to go down for the count, too."

"I was wondering why Diaz wasn't here."

"Yep. He sat in his car breathing all those germs for like an hour just trying to get Gomez home. Coach is next to get sick and none of us wanna be on a plane with him when it starts coming out both ends."

By the time we drive up to the hotel entrance, we're practically howling with laughter. I like my new teammates, but I miss the guys I used to play with. We had a connection and a camaraderie I may never experience again.

Pulling ourselves together, we climb out of my new vehicle and I hand the keys to the valet making sure to tip him. It's not that I don't trust he'll take care of my new car. I guess I just understand the value of being a good tipper now that I've seen what that money is used for sometimes.

"Thank you, sir," the valet says, his eyes lighting up at seeing the Benjamin.

"No problem." I clap him on the shoulder. "Thanks for doing this."

Meeting Liam on the other side of the car, I see his confusion about me taking him to a hotel.

"This is a hotel," he says as we make our way through the sliding doors.

"An astute observation."

"Why are we at a hotel? I thought we were going to a local dive."

"Relax, dude. I'm not here to have my wicked way with you. I wanna introduce you to someone."

We wind our way through the lobby. It always impresses me how the designers were able to bring the outdoors to the inside in a way that feels calming and peaceful.

My awe is short lived, however, since it doesn't take long to reach our destination.

Instead of grabbing a table, we sit at the bar, further confusing Liam. All of this is out of character for the guy he used to know. But this is a different kind of situation. If he's perplexed now, he's about to get the shock of his life.

"What can I get ya?"

It's not Lacy serving us, but I know she's here somewhere. That's okay. I can wait. The anticipation of what's happening is clearly killing Liam which only makes it more fun for me in the end.

"I'll take an IPA," I say.

"Draft?"

I nod in acknowledgement as Liam says, "That seems awfully light for you. Don't you normally drink scotch?" More bewilderment from my friend.

"I'm driving your ass around, remember, so I can't go heavy. Drink up."

"Whiskey. Neat, please."

The bartender nods and we settle in to wait. When I hand over my credit card to start a tab, that's when Liam finally cracks, cocking an eyebrow at me.

"Okay what gives? You're voluntarily paying tonight so I know something's wrong."

"Nothing's wrong. I figured you might like me to treat you this one time before all the bombs I'm about to drop on you."

He crosses his arms over his chest, like he's prepping himself for the worst. "That sounds ominous."

"Quite the opposite actually." I grab my phone from my pocket and swipe it open. Quickly, I pull up the picture of Sutton and slide it across the bar for him to see.

Liam studies the picture for a few seconds longer than I anticipated. "Who's this?" he finally asks.

"My daughter."

Liam's wide eyes go back and forth between the picture and me. "No shit?"

"No shit."

The bartender places our drinks in front of us and I take a sip of my beer. Liam doesn't even notice his whiskey, still looking at the picture, completely taken aback. Bomb dropped and mission accomplished. Man, I miss messing with him. He's so easy.

"How the fuck did that happen?" he finally asks.

I roll my eyes. "Well when a man and woman like each other—"

"I know that part, douchebag." He shoves me. "How do you have a, what, three-year-old?" I nod. "A three-year-old when you've never had a baby."

"Morty."

Liam opens his mouth and then shuts it. "Now I'm confused. Do you have the kid or does Morty have the kid or do you have a kid with Morty?"

"I do. Morty was emailed multiple times by my baby mama when she was pregnant, and he never bothered to pass along the information. I only found out because I randomly ran into Lacy again."

Liam whistles low. "That is some crazy shit. What did Morty say about it?"

"Made up fucking excuses about how many times he gets emails like that and what a waste of time and resources it is to pursue it. It was all bullshit. The least he could do is ask me if I've had relations and if it could be true."

Liam snorts a laugh. "Relations?"

"I got a kid out of it. It feels weird to call it fucking."

Finally noticing his drink, Liam raises his glass to his lips to take a long sip. "And Morty?"

"Fired him that night. I was so pissed that I missed three years of my daughter's life because he made the decision to dismiss Lacy's claims without even asking me. Hell, I'm still pissed."

"I can imagine," Liam says with a slow nod.

What he's not saying is "I told you so," which I'm grateful for. Morty doesn't have the best reputation around the league, but he got the basics of the job done and he came cheap when I was a rookie. That part seemed important in the beginning. Once I realized why he was so cheap, I could have canned him, but I felt bad that I was one of his only real clients. Now I know why.

Lacy finally rounds the corner and I feel my heart pick up speed. It's weird how I feel lighter just knowing she's here. Like my whole body seems to calm whenever she's around. Well, when she's not threatening to kick me in the balls.

She's carrying a few liquor bottles and doesn't notice us as she begins putting them on their proper shelves.

"How long have you known anyway?" Liam asks, not noticing my change in demeanor. Not that I'm jumping up and down or anything.

"A few days. Hell, I just told my own mother today. You're like the third person who knows."

He leans in and lowers his voice. "Then how do you know she's yours?"

"Besides the fact that she's the spitting image of my mother at this age? I don't know man," I answer honestly. "I can't explain it, but I just know. Her mom doesn't want anything from me and is actually pretty pissed I'm back. Or at least she was. She's cooling off a bit. But every time I look at Sutton I just feel like I've been sucker punched. You'll see when you meet her someday. You'll know it, too."

"You're going to get a DNA test, though, right?" Liam looks at me with concern. I suspect I'm going to get that a lot for a while. It's no secret that there are puck bunnies out there who prey on hockey players for the sole purpose of securing a fancy lifestyle. But this isn't that. It's not Lacy's agenda. And we'll prove it soon enough. "You don't want to get attached and then find out later it's not true anyway."

"Oh yeah. My attorney is already working on paperwork so I can get child support started right away and all that legal crap."

Liam shakes his head and furrows his brow. "You seem awfully determined to give away your money."

I glance over to make sure Lacy isn't listening. When I know the coast is clear, I level with my best work friend. "You didn't see the shithole they're living in, Liam. It's a two bedroom for two moms and their two kids. The kitchen looks like it'll catch on fire at any moment. I'm pretty sure I saw a family of roaches building their dream home behind the TV. And I don't like the idea of Lacy walking through that parking lot in the middle of the night."

"So what, you're just going to try to rescue them?"

"Oh hell no. I don't know Lacy well, but I can guarantee she'd have my balls before I could even do that."

"Before you could do what?"

Speak of the devil...

"We were just talking about you."

I flash her my most charming smile. It doesn't work.

"I figured." She places her hands on the bar and leans forward. "What are you doing here, Tucker? I finally got rid of you like three hours ago."

Her words say she's pissed, but her eyes tell a different story. If I'm not mistaken, she's losing some of her anger toward me.

I cover my heart with my hand. "Lacy, you wound me."

"Mmhmm."

"Alright I give," I say dropping the act. "I knew you were working and wanted a good friend of mine to meet you, now that we're all going to be in each other's lives permanently."

She narrows her eyes at me. "That's still up for debate."

Liam laughs at her fiery attitude. "I like her already." Holding out his hand, he introduces himself before I get the chance to. "Liam Tremblay. Former teammate of this asshole right here."

Taking his big paw in her small hand, she gives him the smile I wanted. *Rude.*

"Lacy Hawkins. Former lover and current baby mama."

"Nice to meet you. You've got a cute daughter."

Liam smiles again and I'm starting to get irritated with all the niceties. These two love to give me shit individually so maybe it wasn't such a hot idea to introduce them and let them form an alliance.

Lacy's face lights up at Liam's compliment. "Yeah, she's pretty great. No thanks to this one."

She gestures at me, and I hold my hands up defensively. "Don't blame me. I didn't know. Besides, you gave her a solid base before I could come in and screw her up. Hopefully it sticks."

"Oh good," Lacy deadpans. "Four days in and you're already planning to be the fun dad that never disciplines, aren't you?"

"What could my sweet little baby girl possibly ever do wrong?"

Lacy drops her chin to her chest and looks over at Liam to address him instead of me. Again. "He's going to undo all the good things I've done, isn't he?"

Liam chuckles and brings his glass to his lips again. "Watching him parent is going to be interesting, that's for sure."

Lacy shakes her head as she grabs a shot glass and fills it with tequila before shooting it right in front of us, wiping her mouth and then grumbling, "Lord help us," before turning away and tending to the next customer.

CHAPTER NINE

LACY

I blink my eyes at the continuous smack on my face and begin swatting at whatever keeps hitting me.

"Mama."

A little voice starts to break through my dreams, but I'm still trying to get the smacking to stop.

"Mama," the voice says more forcefully, and I finally wake up enough to realize what's happening. Sutton is patting my face. In the middle of the night. Why is Sutton patting my face in the middle of the night?

Peeling my eyes open, I rub the heel of my hands in my eyes to clear out the sleep.

"What's going on, baby girl?"

I reach over and just as I realize how warm she is, she hiccups a small sob.

"I no feel good, Mama."

Sitting straight up, I grab my daughter. She's burning up.

Fully awake now, I pick her up and race to the kitchen, setting her on the counter before rifling through the cabinet.

"Come on, come on," I grumble until I finally find what I'm looking for. "Ah ha!"

Popping the thermometer under her arm, I smooth down Sutton's hair as she leans against me, her little cheeks bright red.

"Does your tummy hurt?" She moves her head back and forth against my chest. "Does your head hurt?" That gets me a nod.

I snatch a sippy cup out of the cabinet, careful not to jostle her too much as I fill it and screw the lid on tight. She takes it from me and begins drinking but quickly pushes it away, a small grimace on her face like it tasted rotten. It's then I notice her nose is running, too.

I only have time to wipe her face off before the thermometer finally beeps.

103.4.

Quickly I add the degree and realize how high her fever actually is.

Shit. I've got to get some medicine in her and fast.

I find the last of our baby Motrin and suck it into the syringe we got at the doctor's office a couple years ago. There's not enough medicine to make a full dose, but it's at least a start until one of us can get to the store.

"Go ahead and take this baby." She sucks it down and licks her lips. She's so pale and her eyes seem dull. I've got to get this fever down fast.

Scooping her up in my arms, we head toward the bathroom. "Come on baby, let's get you a quick bath."

"No Mama." Sutton starts to cry, her little head laying limp against my shoulder.

"I know baby, but it'll make you feel better."

Setting her on the floor, I run the bath water a little warmer than lukewarm. I need to get this fever down, but I don't want to shock her system, either.

Sutton continues to cry, her wails getting louder when I strip her and put her in the bath.

"It's cold, Mama," she cries, breaking my heart right in two.

"I'm so sorry, baby. We've got to get your fever down. We'll just be in here for a few minutes."

I use a washcloth to run cool water over her back and neck as she shivers. I can only imagine how miserable she is. If there was any way I could change places with her I would.

Having woken her up, Ellie stumbles in, wiping at her eyes from the brightness. "What's going on?"

"She's got a really high fever, Ellie."

I can hear the panic in my voice. Apparently ,Ellie can too, because she's suddenly wide awake, too.

"How high?"

"Over 104."

Sutton begins to cough. It's deep, too deep, sounding like it's coming from the bottom of her lungs. She almost sounds like a seal except for a small wheezing noise when she breathes in. My skin prickles. Something is very wrong.

"Lacy, I don't like the sound of that," Ellie warns.

"Neither do I."

"I think you need to go to the ER."

I look up at her, panic filling my whole body. "I can't afford that."

"She's got Medicaid."

"No, don't you remember? That signature page got lost in the mail, so they denied her and I had to start over. They haven't processed the new paperwork yet."

"Shit."

I turn back to Sutton when she coughs again, her whole body shaking from the force of it.

"I don't think you have a choice, Lacy," Ellie presses. "She doesn't look good."

My brain is spinning. I can't seem to figure out how to make a decision. If I take her and it's just a cold, I'm out hundreds of dollars I don't have. If I don't take her and it's serious, she could die.

"What do I do, Ellie? I can't... you have to decide for me. My brain can't figure this out."

"I know. You're in panic mode. Go to the twenty-four-hour emergency clinic. You know the one? By Piggly Wiggly?"

"I don't know when we'll be back and you have to work tomorrow."

"I'll call in if I have to. Or you'll be back before I leave. It doesn't matter. Take her."

"Ellie," I whisper. "I'm so scared about the money. What if it's nothing and then we can't cover rent because of a virus?"

"Lacy," she puts her hands on my shoulders, knowing where my brain is at. She's been there, too. "I know you are. We've lived like this for a long time. But Tucker is here now. It's time he stepped up."

"Tucker." I close my eyes and drop my chin to my chest. "I forgot about Tucker."

"You need to call him. Like now."

She makes sense. He's Sutton's father and this is serious. I need to call him. But...

"Wait, isn't he on a road trip? Or is that next week? I don't know if he's in town."

"If he's gone, he'd still want to know. He can fly back if he needs to."

I nod, the entire situation feeling like I'm dreaming and not all at the same time. It's so surreal. "Yeah. Yeah, okay."

"Get her out of the bath and get her dressed. I'll get a bag with her stuff ready."

Feeling better now that Ellie has helped me come up with a plan, I quickly dry my daughter off, her poor body still radiating heat. Ellie helps me get her to the car and into her car seat.

Thankfully, traffic is light at this time of night so I'm able to get on the road within seconds. As soon as I hit a stop light, I open the phone and click on Tucker's name, putting it on speaker since I can't get a Bluetooth connection in my car.

It rings three times and I'm about to curse under my breath about not being able to reach him when I hear a groggy, "Hello? Lacy?"

"Tucker." His name comes out sounding like a gasp.

"What's wrong." The groggy disappears immediately. "Lacy, what's going on."

"Sutton is sick. Really sick. I need you to meet me at the emergency clinic."

I hear sheets and blankets rustling around and the sounds of him jumping out of bed.

"I'm on my way."

CHAPTER TEN

TUCKER

The emergency clinic is easy to find, its bright lights standing out amongst all the dark buildings surrounding it. I throw my car into park, thankful I went with the Porsche. That sucker can really get up and go when it needs to and tonight it needed to.

I race through the doors and straight to the desk. The woman sitting at the front desk doesn't look surprised to see my disheveled self.

"Hi, um…" I squint my eyes to see the name on her badge. "…Karen. Hi Karen. My daughter is here. She's three. Sutton. Sutton… Hawkins." Guilt gnaws at me. What kind of a father has to try and remember his daughter's last name?

"Oh yes." Karen is completely unfazed by my panic. "Let me bring you back."

She leaves her perch and the secured door to the back suddenly opens up, her smiling face peeking through. "Follow me."

We pass a few rooms on the right, a long, built-in desk with several staff members sitting on the left. It pisses me off that they're just sitting calmly and not feeling the frenzy that's racing through my body.

"Here we are."

Karen gestures to room number seven and I step inside and take in the scene.

Lacy is trying to hold Sutton who is crying and squirming around like she can't get comfortable.

"It's okay, baby. I know you don't feel good," Lacy murmurs.

She's so fucking beautiful. It's the wrong time to notice something like this, but I can't help it. Lacy, as a mother, nurturing our daughter, hits me in the gut in a way I wasn't expecting. A way that makes me want to take her into my arms and make everything better. I can't do that, though. It's not my place. But it is my place to help my daughter.

"Hey," I say gently as I approach.

Lacy's eyes, filled with tears, turn to me. "Hey." She sniffles. "Thanks for coming."

"Of course I came. Our daughter is sick." Pulling up the chair next to them, I sit down, not quite sure what I'm supposed to do now that I'm here. "Hard night, huh?"

She wipes under her eyes. "I feel better now that we're here. It helps that the staff isn't freaking out so I guess she's not critical or anything. But yeah. This is pretty scary."

Lacy continues to struggle with Sutton. I reach out my hands. "May I?"

She considers for a second before handing our daughter over.

"Hey kiddo," I say gently. "Feeling kind of crappy, huh?"

Sutton calms almost immediately and leans her head on my chest.

I can feel the fever through my clothes and hear her raspy intake of breath. And yet, I can't help realizing this is the first time I've held my daughter. My eyes close involuntarily and I squeeze them tight, trying to hold back the moisture. I didn't expect it to feel like this. This... protective desire. This overwhelming joy.

"What?" Lacy asks.

"Just... Thank you for letting me hold her."

A look of understanding crosses Lacy's face. A connection and realization that we're in this together. When it comes to Sutton at least, we're a team. "Why don't you sit down on the table with her so you can lean back. That way you both can get comfortable."

I do as she says and situate myself on the thin pad. "Have they come to check on her yet?"

"They checked her vitals. Her oxygen was a little low, but I guess not dangerously so, or they would have her hooked up to a bunch of stuff. They swabbed her throat. That's part of why she was so fussy when you walked in."

I sit in awe with my daughter in my arms. I run my hand over her soft hair, down her warm back. I kiss the top of her head, over and over. I can't stop myself from holding her tight. This is where she belongs, right here in my arms.

Feeling her eyes on me, I glance at Lacy. I can't read her expression, but she looks almost baffled. Is it really so strange for me to be here? I want to ask her what she's thinking but I don't get the chance because the doctor finally comes in.

"Hey family. I hear you have a sick one." I start to shift so he can inspect Sutton more fully but he stops me. "You're okay. I can hear her lungs just fine like this." He untangles his stethoscope from around his neck and tucks them in his ears to listen. "Just stay relaxed there, Dad."

Dad. It's the first time anyone has called me that. I wasn't fully prepared for how it would feel to hear myself referred to by that name.

"Daddy?" Sutton murmurs in her sleep and my heart stops.

My eyes immediately shoot to Lacy. She looks as stunned as I do. Then her lips quirk up into a smirk and she shrugs one shoulder as if to say it's okay. That we can run with whatever Sutton wants.

"Okay." The doctor pulls away and slings the stethoscope

around his neck again. "Her swab came back positive for RSV so that's what's going on."

Lacy gasps. "How bad is it?"

"It could be better, but her oxygen levels are okay at this point. You caught it pretty quick, which is good. Do you have a humidifier at home?"

Lacy shakes her head.

"You're gonna need to get one of those if you can. She needs to stay as hydrated as possible and have lots of rest. No going anywhere unless absolutely necessary."

"For how long?"

"A week. Sometimes longer. Does she go to daycare?"

"No."

I can see the wheels turning in Lacy's head. I'm not sure what that's about, though.

"Good, good. We don't have to worry about infecting other kids." He taps a few times on his tablet as he speaks. "It'll be easy to rest at home then. There are no prescription meds for RSV but use acetaminophen for the fever and saline drops are okay for her nose if it bothers her. Hopefully it'll help. Keep her hydrated, get a humidifier, treat her fever like normal and if she has any breathing problems, bring her in ASAP. Otherwise, give her about a week and she'll be right as rain."

"Um, how contagious is she?" Lacy fidgets with her fingers.

"RSV is very contagious among kids. That's why I'm glad she doesn't go to daycare. We don't need an outbreak."

He answers the rest of our questions, mostly about what to look for in case Sutton gets worse, and then leaves us alone. I'm wondering if we need to stay longer because Lacy doesn't look good. Without looking at me, she gathers their things, so I guess we're leaving.

I'm still holding Sutton, not willing to give her up yet, while Lacy checks out at the front.

Karen is at the front, still looking completely unruffled by our near emergency and going through the rigmarole of discharging us. "Do you want to pay it in full now?"

Lacy flinches. "Um, can I pay a hundred dollars now and be billed for the rest?"

"Sure."

She takes the card out of Lacy's hand and with the press of a few buttons, the machine makes a very unhappy sound.

Karen clears her throat and shifts on her feet. "I'm so sorry but your card is declined."

Lacy squeezes her eyes tightly for a second, embarrassment coming off her in waves. "Sorry about that. Can we try it for fifty?"

Now I'm the one who is embarrassed. *What the fuck am I doing just standing here?*

"Wait. Hold on," I interrupt. "I apologize. I wasn't paying attention. How much is the total?"

Karen rattles off a number that's way more than it should be with insurance. Then it hits me.

Does Sutton not have medical insurance?

I table that thought for later and hand over my credit card.

"Tucker, what are you doing?" I know Lacy isn't used to people helping her, except maybe her roommate. But this is different.

"I'm being Sutton's father."

She lowers her voice, as if it's going to make a difference on who hears what we're saying. "Which means you're responsible for fifty percent of her medical expenses."

I lean in and lower mine, too. "And three years of back child support. Consider this my first payment."

Karen looks back and forth at us, wide-eyed.

"Sorry," I say sheepishly. "I'm sure you see lots of family drama working at night."

"I'd actually call this a lack of drama since there's no scream-ing, but it's not my business anyway."

Suuuuuure. I'm sure she'll be spilling the tea about this one with her friends later this morning. Fingers crossed she's not a hockey fan.

Karen runs my card quickly and before I know it, I'm signing the receipt. Now that I'm paying more attention, I realize there's more Lacy and I need to talk about and soon.

"Thank you, Tucker," Lacy says quietly as I hand Karen back her pen.

"Nothing to thank me for." Turning to face her, I shift Sutton in my arms and we move away from the front desk. "You know you can't go back to your apartment tonight, right?"

"Why not?"

"She'll get Kody sick."

Lacy's shoulders sink. "Shit. I forgot about that."

I can see the gears turning in her head. She's stressing over where they're going to stay and probably how they're both going to work in this situation. At least I can help with one of those problems.

"Lacy, you're coming to my place."

She looks like I've given her the shock of her life. "We can't do that."

"Why not?"

"We just met you."

I roll my eyes. "And I have a squeaky-clean background. You know this. I also have a guest bedroom with a bed big enough for both of you, because I'm sure you're not going to want her to be alone tonight, I upgraded my cable with all the kid channels the other day, and I have a stocked fridge."

Lacy gnaws on her bottom lip as she considers me. "I just feel so bad leaving Ellie in a lurch like this. Fuck."

"What do you mean?"

"I'm Ellie's childcare and she's mine. Day care is really expensive, even with the government programs it's more than we can really afford, and without each other, we don't have anyone to watch the kids."

For probably the hundredth time since this whole situation started, I'm awed by how delicately their whole family structure is set up. How in the hell single moms make ends meet and find ways to make things work is beyond me. It's time I step up and do my part.

"Don't worry about that," I reassure her. "I'll get it squared away."

"Tucker—"

I hold my hand up to stop her. "Don't say another word about it. Just come back to my place with me, at least for tonight. That'll buy you some time to figure things out, right?"

She stares at the floor, hands on her hips. "Fine."

"Yeah?"

"Yeah."

I can feel how big my smile is. I hate that Sutton's sick, but I love that I'm going to get to spend some time with the two of them.

After finally situating Sutton in her car seat, despite her resistance to being put down, Lacy follows me home. On the way, I make a mental list of things to get from the store before I can grab a nap. Practice tomorrow, or later this morning, is going to be brutal, but it's worth it.

CHAPTER ELEVEN

LACY

The soft sounds of Sutton's snores are almost hypnotic. Add the fact that her head is on my lap and I'm stroking her silky hair, and I feel like I could fall asleep sitting up.

Or it could be just plain old exhaustion. We're all tired from a long night in the ER and Sutton's continuous coughing and fever. Thankfully Tucker made sure we have enough children's fever reducer to last through Sutton's future children.

I don't know why I'm still watching *Paw Patrol*. Probably because I'm as tired as my daughter is and the remote is just out of reach. I don't have enough energy to move that far.

It's not like I'm paying attention anyway. My mind keeps trying to crunch my bank account numbers and I don't know how we're going to make ends meet. Missing an entire week of work means we're going to go without for a long while. I'm just not sure what is the lesser of two evils—being late on rent or not eating. Maybe our landlord will give us an extension on the rent. Things will be tight for a couple months, but they'll even out eventually.

Of course, this isn't taking into consideration if Ellie has to take the next week off because there's no one to watch Kody. If neither one of us is working...

I sigh and lay my head back against the couch allowing my eyes to fall closed as I think.

I could always ask Tucker for help. Technically he owes me more than three years of back child support. But...

But what?

But I'm stubborn. I don't trust him yet. I don't want to start relying on him only to have him disappear again. And maybe I don't want to appear vulnerable in front of him either.

And yet...and yet.

My mind wanders back to that moment in the emergency center when he was holding Sutton and kissing the top of her head. The love he has for her was so apparent, it made my heart ache for what could have been if only his asshole agent hadn't taken our choices away from us. Would we be a family now if Tucker had known from the beginning? Would we have found a way to make it work?

I think back to our single night together all those years ago, and remember how he made me feel. Our connection was more than just physical. He was everything I never knew I wanted in a man. Powerful and strong, but gentle with my needs. Well, unless I instructed him otherwise. He was considerate of my wants and desires, never pushing me too far and yet giving me exactly what I wanted. He was clever and fun to be with. We just...fit. He was the kind of guy I could see myself falling for.

The kind of guy I could see myself falling for *now*. But too much has happened since then. Too many lives are at stake now if it were to go south. It doesn't matter if I'm attracted to Tucker. It's not just about me and protecting my heart anymore.

For the millionth time since I was cut off, I wish I could call my mom and pick her brain about this. Or my sister. Even as kids, she was always the logical, level-headed one. She didn't let her pride get in the way of doing what's right. She'd be able to help me figure this all out. But I haven't talked to her since I told her I was pregnant. Haven't talked to any of them. My older brothers made sure I knew how sinful they thought I was, and my parents cut off all contact between me and my younger sibling practically the minute they found out. She's only a couple years younger than me but I'm sure her college experience was very different after my own "mistake". I feel bad about that, but hope she's been able to find her way.

I don't have time to dig deeper into my own issues because the door opens quietly and Tucker walks in.

He takes in the scene; me and Sutton on the couch, a small smile gracing his lips. Lips that are way too kissable for their own good.

I shake that thought out of my head. Apparently being tired makes me horny.

"Hey," he whispers and places a bag on the coffee table. If my nose is working correctly, I'd guess he brought Italian home for lunch.

"What's that?" I gesture toward the sack where the scent of basil and fire roasted tomatoes is coming from.

"Lunch. I figured you'd be too exhausted to make anything, so I got some Italian."

I pat myself on the back for my olfactory senses working correctly. Wonder if there's a way to make money off correctly guessing what things are by their smell. Probably not.

"I figured noodles might be the best choice for Sutton in case her tummy's bothering her," Tucker says and gently strokes her hair. "So I got her some spaghetti."

As much as I hate to admit it, I'm moved by his thoughtfulness. It's unexpected, but not unwelcome. Once again, I have to battle my feelings of attraction and focus on what's important here.

"Thank you. That was sweet."

He drops down on the other couch and stretches out his long legs. The dark circles under his eyes look even deeper with the blinds closed so Sutton can sleep better.

"You look exhausted," I finally say.

His head pops up and he blinks a few times. "I'm not complaining."

"I am," I say with a smirk. "I'm sorry I woke you up last night. I can't imagine how hard it was to do your practice...things...on such little sleep."

"Practice things?" he jokes.

"I don't have the slightest idea what you do at work when you aren't on television."

"I'm too tired to explain so we'll just go with practice things." Running a hand through his floppy hair, he shifts on the couch. "Seriously, Lacy. Never be sorry for calling me about our daughter. Emergency or not, I want to know."

I'm not sure how to feel about this. Why has he taken to us so quickly? There was no hesitation on his part, no question, no time to go off and process this huge change in his life. He just jumped right in. I don't understand it. I'm not used to people wanting to help. It's disconcerting.

Oblivious to my internal conflict, he leans forward and begins riffling through the bags. "Hungry?"

"I could eat."

"We've got spaghetti, fettucine Alfredo, and eggplant parmesan."

"Do you always order more food than you need?"

"I eat a lot. Plus I wasn't sure if you're a vegetarian."

I huff out a laugh. "I'm way too poor to be picky about my diet."

He pauses his movements, eyes trained on the coffee table in front of him.

"What?" I'm not sure what shifted his mood so quickly.

"I don't know how to ask this without sounding like a dick."

"I work at a bar. I'm used to people asking shitty questions. If there's something you want to know, I'd rather you be blunt about it."

"Why doesn't Sutton have insurance?"

Speaking of...Sutton cries out in her sleep, likely having a fever dream.

"Shh, shh, shh." I stroke her hair more and rub her back to calm her down. "You're okay. I'm right here."

She settles back into her sleep relatively quickly which brings me back to Tucker's question. It's an easy answer to a not so easy situation.

"Hourly jobs rarely offer insurance plans and if they do, they're terrible."

"I figured that part. But why doesn't she have Medicaid? Do you not qualify?"

This is the part that makes me frustrated so much of the time. It's hard being poor. There are so many hoops to jump through constantly, and if you miss one of them, or someone accidentally drops one of them, you have to start all over.

"She had it until a few months ago."

"Then what happened?"

The same thing that always happens in our shitty excuse of an apartment. "Our mail carrier has a habit of putting the wrong mail in the wrong boxes. It happens all the time. I've complained to the postmaster and they always say they'll talk to that mail carrier but it never makes a difference. Anyway, I always take any mail that's not mine to the right apartment and shove it under the door, but apparently I'm the only one in my complex that has any kind of moral compass. I've had more than one package disappear and then I have to complain to the seller that I never got it. Sometimes I get a replacement. Sometimes I don't. It's obnoxious."

"People are jerks sometimes."

"You're telling me. Anyway, you have to recertify for Medicaid every year. Basically prove that we still qualify. Since I uploaded all the paperwork into the online system for her recertification, they mailed me the signature page."

"And you never got it."

I tap my nose. "Ding, ding, ding."

"Shit."

"By the time I realized her Medicaid had been cut off, it was too late. I had to start the whole process over again. I'm waiting for them to call me to do the interview so I can tell them we are, in fact, still poor."

Tucker wipes his hand down his face like he's distressed by the whole situation. For some reason, I feel like I need to comfort him about it.

"It's going to be fine," I say with more nonchalance than I feel. The whole thing is actually really irritating and taking up more time than I have. "As soon as they call me and process her paperwork, it'll backdate to the day I applied. I might have to file a couple appeals for any medical expenses, but they'll get it taken care of."

"That's not good enough for her." The vehemence in Tucker's voice surprises me. Is he really indignant on our behalf?

"No it's not," I agree. "Welcome to the wonderful world of government services. This is how it is."

"Not for long."

I narrow my eyes, hackles raising at his sudden change in demeanor.

"What do you mean by that?"

"I talked to my attorney today."

Anger surges through me. This is what I was most afraid of when I told him about Sutton. I want to jump up off this couch and scream at Tucker, yell that he has no right to start a custody battle with me. But I don't. Instead, I carefully slide out from under Sutton's head before stalking out of the room and down the hall.

Tucker follows right behind me. "Lacy, what's wrong?"

I ignore him, instead taking our small suitcase off the floor and putting it on the bed, grabbing the pile of dirty clothes I hadn't gotten around to washing yet.

"Seriously, Lacy. Why are you packing?"

"How could you do that?" I say with contempt.

"Do what?"

"Call your attorney."

A look of understanding crosses his face. Good of him to finally put together why I'm so pissed. "Lacy, stop! You haven't even let me tell you why I called him. Let me explain what we talked about."

He puts his hand on my arm, but I push him off and turn around quickly to confront him, arms crossed over my chest, eyes narrowed. "So tell me then. Why exactly did you call your attorney?"

"To order a DNA test."

I point at him. "Wrong answer." I turn back to my packing not even bothering to fold anymore. We need to get out of here.

"For the love of God, woman. Would you please let me finish before you jump to conclusions?"

I don't look up, continuing tossing clothes in the suitcase. "You've got about thirty seconds until I'm done packing and taking my daughter out of here, so you better make it good."

"Last night when I found out Sutton doesn't have insurance, I realized she could be on mine. It's a fantastic plan that wouldn't cost you a dime. But I can't just randomly add someone to the plan. I need proof. I assume I'm not listed on the birth certificate." It isn't a question. He knows I didn't list him as the father. The bed depresses as he sits on it, trying to get in my line of sight. I don't let him. "The insurance company requires proof of parentage, so a DNA test is the only option. My attorney has done this kind of thing before and has the ability to arrange for a private test. here. We don't even have to go to a lab. When the results are back in about a week, I will be able to add Sutton to my insurance because I'll have the proof they need to show she's my daughter."

With every word Tucker says, I feel myself calming down more, my frantic movements slowing. He's not trying to take Sutton away or take over our lives. He's trying to make sure she has access to medical care, no matter what Medicaid says.

I close my eyes and drop my chin to my chest in a mixture of defeat and shame. I can't believe I jumped to conclusions so quickly.

Taking a deep breath, I force out the words that are so hard for me to say. "I'm sorry. That's actually really nice."

"It's not *nice* to take care of my child, Lacy. It's the bare minimum of being a parent."

I nod in agreement because he's got a point. Ellie and I have had this conversation when the topic of her own deadbeat baby daddy comes up. He wants accolades for showing up every once in a while with a package of diapers that Kody doesn't even need. Says he should get credit for at least trying.

But Tucker isn't just trying, he's doing. It's not something I've seen anyone do in a long while and I'm not sure how to feel about it.

I don't have time to think too hard though before a noise in the other room has both of us running for the couch Sutton is sleeping on.

Tucker gets to her first and picks her up, pulling her to his big chest.

"It's okay." He pats her back gently as she coughs. "Get it all out. I got you."

I believe him when he says that. He's got her. But who's got me?

CHAPTER TWELVE

TUCKER

"That was a hell of a game, man." Maverick Hagen taps me on the helmet and pulls me into a hug after the traditional post-game greeting between teams.

"You weren't too shabby yourself. And this stadium." I let out a slow whistle as I glance around Vegas's state of the art arena. "This ain't no dive, is it?"

Maverick and I played together in college and make it a point to catch up whenever we run into each other. He's a good guy. Hell of a center and I suspect a damn good captain. I should probably be offended that I've never be chosen for leadership, what with my impeccable people skills, but honestly, I don't want the responsibility.

He chuckles low. "Can't complain, man. How you doing in Tampa? You liking the change of pace?"

"The pace is fine. It's cool to be so close to the beach. But I also found out I have a kid."

It's the first time I've shared that information with someone outside my team, except for Liam, and I can't help the huge smile. Maverick on the other hand, looks a bit shell shocked.

"I'm not really sure how to respond to that news. Is this a good thing?"

"It was a surprise for sure, but my daughter is just amazing. You got plans tonight? We can grab a beer and catch up. I've got a ton of pictures I can show you."

"As exciting as an entire camera roll of pictures sounds, I can't. This is the one night this week my woman is off work and I'm taking full advantage of having her to myself."

Lucky bastard. I'd love nothing more than to have some alone time with Lacy but considering how much venom she still spews my way, I don't see that happening any time soon.

"I hear ya. Next time you're in Florida, though, it's on."

He points at me as he skates toward his exit. "You got it. Have a safe trip home."

I head to the locker room, knocking a few knuckles with fans on my way through the tunnel. As soon as I strip off my jersey and pads, my phone rings. Weird. I guess I forgot to turn it off. Lucky it's on though, or I would have missed Lacy's call.

We've been on a road trip for almost a week, the girls still hanging out at my house while Sutton gets better. I've been the one to initiate all the phone contact so far, so it's strange for Lacy to reach out. I answer quickly, hoping Sutton didn't have a relapse. "Hey. Everything okay?"

"Yeah."

A strange sense of relief floods me and I wonder if it's a normal parenting thing to always worry about your kid. I should ask Lacy after she tells me what's so important that she reached out.

"I wanted to show you something. Can you switch to a video call or are you in the locker room?"

I look around and of course a few of our nudists are completely oblivious to everyone else around them. "Put your dicks away, guys," I call out. "I have to take this call!"

A few of them have the wherewithal to wrap a towel around

their waists. Maks is not one of them. He struts right over in all his birthday suit glory. "What's up?" He holds his arms out wide. "Don't want your woman to see what she's missing?"

"More like I don't want my kid to have nightmares. Put that shit away."

"Your kid?" Maks grimaces and drops his arms. "Damn boy. I didn't know you had one of those. I'm out."

I shake my head as he walks off to harass someone else, I'm sure.

As soon as we're in the clear, I let her know. "Okay, potential childhood trauma averted."

"You sure?" Lacy jokes. "No other teammates wanting to flaunt their manhood my direction?"

The fact that she isn't angry about the comment regarding her being "my woman" is not lost on me. I know it doesn't mean much that she didn't argue the point, but the fact that it wasn't even a priority for her to clarify with my friends seems like a step in the direction I'm hoping for. That direction being a chance to show her I'm not just a good dad, I can be a good date, too.

"The word manhood is stretching things a bit," I say as I switch to video chat.

What comes on the screen takes my breath away and makes me laugh at the same time. Sutton and Kody are wearing their new jerseys and trying to hit something around the floor with...

I squint to try and get a better look. "Are those giant plastic golf clubs?"

"It's the closest we could come to finding hockey sticks in the toy box."

"Oh, well, clearly I'm going to have to rectify that situation."

"Please don't bring anything labeled a stick into this house. That's always asking for trouble. The plastic hurts badly enough when I get nailed in the shin."

She reaches down, probably to rub her leg and I realize she has a solid point. I'll wait on the hockey sticks.

For now.

I keep watching as the kids chase what appears to be a soft baseball around, knocking each other out of the way as they swing. Lacy's right—their aim is way off. They don't need anything harder than plastic. Still, it's fun to watch.

Suddenly Sutton body checks Kody and he goes flying off the screen. A guffaw bursts out of me. "I see they were inspired by my amazing performance tonight."

"Yes," Lacy says straight-faced. "Because you're so easy to recognize with a helmet and thirty pounds of pads on."

I shrug with indifference. They're at least watching the game. Close enough. "She's feeling better?"

Kody pops back onto the screen and they're at it again.

"Much. Her cough is almost gone, so her pediatrician said we could come home."

My heart plummets as her words hit me right in the gut. I'm not sure why I didn't put it together that they're with Kody and rifling through toy boxes which means they're not at my place anymore.

"Wait. You moved back?"

The screen flips back around and I see Lacy's guilty face.

"Well yeah. We couldn't stay at your place forever."

"Why not?"

I knew the situation was temporary, but it never occurred to me that they'd actually leave. It makes no sense that the reality of the situation slipped my mind, but I was enjoying us all being together so much until I left for the road trip, I stopped thinking about it, and started assuming maybe it would be forever.

"Tucker..." Lacy starts but I cut her off.

"No really. Why not? Why couldn't you live with me?"

She sighs. "I don't think this is a conversation we need to have while you're in your locker room, still wearing your skates."

I know she's trying to deflect, but I won't let up.

"It's something we can talk about when I get home then?"

There's a fiery glint in her eyes and I know I'm about to lose this round. "There's nothing to talk about. This is where we live. As fun as it was to play house, I still have a job and responsibilities."

"And we still share a daughter," I argue.

"Right. We *share* her. Individually. Not jointly."

I feel like I've been punched. Somehow I know this is not about me, it's about Lacy's fear of me and all the havoc I could bring to her life. But that doesn't mean her words don't hurt. But it's not worth the fight when I have over a week left on the road. Nothing will get resolved over the phone.

I nod and purse my lips, tempering my anger before I say anything I'll regret.

"I get it. Listen I've gotta go, so give the kids a hug for me, okay?"

I don't wait for her to answer, just hang up. I'm not happy with the way things are starting to shape up. I just have to figure out how to make this work in a way that's good for everyone.

CHAPTER THIRTEEN

LACY

I open the door quietly, trying not to disturb anyone. These walls are paper thin and Ellie tends to be a light sleeper so I don't want to wake her up. Not that the bass thumping from the apartment down the hall hasn't already done the job, but I can at least try to be considerate.

As I walk through the door, though, I realize my attempts were for nothing. She's wide awake, laying on the couch, staring at the television.

I tilt my head to the side in question. "What are you doing up? Mr. Party-Hard down the hall wake you?"

She sits up and moves her legs so I can take a load off. "No. I don't work tomorrow and I wasn't tired so I thought I'd wait up for you."

"You weren't able to pick up anyone else's shift?"

"I didn't ask."

That's weird. Neither of us worked for a week so I've been freaking out about rent and she seems almost nonchalant. But it's been a long few days and I don't really want to think about it.

"How were the kids?"

Ellie smiles. "They just hate being apart, don't they? It takes them days to stop clinging to each other. They played all night, no fighting. And I thought there was going to be a mini-riot at bedtime when they had to separate."

That just confirms that this is where Sutton and I need to be. As nice as it was to get to know Tucker better, the situation wasn't real. This is. In this apartment with the people we've chosen as our family.

"I'm glad." I punch her on the leg lightly. "We really missed you guys when we were gone."

"We missed you, too. But it was good for you to spend time with Tucker. Get to know the father of your daughter a little bit. Maybe see if that chemistry is still there."

I ignore her suggestion and waggling eyebrows. No way am I admitting to her, or myself that she's bang on. Sexual attraction isn't the most important part of this situation and I'll be damned if I let it get in the way.

So I shrug nonchalantly. "I guess."

"What do you mean you guess?"

I stretch my legs out and clasp my hands, dropping them on my stomach. My feet are killing me. It feels good to not have any pressure on them. "I'm just still so mad he wasn't around, you know? He put me and Sutton in some really terrible situations and nothing he does now can make up for it."

"Is that really fair, though? He never knew you were pregnant. And as soon as he found out about Sutton, he fired the guy who kept the information from him."

I want to roll my eyes, but I can't because she's right. At this point, there's no denying it. "Logically I know that's true, but it's hard to give up the anger when I've held onto it for so long."

"And probably hard for you to let your walls down and let him in."

I look at her quizzically. "Walls? I don't have walls. I just don't trust him."

"But you trust me."

"Because you were here. He wasn't."

"And who's fault was that again?"

I pause and finally get what she's saying. I'm misdirecting my anger. Tucker didn't do anything wrong. If anything, he's done everything right since the second he found out about his daughter.

I look back to the TV. "Fine. You win. I have walls."

She nudges my knee. "Good for you. The first step is admitting it. Now you can start working on breaking them down."

"Yeah, that's not going to be my priority for a good long while. I've got a child to raise and bills to pay first."

"Speaking of..." Ellie gets up and grabs a flat package off the counter. Biting her bottom lip, she holds it out to me. It's clear she's not sure how I'm going to react to whatever this is. "This came for you today."

I take it out of her hands slowly. There's no postage. It's not a priority-mail box from the post office. But it's stamped with some delivery service logo right underneath my name. "Is this going to blow up in my face? Maybe scatter little penis glitter everywhere?"

Ellie laughs and sits back down. "Oh lord I hope not. Kody is getting a little too obsessed with his lately."

Holding the envelope away from my face, I get my fingers in position to open it. "Get the vacuum ready, just in case," I joke.

"We can't afford a vacuum," she mutters.

I pull the tab quickly, practically holding my breath as the top rips open.

Nothing happens.

"Well, that was anti-climactic," I mutter. It's just a small packet of papers and a note. Not a piece of glitter to be found.

Turning the pages right side up, I begin to read.

Lacy-

Sorry I couriered this over but I didn't want the check to get lost in the mail like everything else seems to.

"Check? What check?" I murmur.

Taking the paper clip off, a check made out to me falls onto my lap. I gasp when I see the amount.

"Holy fuck."

Ellie leans over my shoulder and puts her own spin on my bad language. "Oh my shit. We can afford a vacuum now. Who is that from?"

"Who do you think? Tucker."

"For what?"

I look down at the bottom left corner of the check. "Child support."

"Holy shit," she shouts and snatches the check out of my hands to inspect it more closely. "Is this for the whole year?"

Looking back at the note, I keep reading.

My attorney drew up these papers so we could get child support started and get Sutton on my medical insurance as soon as possible. It's great insurance since injuries are so common in my sport, and those benefits will extend to her.

Before you freak out, there's nothing about visitation or custody in the papers. All these papers do is mandate what I'm required to pay you in support every month. That's it. It gives you legal recourse if I disappear (which I won't) and makes it easier to get benefits if I were to drop dead on the ice (which I hope I won't). Everything in here is to protect you and Sutton. It's the least I can do.

While I hope we can get to some sort of custody agreement eventually, Sutton doesn't know me yet. Neither do you. I'd rather us all take this slow instead of forcing relationships in a harmful way. This is my way of extending an olive branch and showing you I'm in this for the long haul. I've already missed more than three years of her life. I don't want to miss a minute more.

If you have time in the next few days, I'd like to sit down and talk. There's more I want to discuss, but not through a note that some random courier dropped off. I want us to work together for the good of our daughter. I'm all in. I hope you are, too.

Tucker

Quickly I flip through the legal pages until I find what I'm looking for.

"Ohmygod," I breathe.

"What?" Ellie looks over my shoulder again, trying to see what I just discovered.

"This is one month's worth of child support."

"What?" Ellie screeches.

"I'm going to get this every month."

Dumbfounded, I look from the paper, to the check, to Ellie, and back to the paper. "What the fuck, Ellie? I can't accept this."

She looks at me like I've lost my mind. "Uh, you can and you will."

"No way." I throw my hands up. "It's like he's trying to make up for not being here by throwing money at us."

"Okay first of all, put the little bricks in your brain away again and really think this through. Lacy," she leans forward, forcing eye contact. "How much money do you think he makes?"

I have no idea so I take a guess. "A lot, maybe?"

"Right. Because he's a professional hockey player. They make bank." She scooches closer. "Forget about what you think his ulterior motives are. Legally, he's required to provide a portion of his paycheck for Sutton's care. *Legally.* That has nothing to do with you or your pride or making amends or anything."

"I know but... This is a lot of money."

"To us it is, because we're dirt poor. But to him? Hang on." She pulls out her phone and begins typing in some numbers.

"What are you doing?"

"Trying to figure something out. Just wait," she says dismissively. As soon as she's done whatever she's doing, she flips screens and opens a search. Just a few seconds later she turns the phone to me. "This is the average salary for a professional hockey player."

My eyes widen. "Wow. That's more than I thought."

"And this..." she closes the screen and holds up her calculator.

"… is what he probably makes based on the check he sent over."

I blink a few times as I try to get my thoughts in order. "What are you trying to say?"

"That he didn't even go above and beyond what the state requires him to pay. He did everything by the book."

"Well that was kind of shitty. He didn't even want to go above and beyond?"

She purses her lips and cocks her head at me. "Or he knew you'd react exactly like this and to make sure you couldn't throw it back in his face, he *did everything by the book*."

Seeing her point, I sigh. "Okay fine. You're right. But what the hell do I do with all this money?"

"I don't know. Put Sutton in daycare and go back to school to get your degree. Or get out of this shitty, roach filled apartment and find somewhere great to live."

"You said you don't mind the roaches."

"I lied. I don't like the crunch they make when I kill them so I just let them go."

That gets a smirk from me. Still, she's our family. I can't just ditch her. "I'm not moving out and leaving you and Kody behind."

"Then rent a bigger apartment that we can all move into. Or start a trust fund for Sutton. There are a million different possibilities." Ellie grabs my shoulders and gently shakes me. "I know it's overwhelming, but this is everything you never dared to dream of, Lacy. You don't have to worry where her next meal is going to come from anymore. You don't have to power through work when you're sick or pass on getting one of those expensive coffees when you're out. Hell, you don't even have to sign up for that Secret Santa tree at the Community Center anymore. Your whole life has changed for the better. Because Tucker is stepping up."

I know she's right but it's so much to wrap my brain around. And so much to process. Sutton will finally be taken care of. I don't have to worry about her anymore. But how long will this last? And what will the fallout be like when it's over?

CHAPTER FOURTEEN

TUCKER

I'm off today. Want to come over and talk?

Lacy's text makes me smile. Her reaching out is a good sign. That means she's not too pissed off about the child support check that I sent over.

Or maybe she's super pissed and she's about to tell me never to contact her again.

Nah. If she was trying to cut me off she wouldn't have reached out and invited me over.

With that thought, I text her back.

Me: I just got done with practice. Want to grab lunch?

Lacy: I have the kids. But if you enjoy fish sticks and mac and cheese, you're welcome to join us.

Me: I love fish sticks! But how about I bring us sushi instead.

Lacy: I would kill for a salmon roll

Me: Consider it done.

I shower quickly, ignoring Maks trying to discuss our offensive strategies while rubbing soap all over our bodies, determined not to waste any time with his shenanigans. I have somewhere way more important to be.

After stopping for gas and lunch, not at the same place, I finally get to their dingy apartment and knock on the door.

Lacy is the one who opens it, and I'm this close to leaning in for a hug, hoping she'll reciprocate, but the kids aren't far behind. As soon as they see me, they run over, hugging my legs and making it harder than it should be to walk in. While Sutton moves out of the way, Kody, just stays attached and the further I walk, the tighter he wraps his legs around one of mine, making me laugh.

Sutton, finally noticing that Kody is getting a ride, yells, "I want to do it too!"

So of course I stop, the sucker that I am.

"Well climb onto my other leg," I offer and the smile she flashes me practically stops my heart.

It takes her a second to stand on my foot, and as soon as she lifts her legs to wrap them around mine, she immediately slides down to the floor.

"Just sit on my foot, Sutton, and hold on tight."

Once she's situated, I continue the very short and yet difficult trek to the kitchen counter. The kids giggle the whole way. Even Lacy looks amused. The look on her face triggering the beginnings of a memory that fades away just as quickly as it comes.

With the kids still attached to me, I begin pulling lunch out of the bag.

I present the first Styrofoam container with a bit of flourish. "Salmon rolls for the lady."

"Ohmygod I could kiss you," she says absentmindedly as she takes the container out of my hands. I'd make a quip about her comment but I'm pretty sure she means she'd kiss the food, not me.

"Fish nuggets and mashed potatoes for the kids."

"Fish nuggets?" Lacy asks.

"Sure. That way we're all having fish for lunch."

"Ah," she says with a nod of her head. "Coordinating foods.

Those mashed potatoes really go along with the theme of today's meal."

"The theme only goes so far before nutritional requirements kick in. Those aren't your regular mashed potatoes." I put one hand next to my mouth and whisper. "They're cauliflower mashed potatoes."

Lacy gags. "That sounds disgusting."

"I didn't bring them for *you*. I figure if we put enough butter and salt on them, maybe the kids won't notice they're eating vegetables."

"Yeah, we'll see how well that goes over."

"Just watch, I'll be making them protein shakes before you know it!"

She shakes her head. "I knew I should have procreated with a man who loves junk food."

I clap my hand to my chest dramatically. "You wound me."

"No I don't."

"Yeah, you're right," I say, one shoulder shrugging as I keep pulling out containers. "It's too late to change that night anyway so you're stuck with me."

I ignore the smirk I see out of the corner of my eye. I doubt she'd appreciate me knowing that I'm growing on her.

The kids finally let go of my legs and are situated on the ratty bar stools, happily dipping their fish nuggets in their faux mashed potatoes.

Success!

Lacy and I have a chance to dig in. Since, they only have the two bar stools, she and I have to stand next to the counter, but I don't mind. It means being able to brush up against her "accidentally". I don't miss the way she sucks in a small breath every time our thighs touch.

"How was your road trip, anyway?" she asks just before shoving some of her salmon roll in her mouth. It's so big, she doesn't have a choice but to chew with her mouth open. It's hilarious.

"It was good. Long. I was ready to come home."

Still not done with her bite, but having a much better time with it, Lacy talks around the remaining food in her mouth. "Are they always that long? It seems like you were gone for forever."

I waggle my eyebrows. "Miss me, did you?"

"I missed your lunch runs."

"Man, you're full of zingers today."

"I'm full of zingers every day."

"I will make a mental note of that and do my best to keep up." I take my own bite, having a much easier time of chewing than she did. Who says my big mouth doesn't come in handy sometimes? "Usually our trips don't last that long. We have a couple two week trips every year, but usually they're around a week at a time. Maybe ten days."

"Mama, I want juice."

Lacy stops eating to give Sutton a *mom look*. It's impressive. Much gentler than the look my mom used to give me, but Sutton is damn near perfect and I wasn't even close, so it's understandable.

"That is not how you ask for something, Sutton."

Sutton looks at Kody, like she can't figure out what she's supposed to do. After several long seconds of her staring at him, he finally looks up from his nuggets and gives her the answer before shoving another nugget in his mouth.

"Say please."

Flipping her curls over her shoulder in a preteen move I am not even remotely close to being ready for, Sutton says, "Mama, I want juice, *please*."

Lacy shakes her head and turns toward the fridge, her hand accidentally brushing up against mine. I freeze at the contact, the unexpected zing raced up my arm. Lacy reaction happens so fast.

She almost stumbles over her feet before grabbing the juice and focusing on the kids again.

"You two are ridiculous, you know that?

"Yes, Mama," Sutton answers with a sigh, like she's exasperated by the whole conversation. It's pretty hilarious watching a three-year-old give attitude over a sippy cup of juice.

"Kody, do you want some, too?" Lacy is already pouring a second cup, not waiting for his answer.

It's a good thing, too. This time Kody looks at Sutton who gives him the same instructions.

"Say please."

"Yes, juice please."

This time I don't bother hiding my chuckle. "No wonder why people think they're twins. They've got that weird telepathy thing going."

"That's not even close to how easily they read each other's minds. I think that" –she points at the two kids as she places the cups in front of them—"that was more about deciding collectively if they're going to remember their manners today or if today's game is all about how quickly they can make me frustrated." She looks at me with one eyebrow cocked. "I'm sure you played that game with your brothers all the time."

"I don't even live with these kids full time and I can still admit, after a few weeks of limited and supervised interaction with these two, I have no idea how my mother survived raising five of us."

Which reminds me of why I needed to talk to Lacy in the first place. I have an idea that I think is pretty brilliant, but I don't know how she's going to react to it. That's not true. I have a pretty strong idea about how she'll react, which is why my gut is twisted in knots. The goal today is not to get a decision. It's to get her to hear me out before putting the kibosh on it.

Finishing off my last bite, I wipe my mouth with the super-thin napkin that came with the food. "Hey uh, so I have something I want to run by you."

She doesn't look up, just shovels more food in her face, likely trying to get as much down as she can before the kids need something else. "Shoot."

"I want to buy you a house."

Her chewing stops as she takes in my words. I'm not sure how to take her silence. She's not yelling or kicking me out, though, so that's a good sign, right?

Finally she swallows. "That's crazy talk, Tucker. You can't do that."

"Yes, I can. And I want to."

Lacy scoffs. "Tucker, your child support check for one month was more than I made last year. I don't need you to buy me a house."

"You're telling me you want to stay here?"

She looks around just in time to see a roach scurry across the wall behind the television. "No."

"Exactly. This is a terrible place to raise kids."

She rears back like I slapped her.

I quickly back pedal. "That came out wrong. Let me rephrase."

"You better."

"You and Ellie have done an amazing job. Sutton is happy and healthy. She's so clearly loved. But you guys have struggled so much. You don't have to do that anymore to prove you're a good mom. You've already proven it to everyone. My offer isn't about rewarding you for that."

I watch as she takes another bite, considering my words. I can practically see her struggle to hold back her automatic instincts, which if I had to guess, would be throwing something at my face.

Finally, she speaks. "That's really nice of you to say. But you want to what, buy me a house as a way to thank me? Are you serious?"

"You do realize I technically owe you almost three and a half year's worth of back child support," I remind her. "Do you know how much money that is? Would you rather me write you a check?"

She holds her hand up. "Oh god no. Please don't do that."

"Don't worry. I left my check book at home."

"You have an actual check book?" she chides. "I thought you were a little younger than my grandpa."

She smirks and I feel it straight in my chest. The playful banter is a good start to hopefully a great relationship. I take that as a sign I can continue.

"Ha ha. It's a phrase and you know it." Leaning against the counter, I cross my arms, prepping for the most important, and probably hardest part of this conversation. "But really, Lace. There's more to this idea. Before you say no, please promise you'll hear all of it and then you can decide."

"Nothing good ever started with those words."

"Normally, maybe. Promise me you'll listen," I plead.

She turns her head, giving me a side eye. "Fine. I'll listen."

That's further into this conversation than I expected to get, so I take a deep breath and continue with my plan. "Ever since I found out about Sutton, I've been looking at houses. Nothing intense, just a little search here and there. Just coming up with ideas for the future."

Lacy closes her now empty container and pushes it aside, leaning back against the counter. I'm going to lose her quickly if I don't get to the point.

"I accidentally found one."

"Tucker—" She shakes her head.

"You told me you'd listen," I interrupt quickly.

She sighs but waves for me to continue.

"The house itself is three bedrooms in the main house, plus a game room, a gym and a media room."

"That sounds huge."

"It is." And now for the biggest bombshell. "And that's why I was hoping we might all live together."

I bite my lip as I wait for the explosion because I already know she's going to need some convincing.

"Are you kidding me? We just met you." She throws her hands in the air.

Here we go.

"Technically we've known each other for more than four years."

Her hands go down and she shoots me a glare. "A one-night stand doesn't mean we know you. How do I know you aren't a serial killer?"

That's an easy answer.

"Because the PR department would have already found out and would be trying to put a family-friendly spin on it as we speak."

She scoffs at my joke. "You know what I mean, Tucker."

"Of course I know what you mean. But I want you to know what I mean." I take a small step closer to her, careful not to infringe on her space. "You stayed with me for a week when Sutton was sick so I know you aren't afraid of me. And if I live there, in the house that I purchase in your name, it means I'm technically buying the house so I have a place to live, too. That way, you don't feel weird taking more money. And it gets Sutton out of this apartment into a real home, without you worrying about how to front the bills."

"Who says I'm worried about the bills? I have a rich baby daddy who can't seem to stop giving me money."

I can't tell if she's joking or mad at me for sending that check. It might be a little bit of both.

"Come on, Lacy. You know that's not what I'm trying to do here. I'm trying to get to know my daughter without separating her from you. To make the transition easier for her. If it gets you into a good neighborhood with good schools at the same time, don't you think that's in her best interest?"

Lacy flinches and I can see I hit a mark.

Looking down at the floor, she whispers, "I can't leave Ellie and Kody like that. They're family, Tucker."

I scratch at my jaw, because, well, there's more. "Yeah, maybe I should have led with that part."

She looks up and narrows her eyes. "What part?"

"The house has a pool."

"Uh-huh."

"That comes complete with a two-bedroom pool house. Ellie and Kody could come with you."

Lacy's jaw drops open. "You know Ellie can't afford to rent something like that."

"Who says she'd be paying for it? She let you crash on her couch rent-free until you guys could move in here. And she's watched Sutton for free for what, two and a half years or something? It's the least I can do. Frankly, I wouldn't mind giving her child support sometimes because I feel like she deserves it for being there when I couldn't, but somehow I think one or both of you would try to castrate me if I cut her a check, too."

Lacy closes her eyes and taps her fingers against the cabinets behind her. I keep my mouth shut as I watch her internal struggle play out in real time. Finally, her eyes pop open and she throws her hands up in the air again, her go-to move when she's frustrated that I'm right.

"Fine. Let me talk to Ellie and see what she says."

I clear my throat, and I know my cheeks are flaming.

"What now?" she says through gritted teeth.

"Um... Ellie already knows."

"What?" Lacy shrieks.

I hold my hands up, hoping to calm her down, and maybe to block her foot if she tries to kick me in the balls. Honestly, this is the reaction I was expecting at the beginning so I'm kind of impressed it took this much time to get here.

"I asked her not to tell you," I try to explain. "This is something you and I needed to discuss first before a decision was made."

"When in the world did this conversation happen?"

"When she called to thank me for paying for Kody to go to daycare when Sutton was sick."

Lacy rolls her head, eventually dropping it into her hand. "No wonder she wasn't worried about rent. She was working the whole time."

"So yeah. That's how the conversation came up." I quickly try to get back on track. I haven't been kicked out yet, so that's a good sign, but who knows how long this will last. "So anyway, if you're in, she's in."

God love the roach that takes that exact moment to stick his head out of the sink drain and prove my point.

Lacy grimaces and turns on the water, effectively flushing him back down to the hell where he came from.

"Fucking hell," Lacy says with a deep, resigned sigh. "I guess we're moving in together."

As soon as we hear the key in the lock, the kids go running for the door.

"Mommy!" Kody yells and latches onto Ellie's leg. Sutton grabs the other one, now that Tucker has taught them the art of hanging on as he walks. Ellie, however, isn't quite as strong and ends up rooted to her spot.

"Oh you guys are so big!" she says with a smile and rubs their little backs as they giggle. "Can you hop off for one second so I can shut the door?"

"Carry us like a monster, Mommy!" Kody shouts.

"I am not strong enough for that." Ellie laughs. "But I can give good hugs and kisses if you let me walk to the couch."

That seems agreeable to both kids as they clamber off and anxiously wait for her to drop her purse and sit on the couch so she can get down to their level. And then they climb all over her, telling Ellie all about their very exciting day of wrestling with Tucker.

"He came over, huh?" she asks me, more than them.

"He had a proposition for me."

She looks over Kody's shoulder as she holds him tight to her and cocks an eyebrow at me. "Really."

I purse my lips in response. "Don't look so surprised. You know exactly what he came over to discuss."

With a loud smack on the cheek, Kody gives his mom one last kiss and wiggles off her lap, ready to play with Sutton again. For the last half hour or so, Sutton's been building some blocks and Kody's been knocking them over. I'm honestly surprised it's kept them both delightfully entertained for this long, but I refuse to say it out loud for fear of jinxing it.

"I knew he was considering discussing the house with you, but I didn't know he had the balls to do it yet."

"Well he did. And why the hell didn't you tell me he paid for Kody to go to daycare while Sutton was sick?"

Ellie points her finger at me and moves it around to circle my face. "Because of this reaction right here. Seriously, Lacy, you're too predictable."

I roll my eyes and toss the brochure in her lap. Yes, brochure. Because a house this fancy doesn't come with just a single sheet of paper telling the sale price and a picture of the master bathroom. Nope. Almost every room is pictured in high gloss color with every amenity listed.

Ellie whistles low as she glances at the pictures. "Wow. This is fancy."

"Yep."

"Great location to raise kids."

"Yep."

"So why don't you sound happy about this?"

I watch the kids squeal as they knock over another tower. The joy on their faces is the only thing that should concern me. Their happiness—and yes I include Kody in that because he's basically my bonus child—is my second priority after their health and well-being. Moving into a great neighborhood with great schools and a backyard they can play in should be a no brainer. But it's not. It feels...dangerous.

Ellie nudges me with her shoulder. "Do you remember when we first met?"

I puff a humorless laugh. "How can I forget. We were living in my car, for god's sake."

"And working at that horrific gas station that always smelled like sewage had backed up."

I grimace. "It usually had. And you're the lucky asshole that always got to leave before the toilet had to be plunged. I swear I got stuck doing that every single night."

I watch as she tries to hold back a giggle but can't. My eyes widen as realization sets in two years too late.

"You did it on purpose, didn't you, you bitch?"

She nods as she continues to laugh. "I wasn't about to get near that toilet after that weird, creepy dude would clog it up every night."

"Ellie!" I yell, which makes her laugh even harder. "Why didn't you tell him he couldn't use that bathroom!"

"He creeped me out. I wasn't going to talk to him if I didn't have to."

"You are the worst friend ever."

My quip makes her laugh even harder.

When she's finally calmed down enough to speak again, her tone turns serious.

"Answer me a question, why did you move in with me when I first offered?"

"What do you mean? We were homeless. You were a godsend."

"I know that part. But what I mean is, why did you trust me?"

I think for a second, pulling back the ugly memories I've suppressed for a very long time. "I don't know that I did, to be honest. I was just so desperate to give Sutton a better life."

"Aren't you still hoping for better than—"

The kids begin squealing as a roach runs out from behind the television, and quickly changes his mind when he notices the kids. The infestation seems to have gotten bigger lately. We're seeing too many of them.

Ellie looks at me. "Better than a roach-infested apartment?"

I know what she's trying to say, but that doesn't mean I want to hear it.

I lower my voice, partly hoping she doesn't hear me and my irrational fears. "What if he turns out to be a serial killer, Ellie?"

"What if I had?"

"Well what if he turns out to be a pedophile?"

"What if I had?"

"Well what if—"

She grabs my hands, cutting off my fears. "What if he turns out to be exactly who he presents himself to be? Kind, generous, loving, and the kind of dad he keeps saying he wants to be? What if he turns out to be everything you never dreamed of because dreaming it was too scary?"

I sniff as my eyes fill with tears. I hate crying. Despise it. It's probably why I've held onto my anger for so long. It's easier to be pissed off than feel devastated by the hurt of being alone. Yes, I have Ellie and Kody, but everyone else has ditched me. Ditched us. I can't let that happen again. I won't let that happen to my daughter. She won't feel that kind of pain if I can help it. And things going south with Tucker means more than just Sutton getting hurt. I would, too. He's too good. Too kind. Too good to be true.

"What if he leaves us again, Ellie?" I whisper.

She leans down a bit, forcing me to make eye contact. "He didn't leave you the first time, Lace."

I know she's right. But these wounds run deep. Logically I know they weren't made by Tucker. I'm sure they were made by my parents throughout my extremely strict childhood, where nothing less than perfection was acceptable. That was long before they abandon their sinfully pregnant unmarried daughter. But that doesn't mean those wounds don't still break open sometimes and bleed.

"You promise you'll come with us?"

She nods, giving me a compassionate smile. "We wouldn't let you go alone. What if he turns out to be a serial killer or something?"

I puff out a laugh and wipe my eyes with my sleeves. "And what if it doesn't work out?"

"Then we take your new monthly child support check and find us the best apartment it can rent!"

I nod again, still feeling nervous, but knowing I have my support system coming with me, which means I don't have to do this alone.

CHAPTER SIXTEEN

TUCKER

We slowly make our way into the locker room, tired from tonight's game in Seattle, but also just tired. We've been on a nine-day road trip and this is the last leg. Tomorrow, we'll finally head home and I can't wait.

Weird. I never thought of the end of a road trip as the best part before. But I guess I never had anything waiting for me at home either.

Once again, Lacy has been amazing while I've been gone, letting me video chat with the kids every day. And yes, it's both of them. I recognize that my vested interest in Sutton is because she's my daughter, but Kody is a great little kid, and I can't deny that he's just fun to be with. Besides, Sutton thinks of him as her brother so it's important that I treat him as such.

The calls have also given Lacy and I a chance to get to know each other a little better. I know the idea of moving in with me has her a bit wigged out, so leaving for a short amount of time is probably what she needed. It's like I was able to give her space without abandoning her or Sutton.

It also means we've been connecting more for a purpose and not just because I like her. Which I do. Like her. A lot.

She's unlike any woman I've ever met before. She's got this strength and resilience about her, and yet she's still so gentle and loving with the kids. And her humor matches mine which is a big thing for me. I know I can come across as a little immature or too sarcastic. But Lacy and I just...fit. We get each other. For the most part our conversations are easy, and it makes hanging out with her that much more enjoyable. And let's not even think about how much my body wants hers. Especially in a locker room full of my teammates.

Stripping my gear off, I wonder if there are any plans for tonight. Might as well make the most of my last night on the road. I don't have to wonder for long, though. Leave it to Maksim to always have a party planned.

"Ready to go hunting for a little tail, Hayes?"

Maks walks by butt naked, already heading to the showers.

I shake my head at his absolute lack of concern about the media starting to enter the locker room for a few post-game interviews. If a uniform wasn't mandatory, it wouldn't shock me to see him naked on the ice, too.

"I don't need to find any tail," I say, knowing I'm much too into Lacy to think about another woman. "But I could go for a few drinks. I'll have to meet you there, though. I've got plans."

Tossing my sweaty jersey into the giant laundry basket, I slide out of my skates and wiggle my toes in relief.

"Plans? What is more important than finding a lovely lady or two to spend the evening with?" Maks looks shocked that I might need things other than women in my life. You know, like food or a nap. If I hadn't seen him eating dinner once or twice, I'd think he got his nourishment from a singular diet of dirty sex.

"Who said my plans weren't with a cute young thing?"

He considers me for a moment, then nods once, seemingly satisfied with my response, then continues his nude trek across the room.

"Now I'm curious." Nick puts his finger in the book he's

reading to mark his page. We've roomed together a couple times on this trip so I've gotten to know him more and he's a really solid dude. "Who do you have plans with?"

I flash him an amused smile as I continue to strip down, although unlike some people, I'll be staying in my skivvies while the reporters are here. "It's still early enough I can video chat with my daughter."

"I thought that's what you meant," he says with a chuckle. "How's that going anyway?"

"So good, man." I can't stop the grin that overtakes me. "She's just amazing. And her little friend she lives with is awesome, too. Kids are a hoot."

"That's what I hear."

"Now that they know I play hockey on TV, apparently they've made it a game trying to find my number. Lacy says it's hilarious watching them try to keep up with all the movement and most of the time they get it wrong. But hey, at least she's interested in what her daddy's doing, right?"

"Do you get to spend a lot of time with her?"

"Actually," I twist around and grab my phone out of my locker, hoping I'll have finally heard some news. "Fingers crossed I'll be spending a lot more time with her soon. Hang on."

Swiping it open, I see the text I've been waiting for from my realtor.

They accepted your offer. Closing date is roughly four weeks from today.

"Yes," I shout and pump my fist. "I got the house."

"You bought a house?" Nick looks confused.

"Yeah. Check it out."

I pull up the link and open to the pictures of the place I'm officially buying for my new family. Handing him my phone, I can't help but gush about how excited I am.

"See the backyard? That was the selling point for me. There's so much room for the kids to play. And that outdoor kitchen is going to be awesome for team parties."

"Nice pool."

"I know. And the fence around it has one of those adult height locks and an alarm so the kids won't be able to break into that area without someone knowing. Of course that means Maks probably won't be able to get back out of there." I shrug. "Maybe I should hire a lifeguard for him. Who knows. And see the pool house?"

Nick whistles low. "Wow. That place is sweet. Planning on having long-term guests?"

"Actually yeah."

He furrows his brows in a question but doesn't tear his eyes away from the pictures, too interested in my new digs. I don't blame him. The place is amazing.

"Lacy's roommate and her son are going to live there. They've all been together since the kids were babies, so I don't really feel right about them having to separate when this seems like a good solution. Plus, she's not much better off than Lacy financially and after all she did to get my girls off the street, it's the least I can do to reciprocate the favor."

I immediately know I've said too much when Nick looks up, interested by that little tidbit I accidentally dropped. "They were living on the street?"

"Shh..." I gesture for him to lower his voice as I lower mine. The last thing I need is for a reporter to overhear Lacy's business. "I didn't mean to say that. I don't think Lacy would appreciate me telling people so keep it under wraps. But yeah. I guess when I wasn't around they hit a really rough patch. Lacy doesn't like to talk about it so I don't know a lot of details." I blow out a breath, trying to shake off the guilty feelings I have from not being around for them during that time. I know it's not my fault, but it doesn't change how badly I wish I could have a redo. Fucking Morty. I could kill the guy. "I don't actually like to *think* too hard about it, either. But that's basically why I'm so excited about the house. I can see my daughter daily now and still help Lacy get some of her dreams back."

Nick finally hands my phone back to me. "That's really cool, man. And really generous."

"Nah. It's just the right thing to do."

I put my phone back in my locker and finish pulling all my gear off. I'm tired and ready to get back to the hotel for my video date.

"You heading to the showers?" I ask as I wrap a towel around my waist.

Nick leans over and looks into the tiled area before shaking his head. "I'm going to wait a few more minutes. You know how I am."

I clap him on the shoulder before walking away because yeah, I do know how he is. He's a great teammate and fantastic goalie. He also likes to keep to himself, and crowds of people aren't his thing. He prefers to read poetry or some shit that bores me to tears than watching the boob tube. I learned that when he pulled out some noise cancelling headphones in our room while I got caught up in the latest binge-worthy dramedy. Nick also waits until everyone else is done in the showers before using them himself. I suspect he knows Maks's issues with personal space and it's his way of avoiding. Most of the time after practice he doesn't even shower at the arena at all. I don't really get it, but if it helps keep him focused on stopping those pucks, more power to him.

"You just missed all the hot water." Maksim laughs a little too hard at his lie. He uses that line regularly, thinking he's hilarious. Wiping the remaining droplets off himself, he stands a little too close to my shower as I drop my towel. I honestly don't know if his lack of personal space when we're naked is a cultural thing, but he seems to have no sense of boundaries. "You sure you don't wanna go now? Shuto said there's a good strip joint just a few miles from the hotel and I could go for some titties in my face to relax."

Six months ago, I would have jumped at the chance. But for some reason, even the idea of a stripper grinding all over me has me turning up my nose. I'm not sure when that happened. I've always been up for a good time. But for some reason, the thought of Lacy in the bedroom down the hall from mine has more appeal than paying for a lap dance.

That's when my thoughts drift to the thought of Lacy giving me a lap dance. Her tall, lithe body swiveling in front of me. Her full breasts just a breath away from my mouth.

I'm assaulted with a memory of *creamy skin in front of me, dark hair pushed over one shoulder as we move to the beat of the music. Our bodies fitting together like a puzzle. Her fruity, floral scent tickling my nose...*

And just like that, it's gone. This time, I'm kind of glad. No one needs me to sport a hard on in the public shower. I think that's a boundary even Maks would like to hold.

"I'm good, man," I say from under the warm spray as I come back to my senses. "Call me when you hit up a real bar." I pull back and shake my head, water flying everywhere.

"Hey watch it!" Maks yells. "I just dried off."

"Learn some personal boundaries in the showers, dude, and you won't have that problem."

He grunts and leaves me to my shower, my thoughts straying as I wonder about that memory. Where was that? And was it Lacy I was dancing with? I try to draw out the memory again to no avail. I'm frustrated by it but decide to let it go for now. If I try too hard to remember, it'll just lock up my memories anyway.

Instead of thinking about it more, I decide to go with the flow and enjoy myself tonight. I've got a huge life transition coming up so there's no harm in taking a break from it all, right?

Or not. Honestly the only lap dance I want is from a certain tall brunette with a sharp tongue and desire to keep me at arm's length.

Nope. Not gonna think about Lacy when I'm in the shower. I don't need that kind of reputation from my teammates.

I turn the handle until the water runs ice cold to shock the horny out of my system, then shut off the shower and towel down. That's when I realize someone else is in here but around the corner, whispering harshly.

Investigating quickly, mostly to make sure it's not some rando trying to get a picture of my junk, I find myself face-to-face with our team captain, Patrick Smith. With the way his eyes widen when he sees me, he looks like I caught him in a compromising position when really he's just on the phone.

"Uh... everything okay back here?"

"Fine." His answer is short and clipped so I know for sure he was hiding, I just don't know why.

"You sure? I thought I heard some arguing back here."

"Nope," he clips out. "Just talking to the wife."

I nod and back away slowly, trying not to startle the obviously skittish beast. "Okay. Holler if you need something."

I quickly leave the showers and head back into the locker room, wondering how the hell I ended up with such weird teammates.

CHAPTER SEVENTEEN

LACY

I yawn as I scroll through the catalogue of classes. I have the night off, which is rare so I wanted to take full advantage of it.

It's a new feeling, not scrambling to pick up shifts. Even when someone tried to get me to work for them tonight, I said I was busy.

Yeah, busy trying to figure out what I'm going to do with the rest of my life now that money isn't as big of an object as it was.

Don't get me wrong. I'm not squandering the money Tucker gave me. But once I was done paying all the bills and stocking the pantry with more food than we've had in a long time, I decided it's okay to not work myself to the bone. But just this once. You never know when life will flip upside down again, and I don't want to be caught without a hefty savings account to fall back on.

I'm browsing through the pre-law program at one of the local universities when my phone suddenly rings with a video message. I know who that is.

Connecting the call, I see Tucker's smiling face. My stomach flips, but I ignore it. I don't need to get feelings mixed up in this situation.

"Hey. That was a good game tonight," I say by way of greeting.

"It wasn't our best," Tucker admits.

"You still won."

"By the skin of our teeth, but we pulled it together. How's it going on your end?"

"Well…" I settle back in my chair, knowing we could be on for a while. Time always seems to pass quickly when Tucker and I video chat. "The kids passed out about half an hour ago, so I guess you could call it a win, too."

I know Tucker calls to talk to the kids, but we've gotten into the routine of chatting about our days, too. I hate to admit it, but I like it. And the more I get to know him, the more I like Tucker, too.

I doubt I'll ever admit my crush to him or anyone. Nothing like bringing something like that out in the open to scare someone away and jinx everything.

Tucker's face falls. "Well shit. I was hoping to catch them before bed."

"You know what time it is, right?"

He glances up, I assume at a clock. "It's only six o'clock."

I stifle a yawn as I think about how late it really is. Well, for me because of the earlier than normal wake-up call I had when the kids found a new and apparently very exciting episode of Octonauts. "Tucker, you're on the opposite coast. It's just after nine here." I chuckle lightly. "You lost all track of time going from coast to coast?"

If it's possible, his face falls even more, and I feel bad that I didn't keep the kids up a little longer. Just thirty minutes. What could it have hurt?

I actually know that answer. It would hurt me tomorrow when they're so tired they're completely out of control.

"Aw, fuck." Tucker rubs his hand down his face. "I mathed wrong."

"Understandable. You do take a lot of shots to the head. Are those even all your real teeth?"

He opens his mouth wide and moves closer to the camera. I make a gagging sound from all the grossness.

"I've still got all my chompers. *Au naturel*, baby."

"You could never show me the inside of your mouth again and that would be okay."

He chuckles. And then the sound turns into something deeper and more like a moan. I cock my head, wondering what is happening. Is it my phone glitching? Or is it...

Tucker, on the other hand, rolls his eyes. "Maksim!" he yells and bangs his fist on the wall. "Keep it down, motherfucker! I'm trying to talk to my kid, here!"

A muffled "sorry" comes through the wall, which is both very nice of him, and oddly creepy that the walls are so thin, even I can hear it through my phone.

"Sorry about that," Tucker says sheepishly. "Maks has been talking about getting laid for days. I guess he didn't waste any time once we got back."

"Reminds me of another night a few years ago," I mumble mostly to myself.

"What?"

"Nothing," I say brightly, ignoring the hurt I feel. The last time I heard someone banging on a hotel room wall, Sutton was being made and we were the ones being too loud.

A small bit of shame creeps up as the truth of that night hits me full force—it was so insignificant to Tucker, *we* were so insignificant to Tucker, he doesn't even remember that night. He doesn't remember the banter and fun we had. He doesn't remember the sex. As opposed to me, who spent years not being able to forget.

"Did you not go out tonight?" I quickly change the subject.

"I was planning to go out later, but it sounds like my drinking buddy is already done for the night." As if on cue, a groan of an obvious finish comes through the wall. Tucker looks that direction and grimaces. "Or maybe I'll give him a few minutes before he's ready to head out again." I shake my head. Some of Tucker's friends are so strange. "Anyway, I grabbed a bite to eat so I could come back here and call you. I guess I should have waited on food."

He looks so sad about missing Sutton, I can't help but try and comfort him. "It's okay, Tucker. She'll be happy to see you when you get back."

"You think?"

"I know. They were trying to find you on the television again. Only they kept forgetting what color your jersey was and kept cheering on some guy from the other team."

That gets a belly laugh from Tucker and I don't hate the sound. In fact, it kind of stirs a part of me that has been laying low for the last few years. The part of me that loves the feel of a man's chest when a laugh rumbles through it. The part of me that loves the feel of a man bracing himself over top of me.

A small flashback of our night together, the part where Tucker is pounding into me so hard the headboard bangs against the wall, races through my brain.

Once he's sheathed, he leans down and kisses me one last time. "You ready?"

I match his eye contact. "I've been ready. Now get inside me."

No more words are necessary. He thrusts once, hard and deep, both of us groaning in pleasure. He more than fills me and I love how he feels, his hips swiveling and thrusting, the athlete in him refusing to hold back.

Shaking off the thoughts of the best sex of my life, I focus back on our conversation. "Yeah it was pretty cute."

"Next time get a video of it. I'd love to see it."

I nod as I stifle another yawn.

"Do you need me to let you go so you can get to bed?" Tucker asks quietly.

"No. I'm okay. If I go to bed too early, I'll be up too early and then work will be a bitch tomorrow. But I don't mind if you need to go so you can go hang out with your friends."

The picture on the screen wobbles as Tucker settles himself against the headboard. I take it that's a no.

"I see those fuckers for hours every day. Unless Maks comes banging on my door and drags me out, I don't need to see them again. Besides, I have news."

"Yeah?"

"We got the house."

I gasp, a mixture of excitement and fear running through me. Seeing the look on Tucker's face, though, it's easy to focus on the excitement.

"Tucker, that's great! Do you have a closing date yet?"

"I asked if we could do it as soon as possible. I think the sellers are going to go ahead and move out next week and I'm going to rent it until we close so it can get a deep clean and fresh paint. All that junk."

"You sound very knowledgeable for being a first-time homeowner."

"I was a teenager when my mom bought her house and the memories of her putting us to work before we could move in are seared into my brain."

"Which is why you're paying to have someone else do the hard work."

"It's like you've known me for years," he jokes, but it falls a little flat for me.

I *have* known him for years. I've followed his career and news about him on and off the ice. In my bitterness, I wanted to see him fail, wanted to see him get embroiled in some sort of scandal. He never did, but that didn't mean I stopped watching. So I know that he's a nice guy, labeled a goofball by his friends. I know he enjoys a night out and tips well, but never goes over the top in a way that gets him into trouble. And now I know that he wants to be a good dad, no a great dad, more than anything. It's enough to make my bitterness and resentment slowly melt away.

Tucker rests one arm behind his head, settling into our conversation again.

"How are you feeling about this move, Lacy. Really. Are you okay with it?"

I blow out a breath and choose my words carefully. I don't want to obliterate his excitement, but I also want him to understand if I get a little snippy until we get settled. If I know anything about myself, when I feel unsafe, my claws can come out.

"I'm excited to get out of this roach motel."

"But..."

I look away, not able to make eye contact. "I don't have the best track record with people sticking around when things get tough."

"And you're afraid I'm going to be one of those people."

I shrug one shoulder. "Things haven't been hard for you yet. I have no idea if you're someone who powers through or runs away."

He nods like he understands but he can't possibly. This is my own issue, I know that. My own lack of trust. It's something I have to try and push through, if for nothing else than for Sutton's well-being. She deserves to have a father and she could do worse than Tucker Hayes in that role. We both could.

"Anyway, let's talk about something else," I say brightly. "When are we moving and how are we going to get there?"

Tucker chuckles and graciously moves on from the heavy part of the conversation.

"I'm hoping we can move in about three weeks. We have a couple home games that week, but it shouldn't be hard to move out of your tiny little place."

"We can honestly leave everything behind except the kids' toys and our clothes. But the furniture? It was all left over from the last tenants or random garage sale finds. I'm sure you have way nicer stuff."

"I have no problem with that. Sounds like we'll just need a teammate, a truck, and a few hours."

"Isn't that just sad."

Leaving behind my entire life, the last several years of supporting myself and Sutton with the help of only one other person, and all we have to show for it is a couple of boxes and "a few hours" of effort.

I'm choosing not to focus on that part, though. I don't want to be dragged down anymore. I want Sutton to forget living in a shitty apartment that sometimes sounds like a war zone when the neighbors fight. I want her to remember being given every opportunity to be the person she was created to be.

First step, sucking up my pride and moving in with her dad. No matter how queasy it makes me feel.

CHAPTER EIGHTEEN

TUCKER

Three weeks went by incredibly quickly, all while dragging so slowly I could hardly take it. The only bright spot was Halloween. Taking two three-year-olds trick-or-treating was possibly the most fun I've had in my entire life.

There were five of us in total, so I convinced the moms to dress up, too, and we went as The Incredibles. Because of her height, Lacy got to go as Mrs. Incredible. Best idea I've ever had.

She looked stunning in the tight outfit and it was all I could do to not stare at her ass all night long and drool.

Now that Candy Day, as I like to call it, is over, I've been antsy about moving in. The bright spot of having to wait a few weeks, however, is that I was able to hire a designer who quickly came in and did some small updates I wanted and changed out a few light fixtures. Plus, she added a few surprises for Lacy that I hope go over well.

Fortunately, the previous owners left the house in such immaculate shape, there really wasn't much else to do. I just wanted to make sure it was all complete before my new family moved in.

My new family. What a wild thought. Six months ago I wasn't even thinking about settling down and now I'm considering school districts and starting college funds. What a weird life I live.

Finally, though, the day has arrived and I can hardly wait to show off our new digs.

I was able to elicit the help of Nick, Maks, and Patrick. Everyone else pussed out, even the rookies. Which is fine. I figure with the four of us, we should be able to get everything done quickly. My part was finished yesterday when a hired moving crew got all the big appliances and furniture I was keeping out of the old place. Today is all about the others.

We pull up in front of the new place, my teammates in Nick's truck, me in my new SUV, Lacy and Sutton in their beat-up old Honda, and Ellie and Kody in her, hell I don't know what that thing is. All I know is it sounds like it needs to head to the used car graveyard, never to be heard from again. The one time I had the balls to actually say that to Ellie, she took it in stride, telling me it gets her from Point A to Point B just fine and anyone who doesn't like it can suck it. I never brought it up again.

Climbing out of my car, I hear a low whistle come from Nick. Hands on his hips, his eyes are trained on my new crib. "Wow. The pictures don't do this place justice, Hayes."

Patrick hasn't looked up yet. He's leaning against the car, texting. Again. I'd bet money it's the wife. She seems to keep him on a short leash. I have the fleeting thought that I doubt they're going to last much longer. I push the thought aside though. Not my problem and there's too much to do.

"We're gonna have some kick ass parties, right?" Maks belly laughs as he claps me on the back.

"Hell yeah!" I reach my knuckles out to bump his at his good idea. "We should have a pool party. Some kind of open house with lots of booze and lots of food."

"Sounds like my kind of party." Maks slaps his hands together and rubs. "Next week work for you? I met a set of twins who seemed up for a good time."

"Consider it done. Let me get settled first and then I'll come up with a plan."

I hear a giggle next to me as Sutton comes through the lush grass with Kody right behind her.

"Is this our new house?" she asks. Her eyes are bright and her smile is huge. I can only imagine that it must look like a castle from her short perspective.

"Sure is," I say with a smile, happy to see the excitement on her face. "Wanna go see your bedroom?"

"Yeah!" she and Kody yell simultaneously.

I turn to Lacy who's slowly strolling our way, taking in the neighborhood, and looking a little overwhelmed. I bet this place seems like a castle to her, too. And a castle has lots of bedrooms which has me wondering about how easy this transition is going to be for the kids.

"Hey Lacy, do they know they won't be sleeping in the same room?"

"Yeah, we told them they would each have their own." She finally stops looking around like the boogie man is going to jump out at any second. "We just didn't tell them a backyard would be separating them. Seemed like a good idea to wait on proximity until they could see it for themselves."

Smart plan.

I rub my hands together, anxious to show everyone our new home. "Well come on everybody. Let me show you around so we can get started."

The eight of us make our way into the house by way of the front door. I hear gasps and murmurs behind me as I lead them into the huge living room area. It's not quite an open floor plan with a wall separating part of the kitchen, but it's close. The huge windows to the backyard make it feel even more open.

"Wow. Is this all the furniture from your last place?" Lacy asks me.

"No. Most of that went into the pool house for Ellie. We wouldn't want you and Kody camping out on the living room floor."

"Thanks, Tucker." Ellie punches me lightly in the arm as she snickers.

"The designer gets all the credit for this stuff. She had a vision and unlimited use of my credit card. Except for the wall décor and other odds and ends. I figured we could decide what pictures and stuff we wanted together. So both our tastes are reflected."

"Awwww..." Ellie holds a hand over her heart. "That's such a sweet thought, wasn't it Lacy?"

Lacy rolls her eyes at her friend.

"I don't know if you guys want to check out the bedrooms, but you and Sutton are down that way." I point down the small hall into what feels like a separate wing of the house. It kind of is. With their bedrooms one way, the master suite a different way, the indoor gym and media room a third way, and this open area in the center of it all, the house is split up nicely. There's no way any of us can really disturb each other, yet we're not that far apart.

"Kids, are you coming with us?" Lacy calls.

The two littles have their faces smashed up against the wall of glass overlooking the backyard, probably conversing about the pool they're staring at. But as soon as Lacy distracts them with words like "bedroom" and "toys", they tear themselves away and race after their moms.

"Seriously, man, this house is awesome." Nick saunters over after exploring the open area with what looks like awe on his face.

"I'm telling you, my realtor, Millie, was amazing. She really came through when I told her what I needed."

"I'll say."

"Listen, I'd love to hang out and shoot the shit, but I have a date tonight so we need to get this show on the road," Maks announces. "Also, you promised beer. Where can I find that?"

I chuckle. "In the fridge, already fully stocked for your entertainment."

Maks heads toward that direction, Patrick hot on his heels.

"The fridge in the kitchen?" Nick asks.

"Yeah, of course."

"Oh." Nick looks surprised but I'm not sure why. "I thought you'd have a beer fridge in the garage or something so you can keep kid stuff in the kitchen."

I shake my head with confusion. "Why do I need to do that? There's room for both. You just gotta clear out some of that beer for the juice boxes or whatever to be able to fit."

"On it!" Maks hands four or five beers to Patrick, then grabs two more while still digging for more liquid treasure.

"I don't know Lacy all that well," Nick says slowly. "But maybe you need to ask her if she's comfortable with that. She's a cool chick, but I get the feeling she's a little protective of her daughter like my sister is of hers, and that would never fly in that house."

Our daughter, I think, feeling the sting of not being considered a primary parent. I keep that thought to myself, though. I know he didn't mean anything by it.

"I hear ya and I appreciate the concern but it's my house, my rules. If I want beer in the fridge, that's where it'll go."

"Your funeral," Nick grumbles.

I'm starting to get irritated by his parenting digs. It's not like he has a kid. What does he know about child rearing, anyway? So far, I've done a pretty good job of jumping in and helping out.

My attention is turned when Maks slams an empty can to his forehead, crushes it, and belches loudly. "Okay men. Let's get this show on the road. My hot date can't wait."

Patrick tosses his own empty in my new trash can. "Yep. The wife apparently made dinner plans for us, so I've gotta get home soon."

Nick and I give each other different expressions that communicate our same thoughts—we're not shocked by Patrick's news. He's either fighting with his wife, or being dragged around by his dick wherever she wants to go, usually spending more money than he thinks is necessary. We learned that little tidbit when their last phone argument played out on our bus to the airport in Toronto. That exchange was not quiet. It was loud and heated and we learned way more information about their floundering relationship than any of us were comfortable with.

Patrick's right about one thing, though. There's no reason to sit around. We need to get the cars unpacked while the kids are entertained.

My friends start tackling the boxes in the back of Nick's truck while I start unloading the clothes from my backseat. I grunt as I try unsuccessfully to grab a couple handfuls of hangers.

"Why...the fuck...did she not put these in boxes?" I groan as I finally get myself somewhat situated. And then a shirt falls on the grass in front of me, tripping me. "Shit," I mutter and just keep going. That'll just have to stay put for now.

I pass a scampering child on my way into Lacy's room. As soon as I walk in, she whirls around, staring accusingly at me.

"What?" I ask a little too forcefully as I lift my arms to put the hangers on the rod in the closet. Half of her clothes fall to the ground in the process.

Well shit.

"This room," she practically whispers.

"Do you like it?"

When Lacy mentioned she didn't want to keep any of her furniture, I took it upon myself to make sure she still has something to sleep on. And since the designer was putting the final touches on the rest of the house anyway, I just let her go crazy in the bedrooms.

"It's...so much. I don't think I can accept this."

I can see the concern in Lacy's eyes and how unsure she is

about my gift. She thinks I'm trying to throw money around instead of actually investing in relationships. That couldn't be further from the truth. I'm throwing money around *because* I'm investing in relationships. It's just an extension of my desire to make up for everything I missed before.

Keeping my tone even so I don't scare her off, I do my best to put her at ease. "I know it seems like a lot but hear me out."

Lacy crosses her arms and tries to put on her defensive face. It doesn't work on me anymore. I can see right through her.

"First, you said you didn't want any of the furniture in the last place and I think it's a nice idea to leave it for the next person. You never know if someone will really need it, right?"

She grunts softly, seeming unwilling to admit I'm right. That's okay. She knows.

"Second, it doesn't go with the new décor anyway. And third..." And this is the big one. "You deserve a fresh start. Things are different now. Hopefully you can breathe a little easier now that some of the financial strain has been taken off you."

"I can afford my own bed Tucker. You didn't have to buy me one," she snarks.

"No, I didn't. And you don't have to keep it if you don't want to. Hell, buy yourself a new one and put this one in storage. Give it away. Sell it. Makes no difference to me. My mom will need a place to crash when she comes to visit anyway, so we can always use it in the media room when she gets here."

Her arms drop to her sides, eyebrows squished together making a divot between them. "Your mother is coming to visit?"

"Not any time soon. I told her she needs to wait until we get settled. She didn't like that, but we compromised and now I send her a picture of Sutton every day to appease her temporarily."

Lacy laughs a little and then looks back at the bed. "I could always give this to Ellie. She still needs one."

I rub my hand on the back of my neck. "She actually doesn't."

Lacy's eyes widen. "What did you do?"

"Like I said, I had a designer with a very clear vision and some practically unused stuff at the last house. Ellie needed a bed, too and I wasn't about to leave her stranded."

"First the kids' rooms and now this. Wait..." Lacy's eyes narrow on me. "You did Kody's room, too, didn't you?"

"Do you really think I was going to let that little maniac go without? What kind of a monster do you think I am?"

I don't wait for her answer, instead heading back to the closet to clean up my mess, chuckling as Lacy grumbles under her breath about dumb asses with too much money.

I find it hilarious that she thinks I'm being irresponsible. She's seen my income. Hell, it's public record. Buying a couple beds and a couch isn't exactly hurting me. But I know this is all new to her and it's going to take time for her to trust my intensions. I can be a patient man and I know it's just a matter of —

My thoughts freeze up on me as I take in what I'm holding. The dress on the hanger, I know this dress. It's slinky and black and, yep, turning it around reveals no back at all.

Suddenly my mind is flooded with memories of one of the best nights of my life. The night of my first professional hockey game.

The night I met Lacy in that club in the hotel.

"I'm Lacy." She leans in to say her name just loud enough I can hear her over the music. She's close enough I get a quick whiff of her subtle fruity and floral scent.

"Tucker," I respond, hoping I smell just as good as she does.

"Wanna dance?"

She scoops her dark, wavy hair forward, exposing the broad expanse of her bare back. All the smooth, creamy skin is distracting and I almost forget how to move my hips. I put my arm around her waist and encourage her to get closer, to let me take the lead on the dance floor, just like I plan to do later.

If she'll let me.

The longer we dance, the more our hands are free to explore. Her hands on my thighs, pulling me in tighter. My hands on her hips, keeping her where I want her.

My breathing picks up as I'm assaulted with the memories I've been trying to draw out for weeks.

"Last chance to call it a night," I mumble against her lips, my way of making sure she's all in before talking ceases.

"If you don't fuck me soon, I'm going to go find your weird friend and check out his moves instead."

The single night we spent together was arguably the best sex I've ever had. I remember when I left her alone in that bed the next morning, thinking how unfortunate it was that life wasn't different then, that I could fall for Lacy if circumstances were different. And then I locked that memory away.

Until now.

It all comes rushing back to me. The softness of her skin. The sounds she made as I thrust deep inside her. The laughter when my teammate Liam pounded on the hotel wall because we were making too much noise.

I remember.

"Trust no one," she'd said so many times that night.

She was right. We'd just met so I held parts of myself back. So did she. And now—now life has thrown us back together. The woman of my dreams, the one I refused to remember because there was no point, she's here. And she's the mother of my child.

Stunned, I stumble my way out of the closet still holding the dress.

Lacy turns away from the box she's unpacking and freezes, much like I did, when she sees me.

"It was a club inside the Sumke Hotel."

Her eyes widen, knowing I remember.

"You were wearing this dress and every time you turned around, your back was completely bare."

I take two small steps toward her.

"You were there with friends, but they didn't really hang around, too busy dancing with each other."

Two more steps.

"Your body fit next to mine exactly, the perfect height for a guy of my build, and the softness of your skin practically undid me right there on that dance floor."

Two more steps.

"We both knew what we wanted, and we both knew it would be one night only. *'Trust no one'*, you'd said, not even you."

I'm standing in front of her now, close enough to see tears shining in her eyes. I don't understand why it's so important to her that I remember all those details, but clearly it is. It was. And for the first time I feel like a wall is coming down from between us.

"After the best night of my life, I set an alarm for you and left, wishing there was a way to see you again but knowing it was impossible."

"You remember," she whispers, a lone tear sliding down her cheek.

I nod, wiping the tear away with my thumb but leaving my hand right where it's at. "I do. I remember everything. And now, here you are. Living with me. Sharing a child with me. Like everything shifted so I could finally get to know you again. Get to see if what we had then could be something more."

"You left and you never came back." A small sob bursts out of her and my heart cracks open, a deeper appreciation of how guarded she is, and how hard I'm going to have to work to break through her walls.

I lean down, pressing my forehead to hers, dropping the hanger and clasping her face in both my hands.

"But I'm here now. And I'm not going anywhere."

I breathe her in, letting the emotion wash over me. The woman I felt a connection with so long ago is here. And she's never going anywhere. Not as long as Sutton is around. Any lingering desire I had to be a professional bachelor fades away. I knew before now I was in this for the long haul but having such vivid memories of how our story began just cements it for me. And not just because of our daughter. Lacy has always been the only one I've wanted. And not just physically.

It just took until now to remember.

Her hands hold on to my arms, as if they're helping keep her upright. My eyes zone in her lips and I couldn't stop myself from leaning in if I wanted to. But I don't. I want Lacy, need her, with a ferocity I didn't know my body could feel. We are just millimeters apart and nothing else matters except us. This moment when I succumb to something bigger than me, bigger than her, bigger than any of us. Like the universe heard me all those years ago and is giving us a chance to have all our dreams come true.

I barely register the patter of little feet racing down the hallway as I lick my lips, ready to claim a piece of the woman who can simultaneously bring me to my knees and lift me up, just with a smile.

"Mommy!" Sutton comes screaming into the room and we pull away quickly, ending this moment for us. This time.

Lacy wipes under her eyes, pulling away slower than I would expect under these circumstances which makes me more pleased than I should admit.

"What's up, baby girl?" Lacy asks with a sniff.

Sutton assesses her mother for just a second, likely trying to figure out why she's crying, before the excitement of the day takes over again. "Can I play on the swings?"

"There are swings?" Lacy glances back over at me, her lips tilting up.

"Outside, Mommy! By the pool! Can I go swimming?"

I chuckle at Sutton's enthusiasm. Looks like she's going to be spending a lot more time outdoors. I like that.

Lacy shoves her hands in her back pockets and looks at me. "How safe is the backyard? I assume it has a privacy fence?"

Looks like Lacy is back in mom mode, our near kiss either forgotten or shoved aside. It stings a little, but this isn't over. I just know it.

"Privacy fence with latches that are extra high so kids can't reach. Full fence around the pool with a double latch system. And you can see the entire yard from the living room and kitchen."

"Then I guess you can head to the swings, kiddo. Is Kody going with you?"

Sutton is already gone, running down the hall. "He's by the window," she calls over her shoulder, leaving Lacy and me alone again.

"You okay?" I ask gently and push a strand of hair off her face.

She glances down, then tilts her head to look up at me. "Yeah. I'm good. I guess this day is more emotional than I thought it would be."

I pull her to me again and hold her close. She doesn't resist.

"We're in this together, Lace."

And I mean it. Nothing is going to take me from my girls again.

"How was sleeping in the pool house?" I ask Ellie who isn't here for our morning coffee.

It's weird to be talking to her on the phone, especially since she's only a hundred yards away. It's not like I can't walk around the pool and have this same conversation in person. But I'm lazy and would rather sit at my new kitchen table, overlooking the back yard. Tucker is off at practice so I don't even have to put on pants.

Not that I need to be fully clothed. Now that he remembers the first night we met, everything feels like it has changed. Like something about having a history together, however short lived it may have been, means a deeper connection.

Or maybe I'm just horny and Tucker is hot. I'm not completely sure of what I'm feeling, but know I wouldn't mind us having another night together. From the way Tucker kept throwing glances my direction after all his memories came back yesterday, I don't think he'd mind that, either. But kids live here, *so hands off, Lacy*. You aren't twenty anymore.

Ellie practically moans in response. "That bed is the most comfortable thing I've ever slept on. It was like laying on a cloud all night. That man of yours didn't spare any expense on mattresses, did he?"

"First of all, he's not my man."

I push aside the thought of Tucker thrusting deep inside of me, instead focusing on the problem right in front of me.

Frowning inside the fridge, I can't find any milk for my coffee. Instead, all I'm seeing is various kinds of beer and cheese. Not sure how Tucker got the entire house decorated for a family, but forgot food. Looks like I'm going to need to make a grocery run today.

Ellie mumbles, "Yeah right."

I ignore her and finally find a small container of milk in the very back that I can use to doctor my coffee.

"Second, we must have gotten the same mattress because I almost had an orgasm just from laying down on it."

"I knew we were dirt poor, but I didn't realize how bad off we were until the air conditioning kicked on without making a *thunking* sound first."

I laugh because she's not wrong. "Isn't it nice to be in a place where the windows and doors are sealed tightly and there isn't that never ending stickiness of humidity?"

"I could fucking kiss you for making a baby with him."

Plunking myself down at the kitchen table, I take my first sip of my magical caffeine juice.

"That's how the baby was made in the first place, Ellie, so hands off. There are too many kids around here as it is."

Well not actually here. They're outside on the swings again while I sit here watching from the comfort of the air conditioning.

I can almost hear Ellie giggle at my comment except she doesn't giggle. Neither of us do. We specialize more in sarcasm than actual jokes. She must have slept *really* well last night.

"Speaking of kids," she asks. "How did they do last night?"

"Are you kidding? That bunk bed contraption thing was a huge hit. I didn't think they were ever going to sleep. They kept running up the stairs, bouncing across the bed, and sliding down the other side. They finally knocked out together on the bottom bunk. Did you see that's a full-sized mattress? So much for having two different beds for sleep overs."

"Don't sound so shocked. If I had a slide in my room, I'd stay up all night using it, too. You'd probably find me passed out on the floor at the bottom of it."

"I have found you passed out next to the toilet after a night out before."

"Life is too short to waste." I can imagine her waving her hand at me, dismissing my criticism. "On nights out or room slides."

"I admit, I am kind of jealous Sutton got the good bed. All I got was the world's most comfortable mattress."

"Seriously, though. Did you see Kody's room?"

I think for a second, knowing I toured the pool house. Did we get sidetracked in the kitchen? "Now that you say that, I don't think I got that far." Suddenly I feel the intense desire to see what I missed.

Jumping up from the table, I shove my feet into my discarded slippers and carefully slide the back door open making sure not to spill any of the liquid gold in my mug.

The kids are laughing as Kody tries to push Sutton on the swing. It keeps twisting and going sideways, ultimately knocking him over every time it swings back. They're getting way too much entertainment out of it, but at least they're having fun.

"Do you need more coffee?" Ellie asks and I know she can see me coming through the window.

"You plan on greeting me at your door with a fresh pot?"

"Hell no. I'm fancier than that. I found a carafe in the cabinet."

Sure enough, I barely make it to her front stoop—who knew a pool house would have an actual stoop?—when the door flies open, Ellie holds a fancy looking pitcher in one hand.

I click my phone off and slide it into the pocket of my night-shirt and hold out my mug for a top-off. She immediately complies.

"The fanciest part of this scene is you wearing your ratty bathrobe while holding a decanter that's worth more than my car."

"Your math is so far off," she says shutting the door behind me. "It's worth more than both our cars combined."

"Cheers to that."

We clink mugs and sip simultaneously, beginning to feel more human now that we're on our second dose.

I follow Ellie into her new humble abode, noticing details I didn't see yesterday during the chaos of moving. Like the beautiful light fixtures over a solid wood dining table. And the marble countertops in the kitchen. And the huge windows that overlook the backyard just like mine do, except from the opposite angle.

"This place is unreal," I marvel. "Do you think he had the designer do all this?"

Ellie shakes her head. "Nope. I looked up the pictures while they were still online and this is exactly what it looked like. I mean the couches were changed out but except for the bedrooms, this is the furniture it came with and everything. That dining table was left by the previous owners."

"And I thought we lucked out finding a ratty couch that only smelled a little when we moved into our apartment."

"Welcome to the lifestyles of the rich and famous, baby. Fully furnished means something completely different now. Speaking of..." she gestures for me to follow her down the hall where there are two bedrooms and a full bath between them.

The room on the left looks a lot like mine, except smaller. And Ellie hasn't made her bed yet while mine was done the second I got up. Force of habit from my childhood, I suppose.

The room on the right...

"Holy. Shit," I breathe, not believing my eyes. "Does he have a real fire truck in here?"

I don't think it's real because it's small enough to fit in this room, but the likeness is uncanny, down to the paint job and logo.

"It might as well be. Check it out." Ellie moves closer to give me the up close and personal view. She opens a double door on the side of the truck and.... "Voila. Bed number one is in here."

"No way." I push her over so I can see inside and sure enough, there's a twin mattress and some shelves built into the side.

"Yes way. He can get in through this door. Or he can get in the front of the cab and climb through that sliding door to get back here. And if he doesn't feel like sleeping on the bottom..." She gestures to a ladder at the back of the truck. It looks just like they have in real life, except smaller.

"This is the coolest bed I've ever seen," I muse.

"Yeah, well, it's not going to be cool forever. The siren really works."

"Oh shit," I say with a laugh.

"And it's loud. There's a reason I let Kody bunk with Sutton last night and it has everything to do with how many times I thought emergency services were on their way yesterday. I could kill Tucker for that part."

I sigh as I peek out the window to see the kids happily playing in the yard still. I love that they have grass and a swing set and a pool. But I just can't get over this feeling that it's all going to be short lived.

"What's wrong?" Ellie always could read my moods.

"Am I the only one who feels like this is too good to be true. Like this whole thing is just a fluke and is going to end badly."

"That's just your trust issues talking again." Ellie tries to be dismissive about it, but her words fall flat.

"Seriously, El. What happens if we get too comfortable and have to leave again?"

She shrugs like it doesn't concern her in the least. "We leave again."

"That doesn't bother you?"

"Not really. I'm living in an amazing place rent free for the next however long so I can bank almost everything I make. Really beef up my savings for when I need it. You should be doing the same. Better yet, you should be banking child support and going back to school to get that law degree you always wanted."

My finger taps the side of my mug absentmindedly. "I'm not sure I really want it anymore."

"What? Since when?"

I glance out the window again, watching the two kids I love more than anything as they giggle and squeal and enjoy their childhood. It's not something I want to miss.

"I guess since recently. Law school is tough and takes a lot of work. And then interning at a law firm and studying to pass the bar. I'm not sure I want to miss out on Sutton's life any more than I already do."

Ellie narrows her eyes, assessing me. "Why do I feel like you have a guilty conscience for wanting to stay home with her for a while?"

"Because I do. What kind of message is that sending to her? That I'm putting off my career ambitions to be Suzie Homemaker?"

She lifts her hand loosely, palm up. "One that says you have a choice to do what makes you happy regardless of what anyone else thinks."

"And what happens if it doesn't work out between me and Tucker?"

Ellie takes a quick sip before laying into me. "You sure have a lot of what-ifs for someone who moved in yesterday. Let me add some more. What happens if Tucker dies. Or gets horrifically injured in an accident. Or you fall in love and then he comes out of the closet. Or he invests all his money in bad business investments..."

"Okay, okay, I get it."

Ellie moves closer and puts her free hand on my shoulder. "Lacy, there's no guarantees on anything. Not on this. Not on the future. Hell, there were no guarantees when we moved into that shit hole together, but we took the plunge and did it anyway. I know you have a hard time trusting people. I *know* that. But you're looking for red flags where there aren't any because you're scared."

"But—

"No buts," she interrupts. "If you want to quit working and stay home with Sutton full time, go for it. I'm not going to be mad about the free childcare." My lips quirk up a bit recognizing her attempt at humor. "And if you want to put the kids in daycare and go back to school, do it. Let's say you get halfway done and the bottom drops out here and you have to go back to work. So what? You're still closer to your degree than you are now, right? And if the bottom doesn't drop out, you end up with everything you ever wanted. Maybe more. The future is going to happen one way or the other. Are you going to take advantage of this time you have? Or are you going to stay frozen and have regrets later?"

I recognize that she makes a lot of sense. But I also know I've spent a lot of time trying not to turn into my parents. I know it in the way I parent with grace and forgiveness and not an iron fist demanding perfection. I know it in the way I'm quick with loving words and slow with criticizing the kids. And I know it in the career path I thought I wanted to take. I don't want to become my mother.

She was a stay-at-home mom, living under the rules of her husband. While she used to say it's what she wanted to do, I knew better. I could see it on her face when we'd watch television and a career woman who had the best of both worlds was spotlighted. I knew she craved more than to just follow my dad's rules, only having purpose if he gave it to her. It always made me so angry she felt like life couldn't be any other way. Even now, when everyone is out of the house, she's still never done anything more with her life. Or at least that's what I've been able to deduce from stalking the little bits of social media my family has. I don't want that for myself. And I don't want Sutton to ever think she has to have that either.

Ohmygod.

I'm exactly like my mother—frozen with fear at the unknown. Wanting something more, but passively letting it pass me by instead of taking what I want. Too worried with what could happen if I put myself out there and not worried enough about missing out.

The realization hits me like a punch to the gut. The idea of being the same kind of mom to Sutton that mine was to me makes me sad. And yet, I was forced to dig deep over the last four years and now I have a strength my mother never found. I also have something she never had—the support of a very best friend.

Taking a deep, resolved breath, I turn back to Ellie. "You really don't mind putting the kids in daycare for a few hours a week?"

Her responding smile is all I need.

We glance out the window to see the kids twirling around until they're so dizzy they fall to the ground.

"I think maybe some structure and planned activities might be good for them," she says impassively and brings her mug to her lips again.

I just laugh, feeling a huge weight lift off my shoulders.

CHAPTER TWENTY

TUCKER

Somehow, some way, our team was graced with a miracle.

We have Thanksgiving Day off.

I have no idea how it happened, although I'm sure it was just luck of the draw. But to make things even better, today is unseasonably warm, even for Florida. *And* I have a brand new house that I'm ready to party in.

Add those three things together and a joint Thanksgiving/housewarming party was born.

This place is packed with people since basically the whole team is here. There are a few stragglers missing, mostly those who have family in the area. But since we leave early tomorrow morning for our next road trip, this was as close to a family holiday as most of us could get.

Speaking of family, I wonder where mine went?

"Hey man. Here's a refill for you." Nick places a beer down on the countertop next to my amazing outdoor grill. "Can I help with anything?"

As I suspected when we signed the contract, this outdoor space is the perfect place to host a bunch of people. The lounge area is comfy and comes complete with a huge outdoor television, there's lots of space in the backyard to move around and play cornhole, and this outdoor kitchen is a dream with an oversized grill with a burner for the non-grilled foods, a built-in fridge, and enough counter space for the food to be spread out buffet style.

I glance over my shoulder to tell my teammate I'm good, but Lacy catches my eye. She's standing next to the pool looking more like a lifeguard than a partygoer. I wonder what that's about.

"Actually, I think I could use a hand." I give Nick my spatula and contemplate giving him my apron but quickly decide against it. It says "Kiss the Cook" and I'm hoping I'll be able to convince Lacy to follow up on that. "Can you take over the grill for just a few?"

"Sure. Is this the last of it?" He presses down on one of the patties and the juice that squeezes out drips into the flames, making a satisfying sizzle.

"I think there's one more platter of hamburgers in the fridge if you don't mind."

"Yeah, no problem."

"Thanks, man."

I jog over and let myself into the pool area, wandering to the far side. Quickly, I figure out where the kids are by the squeals. They're having a blast swimming around in their little floaty vests, wiping water out of their eyes from the waves generated by so many people in the water at once.

Lacy, on the other hand, is standing with her arms crossed, her teeth digging into her bottom lip.

"Hey. What are you doing?"

She doesn't look up, her eyes trained on the water. "Watching the kids."

"You don't want to get in?"

"I don't like swimming when I'm on my period."

"Ah. Yeah. I get it. Don't want to risk a shark attack."

She punches me on my arm playfully, tearing her eyes away

from the kids for just a second. When she turns back, she's not happy about what she sees.

"Hey watch out!" Lacy yells when a game of chicken goes wrong. Patrick and his wife, who I've never seen up close and personal before, get knocked over and she practically falls on top of Kody. "There are kids in the pool! Don't they see we have kids in the pool?"

"They'll be okay," I say gently, trying to help ease her anxiety. I've never seen her this nervous. "They have their floaty vests on."

"That doesn't mean they won't be dunked unexpectedly and get water in their lungs. Dammit, he did it again." She shifts back and forth on her feet, and I wouldn't be surprised if she jumped in regardless of sharks. "Hey! Mr. Hockey Guy! Watch behind you!"

"Mr. Hockey Guy?" I snicker.

"I don't know his name. Tucker, go get the kids." She waves her hand their direction. "This is stressing me out."

"Yo, Patrick!"

Our captain shakes the water off his face, glancing up at me, shading his eyes with one hand and holding a beer can in the other. He and his wife went underwater, but somehow that beer stayed dry. Go figure.

"Can you grab my kids and steer them toward the edge?"

He looks over his shoulder and startles like he's suddenly noticing there are children in the pool with him. Dumb ass.

"Thank you," Lacy says as she pulls them from the water, the relief evident on her face.

"I want to swim, Mommy," Sutton complains and turns to jump back in, but I'm faster and grab her by the back of the vest.

"No more swimming," Lacy says sternly. A much more compliant Kody lets her get him out of his vest and wrapped in a towel. "We're going to have some hot dogs. Plus it's too dangerous right now."

I cock an eyebrow at her. "Don't you think you're over exaggerating just a bit?"

Just then, a wrestling match between Jake Vision and Anthony Stutteville ensues. They dunk each other around a few times knocking into other people, including two women that I've never seen before. I guess they're someone's "plus one". Or maybe "plus two". Who knows? Regardless, the women suddenly decide they want in on the action and as soon as the guys notice the women wrestling, they stop to watch. The one in the red bikini finally gets dunked, her friend in white raising her arms in victory. And as soon as red bikini comes up, we get a clear view of her boob before she rights her top.

"Oh good. A family friendly dinner and a show," Lacy says sarcastically and purses her lips at me, obviously pointing out her concern has been proven. "You did remember dinner, right?"

"Uh...." I scratch the back of my neck as I try to remember if I thawed out the hot dogs while I was grilling everything else.

"Tucker..." Lacy shakes her head and wraps Sutton in a bright yellow towel.

"Sorry. Just an oversight. Nick is manning the grill right now, so I'll get the hot dogs ready while you get the kids changed, does that work?"

That seems to appease her, and she starts to guide the kids off the warm pavement and toward the house. "Fine, yes. That works. Also, your friend Nick is really nice, by the way."

"Yeah, he is. Not everyone is willing to use his truck to help us move and then help out at a party instead of..." I gesture to more rabblerousing happening in the pool. "...whatever they're doing. He's a great goalie, too."

Lacy ignores the raucous behind us. "He's the goalie? That's so weird. I never put together his position and his name. I only see you guys in all your pads so I can't tell who anyone is. That's kind of cool to know the man under the mask."

"I've gotten to know him a little better when we room together sometimes on our road trips. Did you know he's the first person I told about Sutton?"

"Really?"

"Yeah." I smile at the memory of when I first started sharing my joy with people on the team. "He was really excited for me so I'm glad he's been able to hang out a bit and get to know her."

"Me, too."

We step into the cool house and kids immediately stop in their tracks, their teeth beginning to chatter.

Lacy encourages them to move forward. "Come on, friends. Let's get you warmed up."

"O-o-o-k-k-k-a-a-a-y," Kody chatters and they all amble down the hall, trying not to trip on the towels that are bigger than they are.

I, on the other hand, find the hot dogs exactly where I left them—in the freezer.

Oops.

Thankfully, it only takes a few minutes to thaw them in the microwave before taking the reins back from Nick and popping the kids' food on the grill. The timing is pretty perfect, as they're just about done when the kids come scampering outside again.

"Sorry that took us so long." Lacy plops down in a vacant chair as the kids run toward the swing set. "We would have been out here sooner except I was arguing with them over why they couldn't wear footy pajamas in ninety-degree weather."

"You're such a buzzkill, Mom," I joke making her shake her head in amusement. "No but seriously, it's fine. Hot dogs are coming off right now."

I use my new tongs to pull them off the grill and pop them right into the waiting buns.

"Um..." Lacy scrunches her nose.

I look down at the food, feeling like I'm missing something. "What?"

She grabs another plate and holds it out in front of her. "You might as well put them next to the bun, not inside them."

Wait, what? "They don't eat hot dogs and buns? I thought that was a staple of childhood nutrition."

"Oh they'll eat them. Just not together," Lacy clarifies, then adds, "And the ketchup goes on the bun, not the hot dog."

"Why?"

"Because they're three?"

"Kids are weird, man," I say with a shake of my head.

"You haven't even learned the half of it yet."

Once the plates are ready with hot dogs and *ketchup buns*, Lacy calls them over to eat. It only takes minimal encouragement, and as soon as they sit, I see why. They're starving. Probably from exerting so much energy trying to stay alive in the pool.

I dig into my burger, not at all interested in having what the kids are eating again. I've been doing that too much lately. I need to get back on track and a giant dose of real protein is exactly what I need.

"No, Kody, no!" Lacy suddenly yells and reaches over the table to grab an open beer out of his hand.

"Where did he get that," I ask, trying not to laugh at the fact that Kody almost had his first serving of Coors Light.

Lacy shrugs. "There are beer cans and bottles everywhere. It's not hard for them to get into it right now. Why do you think I'm watching them like a hawk?"

"Oh." That's my only response. I guess I didn't notice, but a quick look around confirms she's right.

"I thirsty," Kody whines.

"I know, baby. I'll grab you a drink."

Lacy runs inside and comes back with a couple juice boxes, making quick work of shoving the straws in and placing them on the table. Then she tucks into her food again.

Suddenly I feel someone kick me under the table. Assuming it's one of the kids, I look down only to see Lacy's foot connecting with my leg.

I furrow my brow and take another bite. "What?" I ask around my food.

She gestures across the way where Maksim is sitting on one of the loungers. Somehow, that asshole was able to find himself two dates for today's event, unless these are the twins he was talking about the other day. I guess they've all loosened up from heat and the booze. At least I assume that's why they've started a three-way make out session.

I roll my eyes and continue shoveling food in my face. Lacy kicks me again.

"What?"

"You gonna stop him?"

"Oh don't worry," I reassure her. "He's not an exhibitionist. Just likes to make out for a while."

Lacy pauses, a tortilla chip halfway to her mouth. "But we have kids sitting here."

I gesture to the kids in question who are smiling at each other like ketchup buns are the best thing they've ever tasted. "Their backs are to them."

"Tucker, seriously?"

Lacy's starting to get really irritated but I can't figure out why. No one is falling down drunk, and the only nudity was accidental. No one is acting creepy around the kids or offering them candy to go off into a dark corner. From where I'm sitting, this is about as family friendly as it gets.

"I don't understand what the big deal is, Lacy."

"They're three," she says forcefully. "They see everything and then model all that behavior. You really want them to pretend to make out with each other because they saw it on their back patio once?"

I go completely still as I digest what she's saying. "You think that'll happen?"

"My little sister and her best friend were pretending to be in the movie Tangled when they were four. My mom about lost her mind when she walked in on them practicing the kissing scene. And that was on television. Yes, yes I think ours will try something they see in live action."

I guess that makes sense. "Huh. I never knew that. Hey, Ivanov!"

Maks tears his lips away from the woman I now refer to as Date One to answer me. "'Sup?"

"Knock it off. I got kids, man."

To their credit, Date One and Date Two pull away looking a little sheepish. Maks, on the other hand, looks more frustrated than anything.

"There you go," I say with a nod at Lacy. "Problem solved."

Just then another partygoer runs by screaming, being playfully chased by Roger Shuto. We watch as he catches her, and wraps his arms around her, grabbing a handful of boob and squeezing, while she laughs.

Lacy drops her burger back on her plate and stands up. "That's it. We're done here."

"There wasn't even any skin."

"Nope. I'm not exposing them to all this just because you don't see the big deal." She gathers not only her plate, but the kids' as well. "Come on guys, I've got some cookies inside and a new movie."

Sutton and Kody jump up at the word "cookies", ready to follow her anywhere. But I'm starting to get irked. This is a family party. We should all be hanging out, enjoying our friends.

I follow her inside, bringing the kids drinks with me.

"Come on, Lacy. This is a little over the top. We're just trying to have a nice, fun Thanksgiving before being away for a week."

She drops the plates on the counter and whirls around to face me, fire in her eyes. "This isn't Thanksgiving. We're eating burgers."

"They're turkey burgers."

"Are you serious right now?"

"I don't understand why you're angry."

She looks away and takes a second to get her breathing under control. "When you said you wanted to have a housewarming party, I thought you meant some of your teammates coming over and hanging out, meeting me and the kids and having a nice time."

"And they are."

"No, *you* are having a nice time. *I* feel like the girl who accidentally got invited because she happens to be the prom queen's cousin."

I put my hand under my chin and bat my eyelashes, trying to break up the tension. "Am I the prom queen?"

She pushes off the counter and walks right past me, watching the kids race down the hall to Sutton's bedroom. "This isn't funny, Tucker. No one except Nick has spoken two words to me or the kids, it's not like you've introduced us to anyone, there's booze everywhere that Kody keeps trying to drink, and the beginnings of an orgy are happening right there on the back patio."

I throw my hands in the air and then place them on my hips. "What do you want me to do? Kick everyone out?"

"Yes. Or maybe just put a few boundaries up about what happens in the house where we're raising your daughter."

"These are grown men, Lacy. I'm not giving them a list of rules."

"Then maybe you guys need to party somewhere else."

My eyes narrow. I won't let up on this. These are my teammates. My friends. We're finally gelling on the ice and I don't want to lose the camaraderie we're building. "I'm not kicking them out of my house."

"Then it looks like you can have your 'family Thanksgiving,'" she says with air quotes, "without your family."

The back door slides open with an unnecessary bang and Maks comes strolling in, one arm over each of his dates. Their hands are running up and down his bare abs as they smile up at him seductively.

"Sorry to interrupt." He's not sorry and we all know it. "Do you have somewhere that we can get some, uh... privacy? Sherry here has something she needs to show me. Something about a talent she has with her tongue."

Lacy crosses her arms and glowers at me. "Would you like to offer up your bed, my bed, or your daughter's bed?"

"Don't worry," Maks interjects. "I'm very clean and always make the bed afterwards."

Looking me straight in the eye, Lacy says, "Ours are taken. I guess it's your bed that's going to get all the action."

Then she storms off down the hall, leaving me to deal with Maks and his continual lack of boundaries.

Guess I can get rid of the apron now. There's no way I'm getting that kiss today.

CHAPTER TWENTY-ONE

LACY

The kids were sad to see Tucker leave for another extended road trip, but they were the only ones. I'm happy to have the space.

After the debacle that was our Thanksgiving party, I need the time to get my nerves under control and figure out how we're going to make this work. I knew learning to co-parent was going to be difficult, but I had no idea how little Tucker actually knows about raising kids.

He has no sense of how to keep them safe and healthy. Even worse, as much as he loves them, it's like he hasn't figured out how to make them a priority. He's still stuck in some of his bachelor ways and that is a huge problem.

I will give him credit for having the love part down. He seems to enjoy pre-bedtime snuggles and is always willing to get down on the floor and play with the kids. And my biggest pet peeve that probably isn't doing as much damage as I fear—he spoils them. If Sutton said she wanted a pony, I guarantee Mr. Ed would be hanging out in our backyard by morning.

That's how we ended up with this huge, white Christmas tree set up next to the fireplace that is unusable because it's too hot outside. One of the kids, I'm not sure which one, brought up

Santa last night and the conversation spiraled into making sure they have a house decorated in as much Christmas spirit as possible.

I woke up after Tucker had left, and this monstrosity was already here, boxes of decorations scattered around the room for us to use. The kids are delighted. Me, not so much.

"You are such a sourpuss," Ellie says as she drags another box over so we can open it and see what treasure is inside.

I don't bother reaching for it, knowing she's leaving for work in a few minutes and I'll end up doing the whole thing. Might as well rest up.

"I am not. I'm just not a huge decorator and you're leaving. I'm not excited to do this all by myself."

"You're not by yourself. You have them." She gestures to the kids who are decorating each other with tinsel. "Okay so maybe you'll end up doing this by yourself."

"We're going to find tinsel everywhere for months, aren't we?"

Ellie tries to rip open the box but only gets about halfway before the world's most indestructible tape stops her progress. "It's worth it for that moment, right there." She gestures her head as she continues to struggle.

I sigh. "I suppose you're right."

Finally abandoning the box, which still isn't open, Ellie settles in next to me and puts her feet up on the coffee table. "What a difference a year can make, huh? Last year we had that tiny, beat up old tree reminiscent of Charlie Brown's Christmas, and this year," she waves her hand in the general direction of the very full fake fir tree. "This is what we get to gather around."

"Seems like a lot of things have changed over the last year. Really everything has. Not that it's bad. It's just... fast."

"I can't believe you finally quit your job," she muses. "Took you long enough."

That is an understatement. The minute Tucker presented me with the child support papers, I knew my options had opened up and I wasn't sure what to do with that. Not only did it seem too good to be true, but I was so deeply intrenched in the panic of going without, it took a while to realize we're not living paycheck-to-paycheck anymore. We're not even living child support check to child support check. With just the last two payments, I've set aside enough to pay for a year's worth of rent and utilities in a good apartment in a decent neighborhood. And my next payment should be here by next week.

It's mind boggling.

But it also made me finally wrap my brain around the fact that I'm now in a position to reach for my dreams and I need to take advantage of that. To show Sutton how to take opportunities you've been given and run with them. To work smarter, not harder.

I'm working on that last one. The guilt I feel when Ellie goes to work is still there. But slowly I'm coming to recognize that by taking advantage of my opportunity, I've been able to give her breathing room, too. Remembering that helps keep the remorse at bay.

"I just need to figure out what I want to do now." I wrap a strand of hair around my finger and check out my split ends as the kids throw tinsel on the tree instead of each other. "I'm trying to allow myself time to rest and get my head on straight, but I'm not used to sitting around. I need to figure something out soon."

"So no idea about school yet?"

"I might have an idea. I just need to weigh the pros and cons first."

Ellie pats my thigh and pushes up from the couch. "That's your assignment for tonight. Registration for next semester starts soon, so you need to make a decision."

"Yes, Mom," I joke but of course Ellie runs with it.

"Good girl." Reaching down, she kisses both kids on the top of the head. "I have to go to work but I'll be back later, okay?"

"Awww," Kody pouts but isn't too distressed. Not that he ever is, but that tree is a huge distraction for him. He and Sutton give his mom a quick hug around the legs and back to the tinsel they go. That one big silver blob at the front of the tree is going to look amazing.

Ellie grabs her keys, kisses me on the top of the head too, and calls, "See ya," over her shoulder as she heads toward the garage where her car is parked.

Yes, she gets her own space, but with a five-car garage, there's room. The kids aren't the only ones who are spoiled.

Taking a deep breath, I force a burst of energy through me. "Okay guys." I stand up and begin looking through the boxes. "Let's see what kind of decorations we have."

I'm not sure where everything came from, but every box is full of Christmas balls and icicles and ribbon, all in shades of silver and blue. It reminds me more of something you'd see on display at a fancy hotel than like a family tree.

The kids get even more excited by all the shiny things and after about three seconds of hesitation, I show them how to hang some of the fancy silver balls on the branches. They pick up the instructions pretty quickly, but I have to show them how to spread things around because they seem to want to use the same branch every time. I don't mind. It gives the tree some character. And if this is going to be a family Christmas, the tree can still be pretty, but we're going to glam it down a little.

I'm rifling through boxes, pulling out packages and opening what I want when the doorbell rings.

That's weird. I wonder if Tucker is expecting another package.

I carefully step through the maze of decorations and packing material to go to the door.

"Okay you heathens, you can keep putting up the silver balls, but be careful."

Not surprising, they ignore me.

Finally free of bubble wrap and box dividers, I don't bother to peek out the window before swinging the door wide open.

Standing in front of me, is the last person I expected to see. "Muriel?"

My heart starts beating fast, my breathing picking up.

Could it be? Is it really my baby sister standing in front of me?

She smiles tentatively, tears shining in her eyes. "Hi Lacy."

I launch myself into her arms, crying and stroking her hair as we cling to each other. She looks the same as I remember, with her long dark blond hair and crystal brown eyes, but any last remnants of baby fat have fallen off. She feels different than the last time I hugged her too, no longer a lanky teenager but a woman.

We stay like that for who knows how long before I finally pull away, wiping the tears off my cheeks while they continue streaming down hers.

"Are you really here?" I look her up and down, still not convinced she's not an apparition. "I mean you are. But how did you get here? How did you track me down?"

She wipes at her eyes, and I marvel at how much they look like mine. I'd forgotten. "I went to your last known address and asked around. It didn't take long for someone to spill that they saw you leaving with this hockey star. Your neighbors may have kept to themselves at that apartment, but they knew a whole lot of gossip."

I huff out a watery laugh and sniffle. "Come in, come in." I pull her inside, keeping one hand on her arm so I don't have to stop touching her. We spent eighteen years sharing a bedroom. Having her here feels like reattaching a part of me. "The kids and I are decorating the tree. Badly, but we're making some progress."

Muriel stops and looks at me, eyes wide. "She's here? My niece? I get to meet her?"

The gravity of this moment hits me full force. This will be the first time someone in my biological family meets my daughter. And she came here willingly to do so.

I pull my sister close again, still unable to believe that this is happening. "Of course you do. Sutton's going to love you." I grab her hands and tug her with me. "Come on."

The living room looks exactly like I left it—in complete and utter chaos. But the kids are giggling and almost all the silver balls are hanging on the lower portion of the tree, so progress.

"Hey kids. Sutton. Kody." It takes a few times of saying their names before they finally stop ignoring me. "Look who's here."

Tearing their gaze away from all the shiny things, I can see the gears turning in their brains.

Kody is the one to break first. "Who this?"

"This is your Aunt Muriel."

I hold my breath as they look skeptically at her. Eventually though, Sutton reaches down to pick up her stuffed dog that was forgotten on the floor in all the excitement this morning.

Holding it up, she says, "See my puppy?"

"I do," Muriel responds, her eyes shining as she gazes at my daughter. "It's a very nice puppy."

Sutton's nod indicates that was the right answer, but it doesn't change the fact that the kids are still less interested in yet another adult in their lives and more interested in decorating. Which is fine. Muriel and I have a lot to talk about anyway.

Tossing boxes out of the way, I make a path to the couch.

"Come have a seat. Oh my gosh, I still can't believe you're here," I breathe. My whole body feels like it's vibrating from the excitement. I've missed Muriel so much.

"Lacy?"

"Hmm?" I look up to see her still staring at the toddlers.

"Do you have twins?"

"Oh." I laugh lightly. "No. That's our friend Kody. He lives in the pool house with his mom, my best friend, so they think they're twins. We stopped trying to correct them a while ago, so just go with it."

"Oh. Okay." Muriel continues to watch them, likely absorbing every giggle, every frown, every lightbulb moment they have. Her expression seems to match what I'm feeling.

I'm so sad she's missed the first three years of Sutton's life, but I'm filled with such joy that she's here now. That she's back. That she's here to be a part of our lives. I think.

How long is she here for? Is this just a quick trip? Do Mom and Dad even know she's in Tampa? How soon does she have to leave? The questions start infiltrating my mind.

Patting her arm, I lean back on the couch. "Tell me how things are. Really. What's been going on with you for the last few years?"

She finally pulls her gaze away from the kids to look at me. "Well, college was hard."

"How so?"

She hesitates and I already know I'm going to cringe at her answer.

"After you got pregnant, Dad got even more strict than he was before."

"Oh no." I close my eyes, feeling the guilt of being the one that ruined it for her. Or at least, my actions being the catalyst.

"Yeah. He was determined that I wouldn't go down the same path."

"The sinful slut I was, and all that."

Muriel looks back and forth between me and the kids, eyes wide, and I don't have to be a psychic to know what she's thinking.

I take a quick peek at them, making sure they aren't trying to climb the tree because Kody probably would, and wave my sister off. "Don't worry. They won't pick up on the word slut. They hear way worse than that."

"Really?"

"Yeah. I'm not a perfect parent, but I try to let things that don't matter in the long run go. I don't want her to feel smothered like we were. Speaking of, so Dad pulled back what little reins you already had when you went off to school?"

She nods. "Remember Nosy Rosy? From church?"

Do I ever. She was the biggest tattletale. No one could stand being around her because she always told our parents what we were up to, even if it wasn't bad. Nothing was secret around her. Not even when the pastor forgot to wash his hands after using the restroom one time. He never made that mistake again.

"Don't tell me they made you start hanging out with her."

"Worse. They made her my dorm roommate for the entire four years of college."

I groan and pinch between my eyes. "Oh no. Oh Muriel, I'm so sorry. Were you just miserable?"

"Yes and no. It was hard at first because I was so looking forward to having some freedom, to come and go as I pleased, so it was stifling. Basically like living at home except with someone else cooking."

"But?"

"But someone, and I'm not sure who, convinced Rosy to go to a party one night and from then on, I rarely saw her."

I bark out a stunned laugh. "She what, just became a party animal?"

Muriel shrugs. "That's the only thing I can figure. I didn't try to track her down and ask or anything. All I know is she stopped caring what I was doing, and I was fine with that."

"I wish I could say I'm surprised, but it always seems to happen that way, right?"

"I guess. I mean, by the time she flew the coop or whatever I was already up to my eyeballs with upper-level classes and an internship so it didn't make much of a difference. But still, I'm glad to finally be done and free of that threat."

Pride swells in my chest. My baby sister is a college graduate. She's already accomplished things I still have on my list. She's done so well.

I reach out to touch her again because I can't stop making sure she's really here. "I'm so proud of you. What was your major? And what are you doing now? Are you just here for a couple days or what?"

"Actually, I moved here."

My jaw drops open. "Here?" She nods. "To Tampa."

She nods again, this time biting back a smile. "I have a marketing degree so I'm on the hunt for a job in that arena. But this is where I want to be. Closer to you. And my niece."

My hands cover my mouth, trying to hold in the overwhelming emotion I feel. "Really?"

"Of course. I've missed you so much and I want a relationship with you and Sutton. That's her name right? Sutton?"

"Yes. But what about Mom and Dad? Aren't they mad?"

"Of course they are." She says it so nonchalantly, I have to wonder if they know she's here, but don't know she's *here*. In my house. "They wanted me to graduate and go straight home to be married off to some awful parishioner who spouts off about having a relationship with God, but has a closet addiction to child porn. I didn't even remotely want that."

Sadly, she tells the truth. More than one of our church friends did exactly that. Some of them were barely out of high school before getting married and popping out babies. Sometimes I wonder if we were actually raised in a cult, albeit not a well-run one.

"But what are they going to do?" Muriel continues. "College is over and I saved almost every penny from the job I had so I could have a little nest egg while I job hunted. I don't need them to front the bill anymore. They can be part of my life or not. That's up to them. The boys already cut me off, but no surprise there."

It makes me sad to know our brothers have given up on both of us. When we were young, I thought they hung the moon. They were our protectors and our playmates. Now, they're strangers who put ideology before people. I hate that. And I hate that my sister gave up the whole family willingly for me. For us.

"Are you sure this is what you want to do?" I ask. "There's still time to make it right. I'm sure they'd take you back if you lived anywhere else except here."

"I *have* made it right, Lacy. I'm showing them that they're wrong. You don't cut people out of your life when they make a mistake, not that Sutton is a mistake. But for all the rules and regulations they like to teach regarding religion, they're missing the part about grace and compassion. I don't want anything to do with that."

I grab my sister's hand, grateful that she loves me so much, she's willing to make a stand. I only wish my parents could see how much damage they have done to our family, but I doubt that will ever happen.

"Anyway." Muriel slaps her hands on her knees, clearly wanting to move on from such a difficult topic. "Need help decorating?"

"Absolutely!"

We spend the rest of the day and well into the evening decorating, cleaning up behind ourselves and just enjoying each other's company. My heart swells as I watch my baby sister get to know my baby girl and see how much Muriel falls in love with the love of my life.

I feel another wall in my heart come tumbling down.

CHAPTER TWENTY-TWO

TUCKER

The lock clicks behind me as I toss my travel bag down on the floor next to the door.

"I'm home!" I yell, marveling at how oddly wonderful it is to be able to yell that into my house, knowing someone is home to hear it.

"Tucker!" A flurry of small arms and legs attack me before I'm able to make it out of the entryway. Amid the tickles and squeals, I'm finally able to pick up both kids, who immediately throw their arms around my neck.

Wow. I didn't expect toddler hugs to be so... *right*.

"Oh man, I missed you guys," I say as I squeeze them tight.

"We...we got a...a Christmas tree!" Kody's eyes light up as he wiggles onto the ground, running over to the tree and pointing at it.

I cock my head to the side, taking in a giant tinsel ball right in the front, and realize none of the decorations go up higher than my arms can reach. Scratch that—higher than Lacy's arms can reach. The top third is completely bare except for the built-in lights.

"Wow. You guys did a great job." I force enthusiasm into my voice.

"It's a bigger tree than I've ever decorated before and I didn't trust them to not follow me up the ladder." Lacy's voice behind me gives me a feeling of being home. Not just at my house, but *home*. It's a fuzzy feeling. One I haven't felt since I lived with my mother, which sounds a little bit Oedipus complex-like if I think too hard about it. "If you don't like how it ended up, you get to fix it, Hayes."

"Now why would I do that?" I ruffle Sutton's hair and put her down. "It's perfect."

I shove my hands in my pockets, not quite sure what to do with myself. Do I hug Lacy hello? Greet her with a kiss on the cheek? I don't know what the protocol is since it's our first time of me returning after being gone and we left on such bad terms.

Thankfully, Lacy decides for me, heading back toward the kitchen but gesturing for me to follow her. "How was your trip?"

"Only lost one game so I can't complain."

"I know that part," she jests. "You know we watch all your games. I meant how was the travel part. Sleeping in hotel beds and airline peanuts and all that jazz."

She gestures for me to have a seat and picks up a knife to continue cutting up veggies.

I gratefully take it. I'm wiped.

"In a nutshell, hotel beds are hit or miss, air travel is over-rated, and I'm allergic to nuts."

Lacy freezes mid chop, glancing over at a bag of cashews off to the side, a look of horror on her face. "Are you serious?" she whispers.

I can't keep up the ruse. I'm a jokester for sure, but even I can't make her feel bad like that. "No."

"No?"

"I'm not allergic to nuts. I was just being funny about the airline stuff."

She breathes out a sigh of relief. "Ohmygod, I almost had a heart attack. My brain was trying to remember if I brought any peanut M&M's into the house or mixed any crushed nuts into the bread crumbs I used on the chicken the other day. I was ready to stab you with an epi pen."

"That's a step up from just stabbing me for being an idiot," I quip, knowing we still need to address how we left things, but not quite ready to go there. Instead, I reach across the counter and snag a small carrot, popping it into my mouth. "Are you making a salad?"

She smiles, and I know she gets why I'm confused. I can't recall ever seeing her eat a vegetable unless salsa counts. "I am. You see this guy keeps throwing all his money at me so instead of having to stick to a strict and unhealthy budget at the grocery store, I got all kinds of healthy options. I think the kitchen looks remarkable with all the different colors of real veggies on the counter, don't you?"

"Absolutely. Just like out of a magazine," I play along. "But you really think the kids are going to eat that?"

"Ha!" she barks out. "Not on your life. This is for us. I figured you'd be hungry, so I've got some of the left-over *nut-less* chicken in the fridge to mix in. I'm not totally sure what an athlete's diet looks like, but it's a start anyway."

I'm touched that she thought of me and is going out of her way to make me dinner. I was nervous about how things would be when I got home, considering the fight we had right before I left. All seemed to be normal when we would video chat and I know her sister's surprise visit was such a huge thing for her that it over-shadowed everything else. But this feels like a real olive branch for me, one that I will gladly take.

"That's nice of you, thank you." I grab a piece of green pepper this time, only she bats my hand away making me almost drop it.

"There won't be any left if you keep munching before it's ready."

"And how long will that be? Do I have time to shower the airplane off me?"

She picks up the cutting board and uses the knife to scrape the ingredients into a large mixing bowl. "Depends on how wilted you like your salad. I just have to mix it all together."

"Then I'll wait."

Making myself useful while she finishes up, I walk around the island to grab a couple large salad bowls and utensils. We both step into the same space at the same time and my hands automatically land on her hips, keeping us from colliding.

We both freeze, the feeling of our bodies next to each other a reminder of that night when we danced just like this. My mind stutters to a halt as my body reacts, my groin tightening from the feel of her, the scent of her, the nearness of her body. I lean in closer, unable to stop myself from breathing her in.

Lacy's own inhalation stutters and my fingers tighten as I battle the urge to pull her closer to me.

A squeal from the other room breaks the moment and I'm not sure if I'm grateful for the interruption so I don't do anything Lacy regrets or not.

Clearing my throat, I move around her to the cabinets. "Do the kids needs plates or bowls?"

"Plates please," she says quietly, likely recovering from her own thoughts. "I was going to make them peanut butter sandwiches, now that I know your face won't blow up like one of those weird fish."

And she's back.

I chuckle. "Well that doesn't sound like a well-balanced meal. They need some veggies, too."

"Which is why I mixed some avocado into the peanut butter so at least they're getting something extra in their diet. Next time I might dice some asparagus and mix that in, too."

I make a gagging sound. "Lacy, that sounds disgusting."

"Oh, my dear Tucker. You have so much to learn about

tricking children into making healthy choices. Just wait until you learn about the Clean Up song. They practically go into a hypnotic state getting all their toys put away as fast as they can."

I actually know this one because my mother used to use it on my brother. But I can never get the tune out of my brain once it's sung, so I push that tidbit out of my thoughts as quickly as possible.

Instead, we gather the kids and have what amounts to a nice family lunch. Or as nice as it can be with the kids eating doctored peanut butter. The conversation revolves around Christmas and Kody and Sutton talk over each other about lights, decorations, and what they're asking Santa for.

When Sutton says she wants a kitten, an idea sparks. I must get that contemplative look on my face all intellectuals have because Lacy picks up on it immediately.

Pointing her fork at me as she finishes her bite, all she says is, "Don't even think about it, buster."

I raise my hands up defensively. "I only have ideas at this point."

"Mmhmm," she hums. "I have no intension of raising an animal. I already have two of them." She gestures to the hooligans who are currently showing each other their chewed up food.

"Who says you'd be the one raising it?" I ask.

"Anyone who has ever had children who asked for a pet as a gift."

I open my mouth to tell her all the ways I can be the one to help out but she cuts me off.

"You spend half the season on the road so don't even try it. Your ideas mixed with your paycheck equals spoiling them rotten. Pull back a bit. You've got a lifetime to go."

Yeah. I do have a lifetime to go. I love knowing that this is just the beginning of our time together as a family. Who knew hearing those words wouldn't scare me, but make me excited? I'm surprised by it myself.

I stab at my salad and decide to change the subject. I think jet lag has me feeling overly emotional. Not that there's much jet lag flying from Phoenix to Tampa, but I'll run with it anyway.

"Speaking of lifetimes, have you talked to your sister again?"

Pushing her empty bowl aside, Lacy leans her arms on the table. "Every day, actually."

I pause my chewing, not able to interpret her expression, and feeling like I need to tread lightly. "That's good, right?"

Seeming to snap out of whatever thought she was in, Lacy's eyes brighten. "Oh yeah. For sure. There's so much catching up to do. It's been great."

I cock my head. There's that expression again.

"Why doesn't your face match your words?"

"What?"

I point my fork at her, drawing it in a circle. "Your face. The look you're giving doesn't match when you say it's been great talking to her."

"I didn't realize I was so transparent."

"You're not. That's why I can't tell what it means. Care to enlighten me?"

She gnaws on her bottom lip for a few seconds before giving me some insight. "It's just weird, having this huge gap of time that I missed. Muriel was a teenager the last time I saw her and now she's...a woman. A grown up. She's not my little sister anymore. She's still younger and all, but she's experienced so much life that I've missed over the last few years."

"Is that a bad thing?"

"No. Not at all. I'm happy she's accomplished so much."

"But...?"

"But I feel a little like I haven't accomplished much of anything."

Lacy's lips twist to the side and her nose crinkles, like she's uncomfortable saying those words out loud.

"I think the obvious is you've successfully kept a child, well, two kids, alive. That's a pretty big accomplishment."

"I know. That's why I didn't want to say anything. I don't want to diminish the fact that I've been raising Sutton. She's absolutely the best thing that has ever happened to me."

Pushing my own bowl away, I wipe my mouth with my napkin. "Lacy, it's okay to have dreams and goals outside of her."

"I know that."

"Do you? Because it seems like you're mincing your words a bit."

She shrugs one shoulder and I know I've nailed it.

"Look, I'm not going to downplay how hard you've worked the last few years, and you shouldn't either. I don't know many women who could have done what you did. If there was a degree in pulling yourself up by your bootstraps, you'd have a Master's by now. Bachelor's at the very least."

"I think it's more like a Doctorate, but whatever," she grumbles playfully.

"I stand corrected. So go get your next degree. There's nothing stopping you. Certainly not me."

"You really think I should go for it? It wouldn't bother you if Sutton was in daycare?"

Just then one of the kids hollers from the living room. Kody has Sutton pinned to the floor, but before either of us can step in and pull him off, Sutton pulls her legs up to her chest, anchors her feet on Kody's midsection and pushes. He goes flying, lands with a thud, then stands up and laughs before running to tackle her again.

"Maybe a little socialization outside of each other would be good for them, hey?"

"I'll be registering for classes today," Lacy deadpans, a blank look on her face as she watches the kids repeat their move over and over.

"Oh, and one more thing."

Lacy's eyes find mine and I cringe, knowing this news might go over like a lead weight. Taking a deep breath, I prepare for her to tackle me next.

"My mother is coming for Christmas."

Lacy's eyes widen, and she shrieks, "What?!"

"I couldn't stop her. She's ready to meet the kids and said the holidays are the perfect time. Not that I'll be here the whole time since I have that road trip..." I tack on under my breath.

Lacy's head falls back and I admit, it's a much milder reaction than I expected. She takes a second or two before righting herself. "I guess I'll register for classes and then start researching how to be the perfect hostess."

"You have like three weeks to get ready."

She shoots me a glare.

"I promise, it's going to be a fun Christmas with my mom here."

Just then, the tinsel ball from the tree goes flying across the table.

Looks like the fun has already begun.

CHAPTER TWENTY-THREE

LACY

Ever since Tucker came into our lives, he's been trying to get us to go to a hockey game. Live. In the arena.

I've resisted because they're usually late games and the kids don't do well with missing their bedtime. But today's game has an early start time, so it won't push their routine by too much.

Also, and I would never admit this to Tucker, I'm curious to see what he does. Yes, we watch all the games on television, but I wondered if it would feel different to be near the ice with him. To see things from this vantage point.

I was right. Not only is hockey way hotter in person, there's something about being in the cold, smelling the ice that made it come alive in a way it doesn't from my couch.

And there was something really sexy about Tucker knowing where we were sitting and making it a point to tap the glass with his stick and smile at the kids every once in a while. The sweetness of the gesture, the acknowledgement that we belong to him, it all made me feel more than I expected.

But I can't kid myself. Tucker always makes me feel more than I expect. He has from the beginning.

Before I found out I was pregnant, I couldn't stop my fixation over our night together all those years ago, wondering and wishing I would see him again at some point. When I found out I was pregnant, that fixation turned to anger and rage.

In hindsight, I'm not sure I was mad at Tucker as much as I was mad at the situation and he was the easiest target. My strength to get through it wasn't because I felt all that strong as much as it was me holding my emotions ramrod straight so I didn't collapse under the weight of all the pressure. But in my dreams, when my subconscious came out to play, Tucker was there and the anger wasn't. Just replays of the hottest night of my life and an overwhelming desire to see him again.

Funny how life plays out sometimes. Now we're still waiting to see him again, only this time, I know he's on his way.

"Are you sure you're okay watching Kody for a little longer?"

I roll my eyes. I've lost count of how many times Ellie has asked me this question tonight.

"Yes, Ellie. It's fine. You know as well as I do that there's no difference in having an extra kid except they bug each other instead of me."

I glance up at the sign above us making sure we're still walking the right way. Ellie is holding one kid's hand, I'm holding the other kid's hand, and the kids are holding onto each other as well. I'm sure we're blocking traffic behind us, but I don't care. I'm more concerned with making sure we don't all get lost from each other.

"I know," Ellie all but whines. "I just feel like you've been watching him more lately. I feel guilty."

"If you were going to work, you'd be fine. You feel guilty because you have a date, not because I'm watching him."

"Maybe a little."

I stop and turn to her, pulling us all in closer so people can get by easier. "Stop with the mom guilt. You haven't had any adult fun in I don't know how long. You deserve one night to see if this guy you've met is actually nice. He could be amazing. Or he could be a douchebag, but at least you get some free drinks out of it. So go. Have fun. And leave the guilt at the door."

She wrinkles her nose as the internal battle wages one. "You're sure? Really sure?"

"If you ask me that again, I'm changing my mind and giving you both kids while I go out."

"Never mind," she says quickly. "I'll get over myself."

"That's what I thought," I say with a nod. "We need to leave you here. This is our turn."

Ellie peers around me. "That's the tunnel down there?"

"I'm guessing by the beefy security guard stopping people from going that way."

Ellie bats her eyes. "Wonder what that security guard is up to tonight. He's kind of delicious, isn't he?"

I shake my head. Leave it to Ellie to have a backup plan in case her actual date goes south.

"Down girl. He's working. Now get out of here before traffic gets any worse and it cuts into your downtime."

There are hugs all around as we say our goodbyes. Kody starts to get a little resistant to his mom leaving, but when I remind him we're going to find Tucker, he quickly changes his tune. He seems to forget her completely once I flash our security passes at the guard and we make our way down to the spot where Tucker told me he'd meet us. I assume this is where we're supposed to be considering other people are waiting against the walls near a door that says "locker room" above it in blazing letters.

A few dozen people with badges like mine mill about, chatting mostly with each other. There are a few straggling reporters as well. I wonder why certain reporters get inside the locker room and these don't.

I don't have time to think about it for long before the locker room door opens and the man we've been waiting for saunters out. I do a double take at the sight of him in a suit. I've never seen him dressed up like this before. Granted, I've never come to a game before and normally it's late enough when he gets home, so we're already in bed.

He's stopped by a reporter before he sees us. He's probably answer questions about what went wrong on the ice tonight, which gives me a chance to take him in without him noticing.

I can't stop from giving him the once over as the fabric stretches over his body, giving just a hint of exactly how strong and powerful he is. When he runs his fingers through his floppy hair, I'm almost surprised the sleeve of his jacket doesn't rip right open.

And then he turns and sees me. The polite smile he's pasted on while explaining tonight's loss changes to a deep, genuine grin. If we weren't in this tunnel right now with people around and the kids hovering, I might jump straight into his arms and suck his tongue right off.

He glances down at the kids and that's all the encouragement they need to run to him and jump in his arms before I can stop them. Tucker just scoops them up and nuzzles into them, making them giggle.

The reporter, a dark-haired beauty who looks like she could have stepped out of the pages of *Maxim* magazine, looks confused. "Who do we have here?"

Without skipping a beat, Tucker says, "These are my kids."

"Your... You have kids?" From the way her eyes keep moving back and forth, it's clear she's trying to decide if this is information she already knew, or if she just stumbled across a new story.

Tucker doesn't notice her confusion, the kids holding his total focus. "Yep. And it's almost their bedtime so if you'll excuse me, we have to get home."

Tucker hands Kody to me and puts his arm over my shoulder, guiding me forward. "Let's go." The seriousness of his tone leaves no room for argument, but as the reporter continues to follow us, calling out even more questions, I understand why.

"How old are your kids, Tucker?"

He doesn't answer. I glance up at him and he gives his head a slight shake, silently telling me not to respond. That doesn't stop the barrage of questions, though.

"Are they twins? How have you kept them a secret for so long? Ma'am." The microphone is suddenly in my face. I hug Kody closer to me, holding his head to my chest and keeping my own head down as we walk. "Ma'am, are you their mother? How long have you and Tucker been together?"

As we reach the exit, two security guards join us from out of nowhere. They don't stop the reporter but at least they flank us as we make our way to Tucker's Cayenne.

We make quick work of buckling the kids in their car seats and finally we're in the safety of the vehicle. I admit, I thought Tucker springing for a Porsche was extravagant, but this sucker is so tight, the noise from outside ceases immediately when the door shuts, even though I can see the reporter's mouth still moving.

As soon as the security guards get her a safe enough distance away, we're gone.

"What was that?" I ask, a tremor from the adrenaline rushing through my body.

Tucker looks to the left before taking a right out of the parking garage. "That was us being found out."

Leaning back against the headrest, I pinch the bridge of my nose. "That was intense. Does that always happen?"

"Nah." He checks his blind spot before hitting the highway. I don't understand his nonchalance. "I've only seen that happen after the Stanley Cup or if there is some big scandal happening. I guess we're the scandal."

"Does that mean we're going to need to beef up security? Are reporters going to start following us?"

I hate the idea of having the kids' pictures being taken and plastered all over the internet for anyone to see. And the idea of having security guards following us everywhere seems so stifling. I know we agreed to try this living arrangement, but this isn't what we signed up for.

Tucker reaches over and grabs my hand, like he can sense my unease. I clasp tightly onto his fingers. "If we have to hire someone temporarily we will, but really Lacy, I think that was all of it. This isn't really a scandal. That reporter just realized she stumbled on a story no one else has. I'm sure my publicist will be calling tonight to see what we want our official comment to be so she can run her story and that'll be the end of it."

That sounds too easy. "Are you sure?"

"Almost positive." His emphasis on *almost* isn't missed by me. "This isn't Hollywood. The level of care about this sort of thing is way less than if I was an A-lister."

He does have a point. All the tabloid magazines and entertainment shows focus on the creative type of celebrities. I almost never see pictures of athletes unless they're dating an actor or musician. That makes me feel better, if still a little curious.

"What is your statement gonna be?"

He glances at me quickly with a smile before turning back to the road. "That depends on how honest you want me to be."

I think on it for a second before coming to the realization that we have nothing to hide. Sutton is his daughter and I'm her mom. Tucker and I get along and we're living in the same house. Sure, some of my old co-workers may wonder how the hell this happened since all they know is I quit my job after coming into some money, so I can imagine what kinds of questions Ellie will have to field tomorrow. Honestly, I don't really care about their opinion anyway. It's not like we were close.

The only people I would wonder about is my family. I hope the news means they would reach out, maybe apologize for how they cut us out of their lives. Then again, I don't want people suddenly sniffing around now that money is involved. Still, it would be nice to know the news would eventually get back to my mother. I don't know if she feels guilty or worries, but maybe it would ease some of her fears knowing we're okay.

"How about we just say that your three-year-old daughter, and our good friend came with us to the game tonight. We can pretend like it was never a thing, they just missed it somehow. Will that work?"

The soft smile on Tucker's face doesn't just indicate he's in agreement. It also does something to my insides.

The Tucker I had a one-night stand with was funny and charming and truly an athlete in bed. The Tucker I've come to know is always laughing and going above and beyond to provide for his family. This Tucker, the Tucker who puts his arm around me to stay close when we're bombarded by a reporter, who cares about my opinion and feelings when determining how to navigate unusual situations, this Tucker has me pressing my thighs together trying to hold back my now raging libido. There is nothing hotter than a man who treats a girl with respect and distinction.

I'm not opposed to having a one-night stand with him, it's been way too long since I've scratched that itch, but I need to be careful around Tucker. My heart is already too involved with this situation. I can't have it broken. I'm not sure I could survive him leaving us. Even more so, I don't want Sutton to have to try.

"I think that's the perfect response," Tucker finally says. "Short. Sweet. To the point. And giving no indication that our situation is unusual in any way."

"Because there's nothing unusual about having twins that aren't twins and two single women living on your property four years after meeting one of them for the first time and making a baby."

He snorts a laugh at the truly ridiculous situation we're in.

"Tucker?" Sutton's sweet little voice calls out from the backseat, interrupting our conversation.

"Yes, honey."

"Are you my daddy?"

My whole body freezes, except for my heart which has started to race. Why would she ask this question? Is it because of what Tucker said in the tunnel? Is it because of our conversation now? Have I said too much? How do I explain this hard truth? And how do I explain what a one-night stand is?

I feel pressure on my hand and look down to see Tucker squeezing it again. Glancing up at him, he mouths, "Relax." That elicits a glare from me which only makes him chuckle.

"One step at a time," he whispers. "No details. Just basic answers."

I blow out a breath and nod, knowing we can't just avoid her questions. She has a right to know who her dad is. I just hope she doesn't wonder why he hasn't been around.

"I *am* your daddy, Sutton. You okay with that?" Tucker asks, lifting his chin so he can see her in the rearview mirror.

"Yeah! You're a good daddy!" she yells.

"Are you my daddy, too?" Kody interjects excitedly. I look at Tucker again and see an expression that probably mirrors my own. We have to be truthful, but this might break sweet Kody's heart and neither one of us wants that.

"I wish I was, buddy," Tucker says gently. "But I'm not."

"You're...you're not my daddy?"

My hands cover my face as my heart breaks for the little boy I consider my bonus child. I can't imagine how he must feel suddenly realizing his best friend has a daddy and he doesn't. Before, neither of them did so they didn't know what they were missing. That's all changed in an instant.

Tucker continues to speak gently, trying to smooth over the sting. "I'm not. But we're still family, right?"

Kody says nothing, only sniffles.

"Like...let me think." Tucker takes a second to pull his thoughts together and I know he's trying to figure out how to soften the blow. "Kody, who is sitting next to me?"

Another sniffle. "Lacy."

"Is she your mommy?"

Sutton giggles and Kody gets a little sass when he says, "No. My mommy went to some mommy time."

"Right. And is Lacy your sister?"

This time Kody giggles, too. "She's too big to be my sister. Sutton is my sister."

Tucker's eyebrows raise and he takes a quick glance at me.

"Let that one go, Hayes," I mutter. "One soft blow at a time."

"But do you love Lacy?"

"Yeah!" both kids yell simultaneously, and I breathe a sigh of relief, figuring out Tucker's strategy.

"Right. You love Lacy because she's your family. And now that I'm here, we're all family, right?"

The kids start giggling and bouncing up and down, squealing about being family forever.

Suddenly Sutton announces, "And mommies and daddies get married to each other!"

We are so shocked by her declaration, it's a miracle Tucker doesn't lose control of the car and run us right off the road.

"Well that's... um... it's..." He begins stumbling over his words as he tries to figure out how to respond.

Delighted at this turn of events, I swivel my body to face him so I can get in on this moment of discomfort.

"What's the matter, Hayes? Do you not want to marry me?"

His eyes widen and his jaw drops.

"Am I not good enough for you?" The way he continues to gape is so much unexpected fun, I have a hard time stopping myself. "Am I not pretty enough or... It's my lack of education, isn't it?"

"It's not that. It's...uh..."

"Married! Married!" the kids start chanting in the back and I can't help but laugh. I admit, I was worried about having this honest of a conversation, but I've also raised these kids. I'm pretty attuned to whether they're being traumatized or not. And it's clear there is no trauma happening with the topic of Tucker's parentage. Which is why it's so easy to let them put Tucker on the spot for as long as possible.

"Okay, okay!" he finally yells as the kids keep giggling. "Listen, some mommies and daddies get married but no one is allowed to get married until they're thirty, okay? That's the rule for all of us!"

I slap my hand over my mouth as more laughter bubbles up inside me.

"Way to deflect and lay down your first 'overbearing father ground rules'."

He winks at me. "It was good, right?"

I shake my head and turn my body around to face front. All that worry about Sutton finding out about Tucker was for nothing.

Well, not nothing. We got some good laughs out of it. Suddenly, it's starting to feel like we're going to be a family after all.

CHAPTER TWENTY-FOUR

TUCKER

For the first time ever, all five guys show up at my place on time.

It's a poker night miracle.

Normally Patrick gets hung up with the missus and we either start late or end up dealing him in when he finally shows up and half our money is already gone. But tonight, all is on track and we're ready to roll.

The very first time we won a home game in pre-season, we randomly had poker night at my house. Coincidentally, the next time we won, we also had poker night plans. When it happened a third time, a new superstition was born. We're convinced, well, Maks is anyway, that if we plan it, wins will come. Anyone on the team is invited and we have a few stragglers come in and out, but for the most part it's just the six of us every time. So here we are, having our very first poker night in my new house.

"Who's ready for me to take their money?" Anthony Stutteville, one of our rookies and one hell of a defenseman, asks as we carry the table out of the deep closet used for storage and, well, this table. He's sporting a good-looking black eye after getting an elbow to the face in a particularly bad scuffle. It just makes his nickname of Tiger, after Tony the mascot of his favorite cereal, fit a little better.

"Only if you have better luck than you did tonight," Becker Bell chides back. Only a couple years into his career, he's got the teams highest number of points this season so far.

"Hey my luck was just fine." Anthony grunts as we flip the table on its side and set it up.

"Really? That shiner says otherwise."

"Who says it's bad luck?" Anthony says like the cocky bastard he is. "All the ladies love a good story that includes my brute strength and what the other guy looks like."

Nick shakes his head. "Does that story include me having to block thirty-two shots tonight because your asses couldn't seem to keep the puck out of my zone?"

"We were just making sure your skills are up to par," Becker says.

Patrick grunts in displeasure as he sets up a couple of chairs, me putting down the others. "His skills are fine. You boys need to step up your game a bit if we're going to make it through the play-offs this season."

Anthony drops down into the chair I just set down and begins organizing the colored chips. "Don't worry, Captain. It was an off night, but we already have poker night scheduled for our next game so as long as Maksim can keep his focus, we'll be just fine."

"Where is Maks anyway?" I ask.

He pops up from behind the counter, a large plastic bowl in one hand and an open bag of chips in the other. "I'm getting the snacks ready."

Becker throws a poker chip at his head. "You fucker. You always get out of helping with this heavy-ass table."

"I have low blood sugar. You know this," Maks spouts off, eliciting a bunch of boos and a few more poker chips thrown at him.

Once everyone has a beer and whatever snacks they think

they need, which mostly means what Maks wants, we get down to business.

For the next hour, cards are dealt, trash is talked, and totals are tallied. Anthony looks like he's coming out on top, which pisses everyone off since it seems to happen every time.

"I swear to god you are counting cards." Becker angrily throws his cards on the table while Anthony leans over to scoop all the chips his direction. He blows Becker a quick kiss and gets a middle finger in response.

"It's because he sits in that same chair every time," Maks says.

We all look around and realize he's right. Every time we play, Anthony sits in the same spot. I wouldn't notice it except there's a gash on the corner from when Nick dropped the table the first time we played.

"Son of a bitch," I gape. "You found a lucky chair."

Anthony looks around innocently. "Oh, did I? Huh. Weird."

Patrick stands up and waves for Anthony to get up too.

"What?" Anthony pretends not to know what's happening.

"Get your ass up," our captain orders. "I've got a high-maintenance wife so I need to quit giving you my money. Get up and let me sit there."

"No way," Anthony yells. "This is my lucky chair."

"Dude, I have kids now," I toss in. "Give me a break and let me sit there."

"Looks like everyone knows about your kids now." Nick points to the television where SportsCenter has been playing in the background. "Look."

We all stop what we're doing and look up to the screen, only to see Lacy and I walking through the parking garage, kids in our arms.

"Well fuck," I breath and crank up the volume on the TV, catching the tail end of the story.

"... three-year-old daughter and, who his publicist claims, is a family friend that joined them for the game. What's strange about this is there

have never even been whispers about Hayes being a family man, so no one knows how he kept this secret for so long.

"I don't know, man," a second host says. "Having been a pro athlete myself many years ago," they all laugh at his jab at his age, "it can be tough raising a family in the spotlight like that. I say good on Hayes for waiting until she was a little older before introducing her to the cameras and fame of it all."

"I didn't introduce her," I grumble. "I got found out."

Nick apparently hears me as he claps me on the shoulder in support.

"No word yet on who the child's mother is, although we can deduce it's the woman in the video. Hayes's publicist is staying mum on her name, but we know Hayes has been spotted with other women over the years so there's some sort of story there."

"Shit." That's not going to go over well with Lacy. Hell, it doesn't go over well with me.

"We'll bring you the latest in the morning as we continue to track down details of this breaking story. Speaking of Tucker Hayes, he had an impressive game last night..."

They move onto the highlight reel and all I can do is shake my head. This isn't how I wanted people to find out I'm a father. And it's certainly not the way Lacy is going to feel comfortable with.

"Don't worry about it, man," Nick tries to say supportively, but it's not working. "They'll get Lacy's name, maybe track down a source who feeds them a bunch of bullshit, and then move on to the next big thing."

"It must be a really slow sports day for that to even have made it to a round table," Patrick agrees.

I rub my hand down my face. "Yeah, I know. It just sounds sordid when other people talk about it. No, I didn't know she was born until she was three. Yes, she was the result of a one-night stand. But that all makes me sound like a dick and doesn't paint Lacy in a good light either."

"So flip the script on them," Maks interjects, still eating. He's like a bottomless pit.

"What do you mean?"

"I mean, you didn't know because your agent didn't tell you, right?"

"Uh huh."

"So flip the script. Tell them the truth. That you met someone wonderful and lost contact with her. She tried unsuccessfully to reach you because your agent was a dick. He's since been fired and you're toying with suing him for damages because you love them so much and are irate to have lost so much time with your daughter thanks to someone else's negligence."

We all sit there stunned at Maks outburst. He's not usually the one to have good ideas. Hell, he's not the one to have any ideas. This is new for him. But it still leaves a couple loose ends.

"I don't plan to sue him."

Maks shrugs. "So what? It gets the heat off you and onto fucking Morty, with the added benefit of making that old man sweat for what he's done. And makes Lacy look like a saint." He says it so nonchalantly I'm a little disconcerted. But then he shovels more snacks in his pie hole and I know the real Maks who could care less about what the press thinks of him is back.

"That's actually a really good idea," Becker comments.

I nod and blow out a breath. "I'll talk to Lacy about it in the morning. That's probably our best option and gets it over with the quickest." I rub my eyes with my palms. "Damn. Where are all the big name guys getting DUI's and shit? I prefer reading about their bad behavior than seeing them try to spin my life into something nefarious."

"Give it until tomorrow. Maksim hasn't gone out to party yet." Anthony shoves our hungry friend, who shoves him back. "I'm sure he'll be more than happy to take the heat off of you."

Maks tips his chip bag my direction whiles he chews, the indication clear—he's up for it.

"Let's not talk about it anymore." I shake my head, ready to forget this for a while. "Someone deal the cards while I go sit in that lucky chair."

Patrick immediately drops down into the coveted seat, making me scowl.

All is forgotten as the cards are dealt, more trash is talked and the ante is upped. The rest of us end up folding, like always leaving Anthony and Becker as the last two standing.

It's down to the wire.

I look back and forth between the two men as they narrow their eyes at each other. The rest of us are silent and I swear I hear the whistling sounds of a cowboy movie right before a shoot-out.

Anthony lifts his hand and tosses four white chips on the growing pile in the center.

"I'll see your bet and raise you twenty bucks."

Becker doesn't even hesitate. "I'll see your twenty and raise you a thousand."

Patrick's jaw drops as Becker tosses ten blue chips in the pile. None of us have ever seen that many go down at once before. Maksim's eyes widen and he shovels cookies into his mouth faster. I lean back, my heart racing like it's my money on the line while Anthony rubs his chin. I have to give it to the man, he has no tell. He could have a winning hand or be bluffing all the way to the bank. There's no way that I've found to determine which it is.

After several long, silent seconds, Nick leans in. "Whatcha gonna do, Tiger?"

Anthony takes a few more seconds to build the anticipation before tossing his own stack of blue chips onto the pile.

"Call."

Nick blows out a breath while I look back and forth between the two of them, my fingers steepled and resting against my mouth in anticipation.

Patrick's gaze finally lands on Becker. "Whatcha got?"

He lays his cards down slowly, smiling like the cat that ate the canary. "Four of a kind."

I clap slowly, impressed with his game. I wasn't expecting him to take it all and I'm excited for him.

The thrill is short lived, however, when Anthony growls, "Not so fast."

The room goes silent again as Tiger reveals his cards.

"Straight flush."

"You've got to be kidding me," Patrick says.

Becker's head hits the table as he realizes he's out close to twelve hundred bucks on this hand alone.

And Anthony, that asshole stands up and reaches his arms out wide. "Woooooo! I am the king!" he yells. "Your undefeated poker night champion!"

There are boos all around and playful shoves as he continues to holler about being the best in the world or some shit we're all trying to ignore as we mentally tally how much we owe him.

A small voice breaks through all the noise and I look up to see Lacy looking disheveled and like she just woke up. Damn, she's beautiful. I could wake up to that sight every day.

"What?" I ask, still smiling from an exciting round of cards.

"I said, what are you doing?"

"Having poker night." I lean over to gather the cards, the guys taking a few minutes to replenish their beers and snacks while they continue to razz each other and decide if we have any more money to lose.

"Yeah, I got that." Lacy's arms are crossed over her chest and I'm picking up on some irritation. I'm just not sure why. "Why are you having poker night here?"

I furrow my brow. "We always do poker night at my house after a winning game."

Her brows raise and I have a bad feeling in my gut. Something is off about this conversation.

Lacy points across the room next to the tree. "Can I talk to you for a second?"

"Oh shit," Anthony mumbles and my friends all grumble about needing to use the restroom or some shit. I ignore them, instead following Lacy like a puppy, a move that doesn't sit right with me.

Once we're safely out of earshot, or at least as much as we can be, she turns on me. "What are you doing?"

"I told you. Poker night."

"And you didn't think to ask me about that before bringing a bunch of rowdy men here in the middle of the night while children are trying to sleep?"

I'm not sure if it's the booze, the fact that I owe Tiger money *again*, or the late hour after a game, but her comment hits me the wrong way. I'm a man. I don't like the insinuation that there are rules I have to adhere to. "Why would I ask you? This is my house."

Lacy rears back like she's been slapped, and I know I said the wrong thing. "So that's how it is."

Dropping my shoulders, I place my hands on my hips, resigned to the fact that my good mood is now gone. "Come on Lacy. That's not what I meant."

I step closer to her, hoping to get a little bit of privacy from the remaining nosy teammates that have gone awfully quiet, which means they're listening.

Lacy takes a step back from me, though. "Seems to me that's exactly what you meant. That whole spiel about this being my house too since you owe me so much back child support was just a bunch of bullshit, huh?"

Frustration bubbles up inside me. I'm getting this all wrong and she's misunderstanding what I'm saying. "I don't understand why you're fighting with me. That's not what I meant and you know it."

"Do I?" she asks, cocking out her hip.

"You're making too much out of this." My irritation suddenly gives way to a flair of anger. "I admit I should have informed you so you'd have a heads up. That was inconsiderate of me. But you can't expect me to just not invite my friends over to my house, especially when it means winning more games."

Lacy laughs lightly. "You're going to justify this with hockey superstition now?"

"Oh man. His woman doesn't get hockey at all," Maksim blurts out behind me.

"Don't you have more snacks to shove in your pie hole?" I pop off to him.

Maks holds his hands up defensively and Anthony hands him a cookie, presumably to shut him up.

"Tucker, there are two children down this hall that are sleeping right now." Lacy gestures that direction. "If I woke up from all your noise, what makes you think they won't?"

"You're a mom. Of course you're a light sleeper." She shakes her head, frustration evident. I take another step closer. "Lacy, the house is insulated enough, and that hall is far enough away, they'll be fine. I grew up with four brothers. If I can sleep through that household, they can sleep through poker night every once in a while."

"Mommy. Are we having a party?" Sutton comes wandering out, clutching her puppy and rubbing her eyes. Kody is right behind her looking just as bad as she does. He wraps his little arms around Lacy's legs and closes his eyes again, falling asleep while standing up.

Lacy gives me an *I told you so* look and the guys snicker.

"Well she just won that argument," Maks states.

I close my eyes tightly, trying not to pop off to him again. He's right, but my ego doesn't like being wrong, especially not in front of the guys who are going to give me shit for who knows how long now.

"Maybe we should move this game into the media room," I admit quietly.

"I know you're new to this whole dad thing, but maybe think things through a little more next time." Lacy picks up Kody, who immediately puts his head on her shoulder, his arms going slack.

My jaw drops, pissed that she'd insinuate anything is more important to me than my kids. "That's not fair."

"Oh, it's not? You mean you thought through the logistics of kids being here when you planned to have a party after they're asleep? Or how about stocking the fridge with beer instead things for kids to drink, which I'm assuming is all we'd find if I opened it right now. You know I had to pry a margarita pouch from Kody's hands today, *again*, because he thought it was a juice pouch?"

"You can't blame me for that one. I didn't even know it was there."

I know I've gone too far when Lacy's eyes flair with anger. My statement seems to be the straw that breaks this argument wide open.

"Well maybe you should have," she hisses.

"And maybe you shouldn't have been sheltering them from things like get-togethers with other people so they would know the difference between alcohol and juice for the last three years."

I don't know why I'm still arguing. Don't know why my mouth won't stop, but it's like every frustration I've had, every angry thought about how unfair it is to have lost so much time with my daughter is directed at her. And she's not even the right target. That doesn't stop my mouth though.

Once again, Lacy rears back. Poking at Lacy for not exposing Sutton to life when they were just trying to survive is a hot button issue I should never touch on. I've screwed up badly this time.

"I'm so sorry," I backtrack quickly. "I didn't mean that."

Lacy leans in, nostrils flaring. "Yes, Tucker. That's what I was doing. I was living in my car and eating two-day-old hot dogs I was supposed to throw out at work so I didn't starve to death, all so I could shelter her from the *real world.*"

Not only is her voice full of more venom than I've ever heard, she's using air quotes. I'm going to have some major groveling to do later. But not now. She's still on a roll and I know better than to interrupt.

"No, I wasn't trying to scrape together money for formula since WIC didn't know what to do without us having an address on record so they couldn't figure out how to help us. No. I was purposely not teaching her about the different kinds of alcohol she couldn't drink."

I squeeze my eyes shut, taking her reprimand. She's reminding me in her own way that the one of us who was living in a fantasy, the one of us who was being sheltered from the real world the last few years was me. Not her. Not Sutton.

Me.

Shame burns through me as my ego completely deflates. I'm a dick, all the way around, I'm the ass in this situation. I feel horrible.

"Lacy," I try quietly but she cuts me off with a hand in my face.

"No. You can fuck right off, Tucker." She grabs Sutton's hand, walking toward the back door. "We're spending the night in the pool house."

I immediately follow her. "Lacy, you don't have to leave. You're right. You're right about all of it. We'll just move to the media room or something."

She looks over her shoulder, giving me the angriest glare I've ever seen. Even worse than the night we met up at the bar for the second time.

"Oh no. This is *your* house so you do whatever you want. We've been fine without you before. We'll be fine again."

The room goes deathly silent as she slams the door behind her. I'm left standing in the middle of the room feeling embarrassed to have been called out in front of my team. But more than that, feeling ashamed at the way I spoke to her.

A throat clears behind me and my head drops. Turning around, I try to make a joke out of it. "So uh...looks like I'm still working on what it means to be a dad, huh?"

No one says anything until Maks finally pipes up. "This party is a real downer. I'm going to hit a club. Anyone want to join me?"

Four big bodies all jump up into action at the same time, making false apologies and excuses about early morning practice. Becker even tosses in a fake yawn for good measure.

Within seconds, they're out the door, leaving me behind to stand here alone in my shame. That's when it occurs to me—I haven't even told her about the news report yet. Groveling may be an understatement.

CHAPTER TWENTY-FIVE

LACY

The sun is shining, there is a nice breeze, and happy squeals come from the kids as they play on the swing set.

None of it matches my mood at all. I'm feeling dejected and alone and not quite sure how to navigate this rift Tucker and I seem to have.

It doesn't help that I woke up to a text from my sister saying my face is all over the news, during the sports reports only, but still being talked about as the mystery woman who apparently has a secret child with local hockey hero Tucker Hayes. It wasn't the news I was hoping to wake up to this morning, but I guess it's not terribly surprising. He's never tried to hide Sutton. Not ever.

From the beginning, as soon as the shock wore off from finding out he has a child, Tucker has embraced fatherhood with a vengeance. I can tell he wants to be a good dad so much. Hell, he jumps in to fix problems as they arise, not even flinching if he has to throw money at it.

Maybe that's part of the problem—the ease of the money.

Sure the stress of wondering where the next meal is coming from is gone and there is something freeing about not having to worry how rent is going to be paid. But that's not all there is to parenting. It also means making your kids a priority, even over your friends. It means seeing things from their perspective so you can anticipate potential problems and prevent them. It means remembering they're not small adults. They're little humans and they still have to grow up before being introduced to adult issues.

And yet, as they laugh and twirl and play, I'm reminded of how happy they are here and how much they love Tucker already. How did everything fall apart so quickly?

Speaking of the devil, the back door opens and Tucker comes through. He's missing his normal swagger. All the confidence he usually exudes is missing.

"Hey." He shoves his hands in his pockets and it occurs to me that he's nervous. Good. He should be after the shit he said to me last night.

"Hey," I reply, refusing to make eye contact, opting to watch the kids instead.

He stands quietly for a moment before the awkward silence becomes too much for him. "How has their day been so far?"

"Well, they've been pretty cranky all day because some jack ass woke them up in the middle of the night having a party."

I catch his wince out of the corner of my eye. "I deserve that."

"Yup."

"And how has your day been? Besides the cranky kids, I mean."

"Well there are a few apartments open in the area that will fit us and match my budget so I guess you can call that a win."

"Apartments? Why are you looking at apartments?"

I finally look over at him. It was unfair of me to throw that out. I'm not seriously considering moving out at this point. Not yet anyway. But in my anger last night and with my inability to go back to sleep, I admit to doing a quick online search of apartments. Having a backup plan helped me calm down a bit so I could finally get some rest. It wasn't enough, but it was better than nothing.

"It wasn't a serious search," I admit. "I don't want to leave but we can't raise these kids in a bachelor pad with people coming in and out at all hours. That's neither safe nor healthy for them."

He pulls a chair up next to me and sits down. "But Lacy, moving? That's a bit premature, don't you think?"

"You suggest I wait until the kids accidentally get alcohol poisoning from mistaking your adult beverage pouches with applesauce? Or maybe after some drunk accidentally wanders into Sutton's room and passes out on her bed while she's on the top bunk? Are those better options?"

"Well no, of course not. I..." He shakes his head and leans forward, resting his elbow on his knees. "I get it, okay? I'm not good at this dad thing."

"Ya think?"

"I mean, I love them and I want to give them the world. I just... I didn't have a dad for very long while growing up. My brothers and I basically raised each other while my mom worked her tail off. It was like living in a frat house sometimes, and it was so full of noise, I got used to it. I still don't really hear it."

"So what, you want us to just get over it? Let the kids watch Maks have a three-some on the patio and learn how to sleep through parties?"

"No. I want you to teach me how to do it differently. Do it better."

Of all the things I expected him to say, that wasn't anywhere on my radar. "Teach you?"

"Teach me how it should be done. My mother was fantastic and I'm sure she did all these things. I just don't remember that part. Teach me what a routine for a kid needs to be and how to set up the house so they're safe. I think I got the locks right with the pool so that's good. But like...do I need to get outlet covers or hide wires? I didn't even think about any of that until last night and now it's all I can think about. I went online and looked up some kid-raising books but I couldn't find anything for three-year-olds, only babies and now I'm not sure what to do. I want to do this right, Lacy. I don't want to lose this little family."

I finally look into his eyes, really look, and see the pleading in them. The longing to be with the kids the right way. Maybe even a longing to be with me.

My heart thumps loudly as I realize we're at a crossroads and I'm the one in control here. I'm the one who decides how this is going to work. I'm not locked into living here, money is no longer an object.

But I'm afraid.

Afraid that Tucker's words are just that—words. That when the luster of having a shiny new family wears off, we'll be disposable. That his fun, fast-paced lifestyle complete with all night get-togethers and loose women will be more important than us. That we'll never match up, never compare, and in the end, we'll lose.

Tucker licks his lips and clasps his hands together, his facial expression devoid of the carefree attitude he normally has.

"Lacy, I screwed up. Several times. I know that. I didn't think and I was selfish and never even thought about the fact that I was probably introducing the kids to things they shouldn't be exposed to. And I never considered your feelings either."

He looks up at me, guilt written all over his face.

"I don't want you to go. I just found you again."

"Sutton or me?"

The words are out of my mouth before I even realize I'm thinking them. I can't take them back, and I'm not sure I want to. I know Tucker is going to be around for his daughter. He's made every effort to prove that to me. Even this conversation shows that he wants to be the best father he can be, he just needs some guidance.

What I don't know is where I fit into that equation, and I hate that it bothers me. I hate that the more I've gotten to know

Tucker, the more I've fallen for him. The more I've begun hoping that his priority isn't just about Sutton, but about me too. It makes me uncomfortable knowing he's holding a piece of my heart. I want to take it back and protect it, like I've done for years with almost every person I know. Like I started doing as a child when I realized I wasn't ever going to be good enough to be loved unconditionally.

And yet, it's true. I want Tucker. I've fallen for him. Not trusting that he feels the same way terrifies me and makes me want to run away. The only thing keeping me from doing just that is sitting on a yellow swing right now, wind blowing in her hair while she smiles brightly at her best friend.

"Both of you," Tucker finally says.

All the air whooshes out of my lungs.

He grabs my hand and rubs his thumb over my knuckles, watching the movement as he speaks. "I used to dream about you sometimes. You wearing that damn backless black dress," he says with a chuckle. "I remember when I left you that morning, you were so beautiful all tangled up in the sheets, still asleep. And I remember wishing we had more time together. Feeling like I wanted to get to know you more. No one has ever called to me the way you did. And still do."

He looks up at me again, a small smile tilting his lips. "I pushed away those memories because there was no sense in hanging onto them, but when I found that dress in your closet, it all came back. All I could think about was how lucky I am to have found you again. To have time to get to know each other. To have the opportunity to be a family with you. I never knew I wanted that until I found out why you threw that drink in my face."

"The Beluga Gold?" I ask with a small smile.

"You really could have used something cheaper and still gotten the same effect," he jokes before turning serious again. "Please don't go, Lacy. Stay and work things out with me. Help me be a better father and let me try to be a partner to you. I just want a chance for us to be a family."

Warmth washes over me as I take in the sincerity of his words. I have no doubt Tucker wants to make this work for all of us. My doubt comes from how long that desire will last. But I owe it to my daughter, and I suppose to myself, to try. I might get burned in the end, but for all of our sakes, I have to suck up my own fears and give it a shot.

I cup Tucker's cheeks with my hands and pull him closer so I can look him in the eye, no distractions, just us. "I spent years hating you for leaving us, blaming you for a situation that was out of your control." He gulps loudly and lowers his lids. "Really what I was doing was protecting myself and trying to protect Sutton. I'm so tired of holding up these walls." He looks back up and I see the hope in his gaze. "I want to trust that we're in this together for the long haul. It's going to take time and we obviously have some things to work out, but I want to try. For her. For me."

I smile at him and pull him closer until our lips are just a hairsbreadth away, and I wait. Wait for him to accept my invitation. Wait for him to be the one to initiate contact. I can't be the one to do it anymore. I can't be the one doing the chasing. I need him to be the one to go the extra mile, or in this case, the extra inch.

Finally, he does. Leaning forward, his lips take mine in a gentle, lingering peck. Sparks don't fly and I don't hear any proverbial explosions, but I feel the warmth all the way down to my toes. A comfort overtakes me that this is right. This situation is exactly as it should be. Tucker isn't going anywhere, and neither are we, even when hard things happen. My body knows it instinctively and my mind is starting to believe it, too.

We give each other gentle kisses for a few more minutes, no tongue, just easy pressure as we tentatively learn each other again, all too aware that little eyes may be watching at any moment.

Sure enough, small giggles have us pulling away, our faces staying close.

Tucker clears his throat. "Hey kids. What's going on?"

"Daddy, will you push me on the swing?" Sutton looks back and forth at us, and I know she's wondering what in the world she just witnessed, even if she isn't asking.

"Sure I will. But wasn't Kody doing a good job?"

We stand and begin walking with the kids into the lush backyard.

"No. We tried to swing but it broke."

"It broke?" I ask, confused as to how that could happen. I've been sitting here with them all morning. It was fine before Tucker got home.

"Yeah," Kody adds. "They don't work."

Tucker and I inspect the swings, which look perfectly fine to us, making their concerns even more confusing.

"Show me where it's broken, baby girl," Tucker says, and Sutton climbs on the swing as quickly as her little three-year-old body can do it.

He helps her get situated and the problem reveals itself pretty quick. She's pumping her legs rapidly making the swing jerk back and forth, but never gaining enough momentum to actually go anywhere.

Tucker grabs the chain and pulls her backwards. "I got you, baby girl," he says lovingly and let's go so she can sail forward through the air.

"Me, too!" Kody scrambles onto his own swing so I can make myself useful pushing him, too.

It's peaceful, just the four of us, enjoying the outdoors on this beautiful December day.

"Thank you, Tucker," I finally say, trying to do better about expressing my gratitude.

"For what?"

"For finding us. For helping us. And for wanting to be with us."

His face softens as he looks at me, somehow still managing to push the swing without getting nailed by it. "Thank you, Lacy. For her. For them. I've never been so happy in all my life."

Oddly enough, I'm starting to feel the same way too.

"Hey kids," Tucker suddenly says. "Let's switch."

They both jump off their swing and Tucker takes a few minutes to situate them with Kody sitting and Sutton pushing.

I furrow my brows in confusion.

"Sit down," he instructs.

"What?"

He gestures to the swing. "It's your turn."

I do as he instructs, pushing myself backward so I can swing forward. Tucker's hands strategically touch my ass every time he pushes me. I don't mind. The swinging motion, combined with the kids' chatter is soothing in a way I didn't know I needed.

Suddenly, I'm stopped mid-air, Tucker holding me to him, his biceps no doubt flexing from the strain.

"I'm sorry," he whispers, his lips next to my ear, making me shiver.

I glance back at him, my heart softening again. "I'm sorry, too. I'm trying to be less...reactionary."

He lets go and I swing forward, the wind blowing my hair back.

"And I'm trying to be more thoughtful."

"We'll get there," I say, with more conviction than I feel, but I'm determined to get past my own reservations, even if it takes time.

"There's just one little bump in the road we're going to have to fix."

I sigh deeply because I know what's coming. "We need to make a statement about the mystery woman and your secret child, don't we?"

"Just trying to give the people what they want, Lacy. And you know they're chomping at the bit for a good story."

I shake my head, resigned to this fate I'm now part of and yet less irritated about it than I could be. There are worse things that could happen than having my face on SportsCenter for a couple days. I know. I've lived through it.

"Life is never going to be boring with you, is it Hayes?"

"Not if I can help it," he says with a laugh.

CHAPTER TWENTY-SIX

TUCKER

It took a couple weeks of hashing a few things out for Lacy and I to get into a better routine, one where we worked together to run the house and made sure the kids were the number one priority.

That's not to say I didn't still have a job to do. Games and practice are what put food on the table, and camaraderie is still part of that. When I explained to Lacy the importance of our superstitions, she told me we were a bunch of idiots, but agreed to help me find a solution to poker night.

We tested out the media room to see how loud things could get before noise made its way into the bedroom area. Turns out, the walls are thicker in this house than I realized. I got the television almost to full volume before she could hear anything at all on the other side.

I admit to feeling a little stupid to not have thought of hosting poker night back there in the first place. Such a simple solution if I had only pulled my head out of my ass sooner, and admittedly, given Lacy a heads up that it was going to happen in the first place.

Regardless, as we settled into a state of domestic bliss, we got into a good groove faster than I expected. We even toured a few daycares and settled on one we all think the kids are going to like when Lacy's classes start next month. We got a few odd looks when Ellie, Lacy, and I toured the places together, but when we explained that Lacy is Kody's current caregiver, everyone seemed to understand.

Except the lunch lady at one of the places we toured. She kept giving me the side-eye and I swear I saw her taking notes every time she looked at us. I'm sure I'll get a call any day now from my publicist regarding my supposed polyamorous relationship.

All things considered, everything seems to be rolling smoothly. The hardest part is Lacy still being a little uncomfortable taking my money, but I made sure to inform the state child support office so they could oversee it all. I think that helped her a bit. It seems to take away the feeling of me providing "charity" and cleared up that this is the bare minimum of what I'm required to do, per state law. So, I was glad to do it.

What I was not glad to do, however, was put my mom off any longer. She'd had enough. I appreciate that she's given us time to get our bearings straight, but after a few months of having a granddaughter she's never met, she put her foot down. She also put me on a guilt trip, reminding me that as an empty nester, she was alone for the holidays.

That one did me in. So here I am, standing inside the airport, waiting for her to exit the gate area.

Once we put out our statement to the media regarding Sutton, the one Maks randomly came up with, the attention died down a lot. But I'm still not interested in having yet another conversation about what a good dad I am with random strangers. So with my beanie pulled down over my ears and some fake glasses on, I do my best to blend into the crowd as I wait.

My size probably gives me away, but at least it gives me a height advantage. I'm easily able to spot my mom over everyone else and she's able to see me, too. As soon as she smiles, the dimples on her cheeks popping, the wrinkles around her eyes crinkling, I wonder why it took me so long to say yes to her visit.

I bend down halfway as she reaches her arms up and wraps them around my neck. "Oh my baby boy. I am so happy to see you."

She hugs me tightly and I inhale the scent that has always reminded me of home. She smells like sugar cookies and ginger, just like a new grandma should smell.

"Welcome to Florida, Ma. Did you have a good flight?"

She hands me her carry-on and wraps her hand around my bicep so we can walk to baggage claim.

"As good of a flight as possible. You know I hate air travel."

"Turbulence still scaring you?"

"Not much this time." That is a surprise. My mom has always been terrified of flying. She does it because she knows that fear is irrational, and she would rather white-knuckle it on an airplane than miss an opportunity to see something amazing. She's pretty strong that way. But that's how she's always done life—white-knuckling her way through the hard parts. I guess you don't have much of a choice when you're raising five boys. "I started a new breathing and meditation program that really helped this time. I stayed very Zen."

"Zen?" I ask with a laugh. "Were you smoking your hookah pipe, too? That's the real reason you stayed calm, isn't it?"

She slaps me on the chest lightly. "You hush. I'll have you know it was the easiest flight I've ever had, which was my goal. Now I can visit my new granddaughter more often."

We get to baggage claim and thankfully the carousel is already moving. The less we wait, the smaller my chance of being spotted.

"Oh good." She points to a bright pink suitcase as it glides by. "That's mine right there."

I have to jog past a couple people to catch up to it, but it's better than standing around waiting.

"I guess we're ready to go," I say as I roll the suitcase next to her other bag.

"Oh no, son. I've got one more."

She points back to the carousel and my eyes widen as I take in the huge pink monstrosity waiting to be claimed.

"Think you may have overpacked just a little? We're in Florida. You didn't need to bring your winter clothes."

"Now Tucker, this is my first Christmas with your family. If you thought I was coming empty handed, you thought wrong."

I should have expected her to go overboard with gifts. I have a sneaking suspicion there are more waiting to be picked up at a local big box store, too. Once again, I'm grateful I picked an SUV.

By the time I turn around, I have to wait for the bag to go through the maze again. In hindsight, I should have taken advantage of the breather while I waited. I vastly underestimated how much shit she can pack.

Struggling to maneuver the suitcase to the floor, I strain every part of my body to wrestle the damn thing. "Did you pack a body in here or something," I grunt. "This must weigh like three hundred pounds."

Leave it to my mother to be proud of her overpacking. "Oh poo. Put a little muscle into it. I know you can. You're a big strong hockey player," she announces much to my chagrin.

Thankfully, the suitcase falls on the floor with a thud right then so the likelihood of a viral video of me playing WWE with a pink suitcase is slim. However, her words weren't missed by several people standing in the area. I'm getting a lot of curious stares and one person even holds up his phone, very obviously taking a picture of me. It's clear by the blank look on his face that he doesn't have a clue who I am, he just doesn't want to miss an opportunity.

I roll the monstrosity to where she waits and give her my best irritated stare. "Thank you for announcing that while I was trying to be incognito."

"Is that what the glasses are about? I thought your age finally caught up with you."

Wrapping my arm around her shoulder, I kiss the top of my mom's head. I've missed her and her sense of humor. "Very funny. Can you roll the small bag so I can get this one?"

"Of course."

It doesn't take long to get to the car loaded, even with her amused reprimands about spending too much money on my Porsche. Once she climbs into the passenger side and the cooling seats kick on, her tune changes. The full-body cooling in this part of the country makes even the strongest skeptic a believer.

As soon as we hit the highway, my excitement starts to kick in. It's clear my mom's does, too.

"Now, is there anything I need to know about Sutton before we get there?" she asks. "I'm so excited to finally meet her."

"Remember there's two of them, Ma. That's the most important part. Kody isn't mine, but I make damn sure he knows he's wanted even if his dad isn't around."

She pats my arm gently. "There's the man I raised you to be. That little boy didn't do anything wrong. No reason to make him feel lesser than."

"Absolutely. The kids insist they're twins and none of us bother to correct them. They're so funny, though. Sutton started calling me Daddy. And now Kody calls me Not-Daddy." I smile at the memory of the first time it happened. I wasn't sure I'd ever stop laughing, which of course encouraged them to keep using the new moniker.

"That is hilarious," Mom agrees. "It's amazing how easily kids sort things out in their little minds to make hard concepts understandable."

"Yeah, they're definitely a pair. Honestly, I can't imagine having one without the other. Is that weird?"

I catch the shake of her head out of the corner of my eye. "Not at all. Families come in all shapes and sizes. Ours didn't look like your best friend's and his didn't look like the next-door neighbor's. What it looks like doesn't matter. Only that you love and protect each other."

"That's what we try to do. Well, sort of. I feel like my role is mostly providing right now, while I get used to the other parts of parenting, but I know Ellie, that's Lacy's best friend, Kody's mom"—my mom nods in understanding—"she really provides the emotional support for Lacy. And Lacy is basically running the house, so, it's weird, but it works so far."

"Can't wait for the tabloids to pick up on it and start sharing stories that you're in a throuple."

I choke on a laugh. "Mom!"

"Don't 'mom' me. You know those rag mags love a good scandalous story. It won't seem so far fetched when the four of them start going to all your hockey games wearing your jersey."

That never even crossed my mind before, but she's right. The family friend explanation worked once, but everyone loves speculation, especially when it's juicy. I better give Lacy a heads up. She handled the last breaking story really well, but it's probably better to tip her off anyway.

Within minutes, we pull into the driveway. Mom looks out the window appreciatively.

"Oh Tucker, it's lovely! So much nicer than that dump you were living in in Texas."

I furrow my brow as I throw the car into park. "It was a twenty-five hundred square foot home in one of the most sought-after neighborhoods in San Antonio."

"And it needed a ton of work you never got around to doing."

I can't argue there. I had grandiose plans that never worked out. What I learned, though, is that I'm not a handyman. At all. This is why I hired someone to get everything ready for us before we moved into this place.

Wrestling with her bags again, I lead Mom up to the front so we can go inside. The door is barely shut behind us when the kids come running. I only have time to drop the bags before they jump into my arms yelling, "Daddy, Not-Daddy!"

"What's this about?" I ask with a laugh. "I was only gone for an hour, guys."

Sutton shrugs a little. "You always catch us when we jump."

My heart squeezes. She has no idea that I'll always catch her, no matter what the situation.

Clearing my throat before emotion overtakes me, I turn to my mom.

"Guys, I need to introduce you to my mom. She's your grandma."

Both kids stare at her, taking her in. I can tell by the way Kody lays his head on my shoulder, he's a little nervous by this situation. And maybe he's staking his claim on me a little as well.

My mom, though, gotta love her, she doesn't skip a beat. She puts her hands over her heart and smiles at both of them, tears shining in her eyes. "My grandbabies! You must be Sutton and I bet you're Kody. Am I right?" Sutton nods. Kody, on the other hand, keeps giving her a critical eye. Mom doesn't even seem to notice. "I've been waiting for so long to meet you two! I even brought presents from my house for you!"

"Mom!" I admonish. "It's not even Christmas yet!"

"Don't you 'mom' me," she shoots back, stroking Sutton's hair and rubbing Kody's back. "These are my grandbabies and I'll spoil them if I want."

Kody's head shoots up from my shoulder. "I have a present?"

I shake my head with humor. The grandma bribing has begun.

"You sure do. I'll get them as soon as Daddy/Not-Daddy takes my suitcase to my room."

I groan. Now she's done it. Just when I thought I'd have a small reprieve from wrestling suitcases again, she says shit like that. The kids proceed to wiggle out of my arms and begin jumping up and down, demanding I take them all to the media room where we've got a sweet set up for Mom's stay.

"Okay, okay!" I hold my hands up, trying and failing to get the kids back under control. "I don't want to run over anyone with this tank, so you guys show Grammy where we're going, and I'll follow you with"—I take a deep breath, resigning myself to my bellhop fate—"with all these suitcases."

"Let's go Grammy!" Sutton grabs one of my mom's hands and starts to drag her forward. Kody is still a little unsure, so he takes Sutton's other hand. I can't help myself and snap a quick picture before trailing behind like I promised.

I only get halfway through the living room when I look over and see Lacy, standing stock still except for her hands that are wringing together. No one except me seems to notice her which is probably good considering she's got a look of fear on her face. Immediately I go on alert.

Abandoning the bags, I round the couch until I'm standing right next to her. "What's wrong."

She attempts a smile, but it's not even close to where it should be. "Nothing."

"Um, that's a lie." Lacy narrows her eyes at me so at least I know whatever is happening probably isn't critical. "Seriously, Lace. Is it my mother?"

She worries her bottom lip for a second before taking a deep breath. "It's stupid."

"Not if you're panicking it's not."

"I guess I just don't have the best track record with mothers."

I raise an eyebrow. "Because you've met so many?"

"Only my own," she grumbles.

And that's when the lightbulb goes off. The last grandmother who was introduced to Sutton slammed the door in their metaphorical face and left them out on the streets. No wonder she's nervous about my mom visiting. I want to kick myself for not putting it together sooner.

Turning her to face me, I run my hands up and down her arms. "Listen, this is different."

"Yeah? Your mom is going to be super cool with the woman who trapped her son into fatherhood after a one-night-stand?"

"You make it sounds so nefarious." I waggle my eyebrows, trying and failing to break the tension for her.

"It was, Tucker."

I chuckle because she's not wrong. It was a pretty wicked night. My laugh does the trick, though.

Lacy shoves me as she tries to fight back a smile. "Stop laughing."

"Sorry, sorry. My mom doesn't need to know the...very dirty details of that night." Trying not to remember those details myself so as to not sport a hard on in front of my mother, I turn serious. "Lacy, my mom brought a present for Kody. *Kody*. Why do you think she isn't going to accept you, too?"

"Because Kody is an innocent and I'm the one who should have known better."

"I am also the one who should have known better. You weren't the only one there. But listen, if it'll make you feel better, I promise if she is anything less than kind to you, I'll get her a hotel room and make her leave."

Lacy gasps. "You can't do that! That's your mother!"

"And you are Sutton's mother, and this is *our* house. No one gets to disregard you or make you feel lesser than in your home."

"Oh," she breathes out and then shakes her head. "I don't ever expect you to fight with your mother over me, Tucker."

"Please. Healthy families fight all the time. And we make up all the time. You think we haven't fought over the last few months as I kept putting off this visit? It was almost daily. That's how she finally wore me down. Listen, she wants to be here. She wants to get to know you and Sutton and even Ellie and Kody. We're family now and she won't be kept out of it."

"That's...really nice in a weird way."

"I know. And I know it's not what you're used to. But try to trust me on this. It's going to be great."

The kids come running back in just then, demand in their voices.

"Daddy, the suitcase! It has our presents! Hurry!"

I glance back at my baby mama who is so much more than that, and I intend on making sure she knows it. "See? Grammy is already spoiling them rotten."

"Daddy!" Sutton yells again.

"I'm coming baby girl."

I pull Lacy close and kiss her on the forehead in reassurance. Then, taking a deep breath, I situate myself with the bags again and follow Sutton out of the living room, curious what these presents could possibly be.

CHAPTER TWENTY-SEVEN

LACY

As much as I hate to admit when Tucker is right, he's right. His mother is lovely.

Holly didn't just introduce herself to me, she hugged me and thanked me for giving her a grandbaby. Then she pulled back and said, *"Actually, thank you for giving me two of them! I'm not giving that little Kody back. He's just too precious!"*

That doesn't mean I'm not still fighting my anxiety with her being here. I can't get over the fear that she's going to change her mind about me at any minute.

Fuck, I hate the aftereffects of parental rejection.

"Mommy! Catch me!" Sutton yells, her new bathing suit is a little droopy in the rear from being in the water for so long. I used to think having a heated pool was a ridiculous luxury in Florida where you can swim for at least eight months out of the year, but even I have to admit, it's nice to be hanging out in the water on Christmas Eve.

Holding out my hands I yell, "I got you!" and brace myself for the inevitable splash when Sutton lands in my arms.

Sure enough, I get a face full of water.

Kody is on the other end of the pool, being spun in circles by Holly. Clearly, he's gotten over his initial hesitation with her.

I wish I could be a little more like that.

"Ooh, my little fish," Holly coos. "You guys are such great swimmers!"

Sutton begins paddling in my arms, trying to swim over to them. "Mommy says when I'm big like Daddy I can take my floaty vest off."

Holly laughs lightly. "Well when you're big like Daddy, those vests probably won't fit you, so I wouldn't recommend trying them on."

"Yeah," Kody adds as he wipes water out of his face. "Daddy's arms are super big."

"He's not your daddy!" Sutton yells suddenly, expressing an anger I've never seen before.

"He is, too!" Kody yells back with as much fight as I've ever seen in him as well. This is such a change from him referring to Tucker as "Not-Daddy". I can only assume this new rift is because Holly is here and Kody wants to make sure Grammy is as much his as she is Sutton's.

"Now, now, kids," Holly says gently, using her grandma voice. "We don't need to fight over who Tucker belongs to. He belongs to both of you, remember?"

"But he's not Kody's daddy," Sutton insists.

"Ya-huh!" Kody yells back, tears welling up in his eyes.

"It doesn't matter Sutton." I turn her around so she and Kody aren't facing each other anymore. I wouldn't be able to do that move successfully if we were anywhere except inside a large body of water where neither of them can touch the bottom, so I'm taking full advantage. "Look at me."

She does, but doesn't remove the pursed lips and furrowed brows. I'm not sure when she became so possessive over Tucker, but this might be a problem if we're not careful and nip it in the bud now.

"We are *family*, remember?" Sutton doesn't say anything, just continues to glare at me. "Ellie's not your mommy. But does she love you?"

Sutton's expression begins to soften as she thinks about it. "Yes. She loves me to the moon and back. She told me."

"Right. And Tucker loves Kody to the moon and back, too."

That's probably a slight exaggeration considering how long we've all known each other, but I can't anticipate Tucker ever pushing Kody away. Not while we have these living arrangements, anyway.

Sutton's lip begins to quiver. "But he's my daddy, Mama."

"And he always will be, baby. Nothing can change that. But that doesn't mean you can be ugly to Kody and not let him be family with Tucker, too."

I can tell she doesn't like that, but she's also considering what I'm saying. I suspect we're going to have a lot of strange conversations for a while. There was no question about where everyone stood when it was just the four of us. It was easy. Each kid had a mom, each mom had a kid. Now there's one dad at an age when they both want one desperately. Leave it to me to make a choice that puts us all in this weird spiderweb of relationships.

The back door slides open and we're greeted with a "Honey, I'm home!"

"Mommy!" Kody shouts and scrambles to the side of the pool as fast as Holly will let him. Sutton also takes off, which basically proves my point, not that she'll pick up on that, but at least I feel like I wasn't wrong in my parenting discussion.

"Hi guys, hi," Ellie says as the kids clamber out of the pool. "How was your day?"

"Well, we're currently fighting over who Tucker belongs to, so that's been a fun time of tears."

"Oooh," she replies with a grimace. "I guess we should have seen that one coming at some point. The kids look okay now, though." Sure enough, all seems to be forgotten as they chatter away.

"Yeah, I'm probably more traumatized by the conversation than they are." That whole 'it hurts the mother more than it hurts you' thought process is more accurate in some cases than I ever knew before I gave birth. "How was work?" I ask as Ellie hugs the kiddos and begins the obnoxious task of trying to wriggle the vests off their wet bodies.

"Basically the same as when you quit. Decent tips. Decent co-workers. Wish I could get something different but it pays well and has good hours. And I got my Christmas bonus," she says with sarcasm. "So why mess with a good thing?"

"They're still trying to pass off a coupon good for one free entrée at the fancy restaurant down the hall as the bonus?"

"Can't wait to spend my whole paycheck feeding everyone else so I can get one free meal," she grumbles.

"Yeah, I don't miss it at all." I make a point of leaning my arms against the edge of the pool and sighing with overexaggerated relaxation.

"Show off," she murmurs followed by "Yes, yes, I'll help you get dressed so we can have a snack, but we have to towel off first," as the kids continue bouncing and chattering about all things Christmas and swimming.

"Hey Ellie, you left before you could meet Tucker's mom this morning. This is Holly. Holly, this is my best friend and the mother of my bonus son, Ellie."

They exchange pleasant greetings, well, as much as they can with two three-year-old's bouncing around. Finally, Ellie puts a hand on top of each their heads. slowing them down for a second so she can finish her conversation.

"It's so nice to finally meet the woman who raised that fine man," Ellie gushes. "He has just taken to this family with no hesitation whatsoever. It's been so nice to have an easy transition."

"I'm glad to hear it," Holly replies. "He's no stranger to lots of noise, what with having four brothers and all."

"Well, he's been a great addition to the kids' lives so far, that's for sure," Ellie adds, purposely forgetting the growing pains we've had recently. Or maybe just grateful he likes to wrestle with the kids because they won't stop hounding her. "Okay, okay," she finally caves. "Let's go inside and get dressed and maybe by then Lacy will have made you a snack. But we need to do it quickly so you and I can get out of their hair, Kody."

Her comment has me furrowing my brow. "Get out of our hair? What are you talking about? It's Christmas Eve. We have movies to watch and cookies to bake like always."

"Cookiiiiiies!" Kody yells and the rambunctiousness continues.

Ellie smiles shyly, her lips twisting to the side. "Lacy, it's your first Christmas as a family. I thought Kody and I could do our own thing this time."

I know what she's doing. She's trying to give us space on this first holiday together, but that's not going to fly with me. I know it's not going to fly with Sutton and I'd be willing to bet Tucker won't be happy if they aren't here either.

Before I can argue with her, though, Holly jumps in. "Oh no, no, no. That isn't going to work for me." Ellie's eyebrows shoot up. I'm sure mine do too. "You girls are like sisters and these kids think they're twins. Unless you have some big plans with your extended family, Ellie, you will be spending Christmas here in this house as you should. Don't stop your traditions on account of me or my son."

Ellie glances back and forth between Holly and I, unease still on her face. "Are you sure? I really do look forward to making cookies with the kids every year."

"Of course—"

"Absolutely—" Holly and I answer at the same time.

The relief on Ellie's face is palpable. "Well okay. In that case,

I'll get these two settled inside so we can start baking whenever you're ready."

"Sounds good." I hold my hands up to inspect my fingers "I'm starting to look like a prune, so we're almost done."

She nods once and begins herding the kids inside when Kody announces, "Mommy! Grammy brought us presents!"

"That's awesome. I can't wait to see them..."

Her voice fades away as the door closes, leaving Holly and I alone in the pool. I'd get out, but I'm finding the water and the sudden lack of noise soothing. Plus, I'm trying to follow Holly's lead and I can't quite figure out what she wants to do.

Why is it so hard to be a good hostess to this woman? She's been nothing but kind so far. More than kind, actually. Maybe it's because Tucker got called away to a random meeting with a potential endorsement he's been trying to nail down for a couple months, so we're here all alone. Not sure why it was so urgent that they meet the day before Christmas. Regardless, this silence is starting to change from being soothing to downright uncomfortable.

Holly finally breaks the ice for us. "Do you have any brothers and sisters, Lacy?"

"I do. I have three older brothers and a younger sister."

"So you're used to a lot of noise, too."

"Not really. I mean, maybe a little. But my parents were really, really strict while we were growing up. The whole 'Children should be seen and not heard thing'. Unless my brothers were arguing about something, it wasn't too loud."

"Do they live here in Tampa?"

"No, everyone except my sister is in Ohio. At least I think they are," I add on, but I'm not sure she caught that part.

"Do you see them a lot?"

I shake my head, hating that I'm the black sheep of the family. I still feel their loss if I dig deep enough, but explaining it to

Tucker's mom? That feels a little sticky. Like she might see the same things in me, the same sins that my family did.

"I was just reunited with my little sister a few weeks ago." Thinking about Muriel makes me smile. "We hadn't seen each other since I found out I was pregnant." My voice drowns out as shame burns through me. I'm essentially telling this woman I want so bad to like me that my own parents don't want anything to do with me, just not in so many words. "But Muriel just moved to the area so I've seen her a couple times and talk to her almost every day. It's been nice getting to know her again."

"She's the only one you talk to?"

I gnaw on my bottom lip and nod. I hate admitting the truth, but she's Sutton's grandmother. She needs to know what she's really getting into with us.

Holly leans back against the lip of the pool. "That's unfortunate. Seems like they're missing out on seeing a really sweet little girl grow up."

A half-smile graces my lips, but I keep staring straight ahead, not sure how to respond. I try to focus on the fact that she already likes Sutton so much.

"Seems like they're also missing out on watching a lovely young woman grow up, too."

My head whips over to look at her faster than I can stop it. Holly smiles at my obvious shocked reaction.

"I have five boys so I know how babies are made. I'm under no illusions about how Sutton came about." She rolls over onto her stomach, mimicking my position. "But I also know my Tucker. The day he found out he had a daughter, he called me. Did you know that?"

I shake my head.

"He was horrified." I bristle. "Not at the idea of having a child," she clarifies, making me relax just a bit. "He was so angry he'd missed out on her life. Just furious that he left you in a position to fend for yourselves when he clearly had the means to make sure all three of you were taken care of. It's a regret I don't think he'll ever get over."

"It's not his fault."

"Just because something isn't your fault doesn't make you feel less guilty. You're a mom. You should know all about that."

She's right. I always felt guilty about not being able to provide Sutton everything she wanted. Guilty about having her on WIC and food stamps and living in a car. It wasn't for lack of trying or because I did anything wrong. It was just a hard life situation we got stuck in. But the guilt will probably always be there.

"I know he doesn't admit to it much, but Tucker usually calls me every day. Just a quick call on his way to or from the rink when he's alone in his car. I've heard what he thinks about you almost every day. If for one second he thought you were anything short of amazing, he wouldn't have been so adamant about you guys living together. I think being here isn't just about getting to know Sutton more, I think it's also about you."

Her words surprise me. "Why? Why would he want to get to know me?"

"From what I can gather, because you've captured his attention in a way no other woman has."

I huff a laugh, trying to dismiss the sudden butterflies moving around in my stomach. "Yeah, well, no other woman has given birth to his child before."

"True. But it's more than that. You are driven and hard-working. You sacrificed your entire life for these children. You hold people accountable when they're wrong, but gave Tucker grace when all the details came into focus. You've raised an amazingly smart and clever little girl on your own with only a penny to your name. I know it's hard to see your situation for anything more than tough, but to the rest of us, it just shines a spotlight on how remarkable you really are."

I blink away the tears that are rapidly forming in my eyes.

"I'm sorry. I didn't mean to make you cry."

"No. It's okay. I just... I was so frightened about you coming to visit. I was so afraid all you were going to see was the whore who trapped your rich son into providing a big house or something."

"Oh please. It takes two to tango. I don't care what society tries to tell us—he is as much at fault for getting you pregnant as you are. From where I'm sitting, you didn't trap him. He owes you this much for letting you suffer for so long without him."

"Wait...but you said it wasn't his fault."

"It wasn't. But he bears the responsibility of surrounding himself with people who didn't have his best interest at heart. I warned him about that scumbag Morty before he hired him. Something didn't feel right to me. But Tucker didn't check with his gut before he hired that lazy ass. Consequently, you were the one hurt. That's not okay and he knows that."

Now I know where Tucker's insistence on taking care of us comes from. It's not a reaction to his guilt as much as it's a trait that's been instilled in him from the beginning.

"Listen, Lacy," Holly continues, "I don't know why your parents don't have anything to do with you. I can't imagine cutting off one of my kids because they made a mistake—particularly when the mistake isn't hurting anyone else, and when not helping will hurt an innocent child—but none of that is about you. You are not unworthy because you had a one-night stand. I've had a couple of those in my lifetime, too. I just got lucky and went home alone afterwards instead of with a child."

She bumps my shoulder, making me giggle.

"Maybe don't tell Tucker about that little secret. I can't imagine it would go over well to know his mother isn't as prim and proper as I pretend to be sometimes."

"Yeah I don't think anyone wants to know that about their mom."

"Probably not. But my point is," Holly continues, "Tucker thinks you're amazing. He is enthralled with you. And if nothing else, he's always been a good judge of character."

"Except with his agent."

"Except with him. I suspect that will be the last time Tucker makes such an egregious error."

"Mommy! Grammy!" The door flies open and Sutton stands in the middle of it staring us down like we're doing something wrong by still being in the pool. "Ellie said you were getting us a snack. We're hungry and we have to make cookies."

"Sorry, baby. Grammy and I got to talking and I forgot."

Sutton throws her head back and sighs dramatically.

"Oh lord, she got her father's dramatics," Holly says as she begins making her way to the stairs. I trail behind her, feeling much more comfortable with her company now.

"Is that where it comes from? I was wondering."

"Oh yes. That is all him."

"Now I need to hear some stories."

"Let's go make these kids a snack and I'll spill all the tea for you."

It's weird how one conversation can change everything, but that's exactly what our time in the pool did. Could this actually all work out?

I feel like a weight has been lifted off my shoulders as I practically glide through the rest of the day, enjoying the company of my daughter's new grammy.

CHAPTER TWENTY-EIGHT

TUCKER

I hate that I got called into a meeting. I had no intensions of leaving Lacy alone with my mom all day, at least not until Lacy gets more comfortable with our company, but for some reason the endorsement contract couldn't wait for a few more days. It's Christmas Eve. It's not like any of this is going to be processed for a few days anyway.

Don't get me wrong. I'm thrilled to be the new face of this small grocery chain. They're locally owned and have a stellar reputation with their employees. They've served the community well and I like being part of that. But seriously. It's the holidays. They could have waited until I wasn't trying to acclimate my baby mama to *my* mama. Hopefully the extra money in Sutton's college fund will make up for my absence today.

"Honey, I'm home!" I call as I step into the living room.

Nothing happens.

That's weird. The kids always come running when I get here. Maybe they're in the pool.

Rounding the living room into the kitchen, I discover that they're not swimming. They're stuffing themselves with apples and peanut butter, their faces covered in baking flour. Actually, the whole kitchen seems to have a thin layer of white powder over every surface. But that's not what I'm focused on right now.

"Tell me you mixed honey in with the peanut butter," I practically growl at my mother.

"Well, hello to you, too." She gives me a half-disapproving, half-amused look only a mother can get away with. "And yes, I did. And before you growl at me again, yes, there's more in the fridge."

I practically race across the room to get it. "Oh man, I love you!"

Tearing the door open, I'm singularly focused on retrieving what was my favorite childhood treat. As soon as I find the container, I want to weep with thanksgiving.

"I haven't had this in so long."

"Now Tucker, you still haven't even said hello to anyone. These are your kids for goodness' sake."

I love how she includes Kody in that sentence. His little face beams as he takes another bite of his peanut butter and honey covered apple.

"Sorry." I lean in and kiss her on the cheek. "Nice to see you." Then I turn to Lacy and kiss her on the cheek as well. "Nice to see you." I walk around the kitchen island and kiss Sutton. "Nice to see you." Lastly, I run the stubble of my cheek all over Kody's neck, probably turning part of my face ghost white from the flour in the process, making him squeal. "Nice to see you. Did I miss anyone?"

"You did." Ellie is sitting at the kitchen table, flipping through a magazine. "But I'll pass, thank you. No reason to make things weird."

I snatch an apple slice off Sutton's plate and dig into my own treat. My sassy little daughter scowls at me briefly but quickly takes another bite, forgetting all about me as she gets a taste of the best treat in the world.

Once my tastebuds are somewhat satisfied it finally hits me

what a wreck the kitchen is. There's flour everywhere, the sink is stacked with dirty dishes, and several racks of sugar cookies are cooling off to the side.

"Looks like you guys have been busy today. Making Christmas cookies?"

Ellie laughs. "Depends on if you call trying to clean up after a couple of independent three-year-olds while they dump ingredients all over the counter making cookies."

I raise an eyebrow at Lacy's giggle. As if she can feel my stare, she glances up at me. "There may or may not be a few rogue eggshells mixed in and I can't guarantee there won't be some pockets of flour."

"Now, now," my mom intercedes. "They did a wonderful job making cookies. Santa is going to love eating them once they're decorated."

Sutton and Kody beam with pride at mom's encouraging words. Lacy, on the other hand, mouths my direction, *That's you, Santa,* making me grimace at the thought of being the only one who has to partake in crunchy Christmas cookies. I guess it can't be much worse than the raw egg shakes I used to drink in high school. I used mind over matter to choke that shit down. I can do it again.

"The cookies are cooling so now you guys are working with meat?" I waggle my eyebrows and my mother smacks me with a towel.

"There are children in this room, Tucker Hayes," she admonishes.

"Sorry, sorry." I'm not really sorry. "I'll rephrase. What are you guys doing anyway?"

Lacy holds up what looks like a hamburger patty. "Your mother is teaching me how to make a Juicy Lucy."

I practically drop the bowl I've been wiping clean with my finger. "No way!"

Her eyes shift back and forth. "Is that a problem?"

"Juicy Lucy's are my favorite. Why no one this far south has ever tried cooking cheese inside the hamburger is still one of life's biggest mysteries."

"We're too busy with Mexican and seafood," Ellie interjects.

She's not wrong. I could eat my weight in either one of those things. Although I admit I have yet to find any enchiladas that are remotely comparable to my favorite restaurant in San Antonio.

"I can't wait for you guys to try these burgers. Once you take a bite into one fresh off the grill, you'll never want to eat a traditional cheeseburger aga..."

My sentence tapers off as something catches my eye. My nostrils flare with irritation and I can barely control myself when I speak.

"Mother," I growl, in complete disbelief she would throw this kind of shade in my home.

"Yes, darling?"

I'm not falling for the sweet tone in her voice. Especially when I narrow my eyes at her and she responds with a twinkle in hers. She *knows* what she did.

"What the hell are the kids wearing?"

"Language, Tucker!"

I ignore her admonishment, much like she's ignored the cuss words that come out of the mouths of all five of her boys for years.

"Mother..."

"Yes, darling?" she repeats. I knew it. This is a game to her. From the way Lacy is pressing her lips together, which I'm sure is to keep from laughing, it's a game to all of them.

"Is there a reason the children are wearing Minnesota Wild jerseys?"

Ellie is the first to break as a laugh bursts out of her. She throws her hand over her mouth and gives a muffled, "Sorry."

"Oh you know," Mom says nonchalantly, but she's not fooling me. "I'm in that Facebook group for hockey moms and my friend

Janet's son plays for the Minnesota Wild so I asked if she could get me some fun swag. Trenton was only too happy to help me out. You remember Trenton, don't you? Trenton Hicks?"

Not only do I know Trenton, I hate him. From the time we were kids, he's always been a cocky asshole.

"I'm sure he was happy to help, just so he could talk smack in my home without even stepping foot inside."

Mom makes a pish-posh noise. "I'm sure you're overexaggerating. They know I just want to make sure my grandbabies know their roots and where they come from."

"Yeah. Tampa. Where they were born and where their dad plays for the Glaze."

She shrugs. "Maybe for now but you have to come home someday."

"That's not the way it works, Ma. You know this."

Really. We've had this conversation multiple times over the years. You go where you're traded and you never make plans to stay for long. Unless you're me and you buy a big ass house, praying you get to stay a while.

"Maybe. But it never hurts to put a little pressure on you."

"And you think turning my entire family against me is the way to do that, huh? Never mind league rules on trades or even the fact that we just bought this house."

"Oh I didn't say you had to come home now. Just...someday."

I shake my head. She's getting way too much enjoyment out of this harassment.

"You like my green jersey, Daddy?" Sutton asks.

Blood roaring in my ears, I turn my head slowly to look at my mother again. "Do you see what you've done?" I ask quietly. How the hell am I supposed to tell my three-year-old daughter that I'd like to rip it off her and set it on fire?

That's when Lacy cracks. Doing a shitty job of hiding her mouth behind her hand, she can barely contain her laugh.

"Oh you think it's funny too, huh?"

She laughs even harder. "The look on your face. I've never seen you so mad before. Over a jersey."

"Seriously, Tucker," Ellie chimes in. "It's a shirt."

My jaw drops. What is the matter with these people? "It is a sign of loyalty and unity."

"It's a shirt," Ellie deadpans.

I glare at her. "Shouldn't you be siding with the man who pays your rent."

She's unfazed by my ridiculous and baseless threat. "I've learned over the years its typically better to side with the *mother* of the man who pays my rent."

"Oooh, yes," Lacy agrees like the traitor she is. "The results are much more long lasting when the mother is on your side."

"And you've learned that from how many mothers you've had to side with?"

"I didn't say it wasn't a recently learned lesson." Lacy flashes me an ornery grin and the cave man in me wants to toss her over my shoulder, drag her down the hall to my bedroom and have my wicked way with her.

I expect my mother to throw shade about living so far from home. This is not a new thing. But dragging my new family into it is not something I anticipated. In a weird way, I can't be upset about this turn of events. This is how we banter. It's how we show love. Seeing Lacy fit right in does things to my loins that no one in this room needs to see right now.

They also don't need to see me cave. That wouldn't fit with the stubborn image I like to present when it comes to this topic. I shake my head with disappointment instead.

"So that's how it is, huh? Everyone suddenly wants to move to Minnesota."

"It would be nice to have snow for Christmas," Lacy says with an ornery smile.

Placing my bowl down, I stalk around the counter and nuzzle my scruffy, floury chin into her neck, knowing she can't do anything about it with hands full of raw beef. The feel of her body next to mine, even with so many people in the room is just...*right*.

"Really?" I rub as she squeals from the tickle. "That's your argument? Snow for Christmas?"

After a few more passes with my chin, her laughing the whole time and trying to wriggle out from under me, she finally caves.

"Okay, okay, I give!" she shouts. "Christmas at the beach! Every year."

I pull back slowly, not wanting to release her just yet but knowing now is not the time to try for a make out session, and grab the baking sheet with patties that are ready for the grill. "That's what I thought."

"Until we move to Minnesota."

She holds out her hands in front of her, anticipating another attack. Instead, I sigh deeply and grab Kody around the waist.

"Come on, Kody. We're outnumbered here. Let's go outside and I'll show you how a real man grills burgers."

As I stalk toward the door, Kody dangling off my hip, he fires the winning shot without even knowing it. "Did you see my green shirt too, Not-Daddy? I like green, too."

My shoulders drop in defeat as I ignore the roar of laughter from the women behind me.

CHAPTER TWENTY-NINE

LACY

Staring at the door, I wring my hands together, trying to decide what to do.

On the one hand, I want to knock. I have things to say.

On the other hand, I'm so afraid of being disappointed. Afraid of the rejection. I know that has nothing to do with the man behind the door, but that doesn't mean my psyche isn't battling itself.

As fate would have it, the decision is made for me when the door flies open.

Tucker is clearly surprised to see me standing in the hall in front of his bedroom, but he's probably not as surprised as I am to see him in all his buff glory. Well, not *all* his glory. He's got some athletic shorts on. But they're low-slung and leaving very little to the imagination. An imagination that has some extremely vivid memories of what he's sporting underneath.

"Eyes up here, Lacy," he says with a chuckle and my gaze snaps up to his.

Sucking up all the bravado I can muster, I give him my best disregarding look. "If you don't want to be ogled, you should have a shirt on."

His eyes light up like they always do when I give him shit. For whatever reason, banter seems to be his love language. Not that there's any love between us or anything. Maybe. On his end anyway. But verbally sparring seems to be a version of foreplay for him.

"I was in my bedroom. Alone. I had no idea I'd have an audience at this time of night." He gestures behind me. "But if my chiseled physique is too much for your wandering eyes, I can always grab something to cover it."

I roll the eyes in question. "Whatever. I won't be here long anyway. I'll try to contain my womanly urges around you."

He opens the door wider, allowing me to step into his space.

"Come on in. I'm going to grab some water but I'll be right back."

That's when I notice the large tumbler he always seems to have sitting around. Somehow, I missed it in my slow perusal of his body. I guess the measurement lines on the bottle aren't nearly as sexy as the lines of that pelvic *V* he's sporting.

Taking advantage of my time alone, I explore the room a bit. It's huge, much bigger than mine, but the color scheme is similar with soothing greys and whites and silvers. The furnishings are all oversized, probably to fit Tucker's extra-large clothes. On the nightstand, right next to a beautiful Crystal lamp, sits a stainless-steel frame. Inside there is a black and white picture of Sutton and me wearing Tucker's jersey. I have no idea when the picture was taken or by whom, but it's beautiful. And it's next to his bed where he can always see it.

Even more surprising, right behind it is another framed picture. I pick it up to get a closer look. This one is of both kids facing away from the camera, arms over each other's shoulders, big cheesy grins on their faces as they look at each other. I've never seen this picture before, but I recognize the kitchen counter in the back, which means he must have taken this in the old apartment.

My heart melts knowing that Tucker's desire to keep the little family I built intact isn't just for show. Behind closed doors, when no one is looking, he's still accepted Kody as one of "our" kids.

The thought makes my knees weaken and I find myself sitting on the edge of his bed, still clutching the frame.

"That was the second time I met the kids."

I glance over at the sound of his voice. Tucker is standing in the doorway, tumbler still in his hand. At my smile, he comes further into the room, closing the door behind him.

The air thickens as the realization sets in that I'm alone with Tucker, in his bedroom, with the rest of the house sound asleep. We're on the opposite wing from anyone else, completely alone.

He places his water on the nightstand and sits next to me, taking the frame from my hands to look at the picture.

"I think you had gone to the restroom or something. Or the bedroom. I can't remember. Anyway, they were giggling about something and then suddenly they were hugging each other like this. And I remember thinking right then that I wasn't a father of one like I thought. I was a father of two."

I suck in a breath at his words. Words that pierce right through my heart in the very best way.

He places the picture back on the nightstand and looks at me, a sheepish smile on his face. "Whether they have the same parents or not, they're brother and sister. That's how they feel about each other and it's how you and Ellie feel about them. And I'm not going to try to divide them up ever. That's not fair and it's not right."

"So what, you're just going to provide for him like you do Sutton?"

"For as long as Ellie will let me. I know she dates and someday she'll probably get married to a guy who wants to be Kody's step-dad. But that doesn't change who they are to this family. That man will have to integrate himself into their already established lives like I am."

I hesitate to believe what I'm feeling, but it's possible I've fallen a little bit in love with Tucker Hayes at this exact moment.

All my life, or at least up until the last five years, I've been trained to believe family is *us against the world*. There is no room for outside influence and anything that might lead to such has to be cut off from the family. I, unfortunately, was the influence that had to be cut out from the family I grew up in.

But here is Tucker, sweet, ornery, overly-generous Tucker, who isn't looking at our situation as weird or unconventional. He's just looking at it as a family. One that we made out of necessity and circumstance, but no less strong and important.

Tucker clears his throat and I catch what sounds like a bit of nervousness from him. "Anyway, I know that's totally cheesy and maybe not normal but I'm not going to ever push Kody away like that. He's the innocent here. So just be prepared that at some point the media is going to pick up on me saying I have two kids and they'll start poking around, probably drawing some pretty weird conclusions about sister wives and all that. If you and Ellie want me to clarify things for them, I will. But I'm okay with just letting them run with whatever they want. Publicity draws butts to seats which helps secure my job, right?"

"You can tell them anything you want. Or you don't have to tell them anything at all. It's your story as much as it is ours."

He nods and clasps his hands together, seeming just as nervous as I am. But why? What about this situation is making me anxious? Is it feeling the heat from his body so close to mine? Is it the feelings I'm suddenly recognizing that I've never had before? Is it the concern I have about why I came in here in the first place? It might be all of the above. Somehow, though, it's making it hard to have a conversation.

Tucker must know I'm struggling because he gives me a reprieve.

"What's going on, Lacy? Are you okay?"

"I'm fine."

I squeeze my eyes shut. I'm not fine but of course my mouth works faster than my brain sometimes.

"Actually, I wanted to make sure you were okay."

He furrows his brows in confusion. "Me? Why wouldn't I be?"

"I guess I feel bad that we had the kids all wrapped up in your rival's logo. I mean, it seemed like we were being funny at the time, but I also know how gross it feels when loyalty is broken, and I don't want to make you feel like that. It's kind of been eating at me all night so I wanted to clear the air about it."

Tucker's responding smile is wide and genuine, the crinkles around his eyes showing exactly how off-base it seems I was.

"My mom has razzed me about playing in Minnesota for years."

"Really? It's not just because she wants her grandkids nearby? Because for the record, Ellie and I talked about it and we'd totally move to Minnesota if that's what you wanted. Neither of us have anything keeping us here."

"Stop. We're not moving." He puts his hand on mine and draws it to him. "When I first moved to San Antonio, Mom came to visit and helped me unpack. It was right at the beginning of the season so I was gone a lot. One day when I came home, she had these giant Minnesota posters hanging up all over my house. Literally everywhere. I found one in the guest bathroom like a month after she left when my buddy had come over and used the facilities. They gave me shit about that for months."

I can't fight the smirk. It appears Tucker got his sense of humor from his mother. I should have figured.

"A couple years later, when we played Minnesota, she came to a game. Did she wear my jersey? No. She got a Minnesota jersey and had my name put on the back of it. Wore it to the game instead."

This time I start laughing.

"It took me forever to live that one down. And not just from my own teammate. The Wild talked trash about it too all night long." He shakes his head. "My point is, don't worry about me. You should be more concerned about the fact that she's using your children to poke fun at me."

"Sounds like she really wants you to come home."

"I think it's less about wanting me to come home and more about making sure I know I always have a place to come home to. That no matter what happens, she will welcome me back with open arms. Decking the kids out in those god-awful ugly ass jerseys was a message from her that she knows I screwed up, and it changes nothing except how many people are welcome. That all of you are welcome home."

"That is..." I blink back the tears that have suddenly filled my eyes. "So fucking kind."

Tucker tugs on my hand. "What? Why does that make you sad?"

"I guess it's just different. When I made a mistake, my family cut me off completely. Disowned me. But your mom, her love is unconditional." I swipe at the stray tear sliding down my cheek. "I've never known anyone like that before. Well, I guess I know you."

"You think I'm like that too?"

"You call Kody your kid. You're exactly like that."

"Good. I like hearing that. My mom isn't perfect, obviously by her terrible sense of hockey style, but she's always made sure we know she loves us no matter what. That's how I want to raise the kids. I hope you want that, too."

"I do. More than anything. I never want Sutton to feel like she can't tell me when she's screwed up. That she's afraid I'll reject her. I never will. I never want to."

"And I won't let you. But I think we need to change one thing."

"What's that?"

"Our verbiage. We didn't screw up when we made Sutton. We screwed..." he waggles his eyebrows suggestively.

"Har har. That was cheesy."

"... but we didn't screw up," he continues. "She was a surprise and I'll never forgive myself for missing out on the first part of her life. But she's perfection in every way. Even when she's an obnoxious teenager and hates us because we're ruining her life, or whatever, I'll never think of her as a mistake."

I swallow hard before asking the one question that still haunts me. "What about me? Am I a mistake?"

Tucker shifts his weight, turning more fully toward me and cups my jaw. The scent of his body wash is overwhelming my senses. I should be afraid, wary, but I'm not. This is what I came in here for, right? To lower the last of my defenses and see if we can build a family and a relationship at the same time?

"You have never been a mistake." He brushes a stray piece of hair out of my face. "You know I used to dream about you. Now you're here and I want nothing more than to get to know you more. Not only because of Sutton, but because of you. You are the only woman I see anymore, Lacy. Even when we're on the road and the guys want to go out and party, no one catches my attention. I'd rather be in my hotel room, video chatting with you, than have my hands on anyone else."

His words break down the last of my defenses. But I have to hear him say it. I have to know for sure. And I have to be brave enough to ask for clarification. "What does that mean?"

Cupping my jaw with one hand, he strokes my cheekbone with his other thumb. "I am falling so hard for you, Lacy. You are smart and strong and sacrifice yourself for others. Most people don't see it, but I do. I see how you gave up your pride and every-thing you had built on your own so I could have a chance to get to know Sutton. You didn't have to do that. No court would have ordered us to live together, but you did it for her. For me."

My heart beats louder as his words invade my whole being, healing me from the inside out. But he's not done.

"You are loyal to those you love, and you never want anyone to feel the kind of rejection you have felt. I love that I don't ever have to worry about my daughter. That no matter what happens to me, she has a better mother than I could have dreamed up for her."

Tuckers rests his forehead against mine and breathes me in. "Whenever you're ready, Lacy. I'm so ready to be all in with you."

The funny thing about everything Tucker said is that I feel all those things about him, too. We react to stressful situations differently, but ultimately, deep down, we're on the exact same page with our priorities and goals. I know there are no guarantees with Tucker. Relationships don't always work out. But I also know if anyone is going to fight for this one to work, it'll be him. And it'll be me.

"I'm ready," I whisper, my mouth so close to his, I know he can feel my breath on his lips.

"Are you sure?"

"I've never been so sure," I admit.

That's all he needs to hear before his mouth is on mine and the frenzy begins. Our tongues begin to tangle as our hands start to explore. My fingers slide down his chest, discovering the ridges of his abs. When my fingers graze the waistband of his shorts, he groans, responding by sliding his hand up my nightshirt and gently rubbing the underside of my breast.

Already about to explode and we've barely even begun, I stand and situate myself between his legs. His hands slide up my calves, up my thighs, and land at the swell of my ass. I pull the nightshirt over my head, leaving me in lacy red panties that he quickly discards.

He leans his head against my stomach and sighs with contentment. Looking up at me, he says those words every woman loves to hear in a moment like this. "You're so beautiful."

"You're not so bad yourself." I drop to my knees in front of him, sliding my fingers into the waistband of his shorts and tugging.

Tucker's eyes widen as he realizes what's happening. "Lacy..." he breathes.

"Trust no one, remember?" He nods but I'm not done. "No one except you."

His features soften at the understanding of my words. I don't trust many people. I've been too hurt for that. But I trust Tucker completely.

He pushes my hair back and shifts his hips so I can slide his shorts down his legs, evening the playing field. He sucks in a breath as I take him in my mouth, enjoying the feel and flavor of him, of this man that I love. *Love.* And trust in ways I never expected.

Tucker only allows it for a few seconds before pulling me off him and picking me up, fusing our mouths together again.

"I know how much that meant to you, what you're trying to say," he mumbles against my lips, just as unwilling to break the physical connection as I am. "But we've already had dirty, raunchy sex."

"You don't want that tonight?"

Using his powerful arms, he shifts us around so I'm on my back on the bed. Hovering over me, he shakes his head. "Tomorrow, I can flip you over and hit it from behind if you want."

"It'll be my Christmas present," I say with a giggle.

"I've got bigger plans than that, but I'm not opposed to mommy fucking Santa Claus tomorrow night."

A bigger laugh bursts out of me. I love that about Tucker. He always has quick little funny things to toss into any conversation. It gives me a reprieve from how deep conversations can get sometimes. That doesn't mean I don't feel things deeply. He just knows how to keep me comfortable when there are a lot of emotions involved. And by the way his smile softens, there are a lot of feelings in this exact moment.

"Tonight, I want to love you, Lacy. I want to take things slow so I don't miss any part of you. And when I'm buried deep inside you, I want you to know I'm claiming you as mine. Not just for the night or the holiday week, but permanently. I don't want to do this any other way."

I try to blink back the tears filling my eyes. One of them escapes, and without saying a word, Tucker swipes it away with his finger.

Resting his forehead against mine again, I take the opportunity to run my fingers through his floppy hair. "I love you, Lacy. So much."

"I love you, too."

As Tucker leans in, kissing me deeply, I wrap my arms and legs around him, holding tightly, not ever wanting to let go. When he kisses my jaw, down my neck, between my breasts, I loosen my grip. When he gets to my stomach, he pauses.

"What is this?" He runs a finger over the faint scar.

"C-Section." His eyes glance up to mine in question. "She was breech, and they couldn't get her to turn around."

"Oh, Lacy," he breathes before kissing all along the scar. "I can't believe you went through that for her. For us." I want to respond but my thoughts can't focus as I just *feel*. The small swipes of his tongue and gentle pressure as his fingers grip my hips distract me from anything else. Especially since he's not done moving south.

As soon as he hooks his arms around my legs and I realize his intensions, I stop him. "I thought we weren't doing that tonight?"

Spreading me open, he licks his lips in anticipation. "Trust no one, except you, remember?"

Before I can respond, he swipes the flat of his tongue up my center, making me moan. His tongue circles my clit a few times before he sucks on it just gently enough to make me writhe with anticipation. I can feel the pleasure building, my core tightening along with my grip on his hair. Just as I'm about to reach my peak, he pulls away.

"No," I gasp. "I was so close."

"I'll get you there again." He climbs up my body, settling himself in between my legs. "But I want to see you. Can I see you, Lacy?"

He has no idea how true his words ring. He's one of the few people who sees me, the real me, and loves me in spite of it. Or because of it. I'm unsure in this moment when all I can do is nod in response.

"Are you ready?" he asks, his forehead resting against mine again, which I'm quickly realizing is Tucker's preferred form of intimate touch.

I peck a kiss on the tip of his nose, widen my legs further, and press my heels into the back of his thighs, urging him to move forward.

Without taking his eyes off mine, he slowly slides into me, as deep as he can get. I pull in a breath as the magnitude of this moment hits me. He's not just deep inside my body. He's deep inside my heart. My soul.

Tucker starts to move, deep thrusts, then shallow, helping our bodies build to the moment we're both needing. He clasps my hands in his, pinning my arms over my head, stretching my body and giving him better access to my neck where he nibbles the skin gently, creating goose pimples all over my body.

"I love you so much, Lacy," he whispers. "I've waited so long for you."

"Me, too." That's all I can get out as I continue to chase my release, moving my hips in small circles, while he continues to thrust deep.

His movements become erratic, and I'm so tightly wound, my insides feel like a balloon waiting to pop. Suddenly, without warning, the explosion hits.

My mouth opens but nothing comes out, just a silent scream as pleasure rocks through me.

Tucker is still above me, his body pressed hard into mine as his own orgasm takes over, leaving him groaning heavy breaths as we stare into each other's eyes.

As I come down from my high, I have the strangest thought that I've finally found my home in this man who stormed into my life and turned it upside down in the best possible way. And when he gently lays his weight on top of me, peppering small kisses all over my neck and shoulder and collarbone, I fall into the deepest, most contented sleep I can remember ever having in my life.

CHAPTER THIRTY

TUCKER

"Daddy!"

The door flies open, startling me awake. My eyes barely open, I catch the fuzzy glimpse of two toddlers, eyes wide and maniacal as they should be on Christmas morning.

"Merry Christmas, kiddos."

"Santa came, Daddy! Can I open presents? Can I?" Sutton pleads. Kody nods vigorously next to her.

I rub my hand down my face, clearing my vision just in time to see my mother come up behind them. Her eyes widen and I look down to make sure my junk is covered up by the sheet.

Yep. I'm good.

"Why is Mommy sleeping in your bed?" Sutton asks sweetly.

Ah. That's why my mother looks like she just swallowed her tongue. Wait, is Lacy covered up? I look over at her and she's on her stomach, covered by the sheet from her mid-back down. Good enough for little eyes. Not a good enough excuse for her being here, however, so I come up with something on the fly.

"We had a sleepover last night."

"She's not wearing a shirt."

"It got hot in here."

My mother fights back a smirk, catching the truth in my words. The kids just shrug. I guess I gave a reasonable answer.

"Mommy!" Sutton screams at the top of her lungs. Lacy pops her head up off the pillow with a gasp.

I immediately place a hand on her back, just in case she forgets she's naked and tries to jump out of bed.

"Merry Christmas, Mommy!" I yell, hoping to divert any more attention away from the lack of clothing in this bed.

Unfortunately, it has the side effect of making the kids even more excited, so they race over to Lacy, who seems to have just realized she's topless as she lays back down slowly and gives quick kisses to the kids, encouraging them to go get Ellie up and tell her to make coffee.

As they race out of the room, my mom just cocks an eyebrow at me and closes the door behind them. Good thing, too. I can't hold myself back from wrapping my arms around this beautiful woman and peppering kisses on her shoulder. No telling where the sheet will end up.

Lacy pushes her hair out of her face but doesn't resist me. That's a good sign. I was worried she'd have regrets this morning. Instead, it seems her only regret is not anticipating the lack of boundaries in this house.

"Please tell me your mother didn't just see me naked in your bed."

I chuckle against her skin. "It would be a Christmas miracle if she somehow missed it."

Lacy groans into the pillow.

"Don't worry about her," I say and rub her arm reassuringly. And also so I can feel her soft skin underneath my palms. I don't think I'll ever get enough of touching her. "My mother has walked in on way worse before."

"That doesn't make me feel any better."

"Really? It makes me feel a lot better knowing she didn't see my naked ass mid-thrust this time."

Lacy pops up, almost nailing my nose with the back of her head. "Tucker! Your mom walked in on you having sex? Like in the act?"

"Not my finest moment. But I was in high school, and it was my first girlfriend. She should have known better than to come a knocking when the room was rocking."

"Oh man, and now I triggered all those old memories. She's never going to like me now."

I give her one last kiss on the shoulder, then climb out of bed, grabbing my shorts from a pile of clothes on the floor. "She already loves you and now that you love me, she doesn't have a choice but to keep it up. You do still love me this morning, right?" I ask it in jest, but deep down, I really need to know it wasn't a fluke. That last night meant as much to her as it did to me.

Lacy smiles shyly. "I do still love you. You still love me?"

I scramble back onto the bed staying on my hands and knees, knowing I'll never leave this room without taking her again if I feel her body underneath me. I kiss her gently. "So much that I should be afraid of how this is all going to play out, but I'm not. Is that weird?"

"Not at all," Lacy says as she rubs my scruff with her fingernails. "I feel the exact same way."

I kiss her again, giving over to the moment enjoying the way our tongues leisurely tangle and our lips fit perfectly. When the head in my pants starts to wake up, I know that's my cue to pull away from her before the kids come back again and get the same kind of eyeful my mother did all those years ago.

Shaking her hip gently, I give Lacy one last quick peck. "Let's go. We've got kids waiting to see what Santa brought."

Lacy gasps. "Santa! Oh shit. Please tell me you ate some of the cookies."

I stick my tongue out and making a gagging sound at the memory. "I remembered after you fell asleep and took care of it. I'm sure I still have eggshells in my teeth to prove it."

Lacy covers her mouth and giggles. "Were they that bad?"

"I wish I could tell you I've had worse, but I can't." I grab her nightshirt off the floor and hand it to her. "The icing would have made it tolerable if I hadn't seen Kody sneeze on it while they were decorating."

"You're such a good daddy/not daddy," she says with a grin.

"Doing my best, babe." I snatch a shirt from my drawer and pull it on. "I'll get them something to eat while you get dressed. No telling how much longer they're going to last before they start climbing the tree."

"I'll just be a minute."

"No worries. Take all the time you need."

As I close the door behind me, I lean against it and let out a deep sigh of contentment. She loves me. I love her. We love each other. That's all the gift I need.

By the time I get to the kitchen, the celebration is in full swing. Coffee has been made, Ellie and the kids are eating some pancakes that either have red and green food coloring mixed in or they're moldy, and Christmas carols are playing in the background.

As I grab a mug, I stop when I recognize the song. Turning to my mother, I purse my lips. "Really mother?"

"What?" she says sweetly.

"*I Saw Mommy Kissing Santa Claus*? That's the song you picked?"

She shrugs. "It seemed appropriate."

Ellie giggles behind her coffee mug.

"*Et tu*, Ellie?"

"What do you mean, *et tu*? It was my idea to put the song on a loop for a while. Just until it gets through Lacy's thick skull that we're all okay with this new reality."

I nod once in understanding. "Solid point."

She holds up her mug as if to toast her thought process and goes back to eating her breakfast. I've just poured two mugs of steaming joe and am getting ready to doctor it when the woman of the hour comes strolling in.

"Merry Christmas everyone." She kisses the kids on top of their heads before making her way to me. Actually she's making her way to the coffee pot, but I can pretend.

Lacy clearly found all my bathroom supplies since her hair is brushed and face looks washed. The faint smell of mint tells me she also used my toothbrush. That could gross me out, but my tongue was in her mouth hours ago and that's basically the same thing anyway.

I finish putting a teaspoon of sugar and three teaspoons of coconut milk in her coffee just as she walks up.

As I hand it to her, a smile graces her beautiful face. "Is this for me?"

"Of course." I kiss her on the cheek. "Merry Christmas."

Her cheeks turn red and she looks down shyly. "Tucker..."

"Lacy." I lean my head forward and make eye contact. "They already know."

"That doesn't mean we need to flaunt it."

I open my mouth to argue but suddenly she turns her head quickly, as if she's listening. She purses her lips as realization hits.

"Seriously, Ellie?"

Ellie stabs another piece of pancake and brings it to her mouth. "It's today's theme song."

"Did you kiss Santa last night, Mommy?" It's a reasonable conclusion for Sutton to come to, considering the background music that's likely invading her psyche.

Ellie holds up a half-eaten cookie, complete with runny icing, and my stomach gives a gurgle.

"By the look of these cookies, I'd say Santa was definitely here," she announces. "Which means Mommy definitely kissed him in appreciation, as well as other things."

"Santa!" Kody yells and the two kids quickly forget about food as they race to the tree, jumping up and down and pointing out all the presents.

"Wait for me," Ellie calls, taking one final bite, grabbing her mug, and then following them into the living room.

These kids have remarkable self-control. My brothers and I never waited this long before tearing into the gifts.

Lacy leans against the counter, holding her mug just inches from her lips. "So I guess everyone knows now."

Matching her pose, I bump her with my shoulder. "I'd say finding you topless in my bed was a dead giveaway."

She covers her face with her hand. "I can't believe your mother saw that," she groans.

Mom doesn't miss a beat, just kisses Lacy on the cheek. "Welcome to the family dear. I appreciate not having Tucker's naked butt flashed at me this time. That's something no mother should ever see." She pats Lacy's cheek gently and joins the others around the tree.

I loop my arm around Lacy's shoulder and kiss the top her head. "See? You earned brownie points already."

She scoffs and shakes her head. Pulling her with me I say, "Come on. The kids have waited long enough."

When we settle ourselves on the couch, Lacy tries to sit on the opposite end but I drag her across the cushions so we're sitting side by side. She narrows her eyes at me, but I narrow mine right back.

"All in, remember?"

She sighs and rolls her eyes, but by the way her lips tip up, I know she's just trying to guard her heart. It's understandable. This is new and we're both a little nervous. I just don't have as many walls as she does. Fortunately, watching Ellie help the kids pass out presents is a good way to distract Lacy until she feels more comfortable with public displays of affection. Especially once the frenzy begins. And I do mean frenzy.

Ellie no more than gives the word and the kids are ripping

wrapping paper and tearing apart boxes like their lives depend on it. I'm not even sure they know what all they're getting with how the paper flies everywhere and lands wherever it wants.

"Holy shit, Tucker. I knew you went overboard but I think I underestimated how much room there is for presents under this tree. Did you save any presents for everyone else at the store?" Lacy jokes, but she's not wrong.

I may have gotten a tad carried away.

"It's our first Christmas together," I argue. "Consider it making up for the three I missed."

Lacy's not buying it. "You're trying to tell me it won't be like this next year?"

She's got a point.

"Let me have my fun, woman. Look at their happy faces."

Sutton holds up a bag of giant Legos, perfect for her age.

"See?" I gesture to my daughter. "I read the age requirements this time."

"They're guidelines, Tucker. Not requirements," she says, amused with my word choice.

"Meh. Whatever. They're happy."

Kody pulls out his own bag of giant Legos and the kids squeal at the excitement of having identical gifts.

"They are happy." Lacy snuggles in closer to me. "We all are."

I look down at her. A soft smile graces her lips and I can't help myself. I close the last few inches between us and take her lips in a searing kiss. It doesn't matter who is in the room. It doesn't matter how many questions I have to field. I love this woman so damn much.

"Tucker Fucking Hayes!" Ellie screeches.

I tear my mouth from Lacy's to see why she's using my self-proclaimed middle name. "What did I do?"

She waves a card and red envelope in the air as she rages. "A year's worth of daycare *prepaid?*"

"Oh that." I say as nonchalantly as I feel. "Merry Christmas."

"Seriously, Tucker?" She reads over the card again, apparently in disbelief which is weird to me. Kody needs somewhere to go while the adults are working and in school. If anything, it feels less like a gift to me and more like a necessity, but by the way Ellie is tearing up, I guess it's good I presented it to her this morning under a tree.

Ellie somehow finds her way through the maze of wrapping paper and discarded toys, so she can throw herself in my arms and hug me. "Thank you, Tucker. This is the nicest thing anyone has ever done for me."

"You need some better friends, then."

She pulls away and smacks my arm playfully, wiping at a few stray tears before turning her attention back to the kids.

Lacy pulls her knees to her chest and settles against the back of the couch. "All inclusive daycare expenses? Big spender."

"Oh that's not what you get for Christmas."

She sits up straight, aghast. "What? Why not?"

"Because it's my job to pay for Sutton's daycare. That's already done. Here." I reach under the couch where her gifts are hidden and pull out a small box. "I wasn't really sure what to get you, but this seemed like a good place to start."

She tentatively takes the blue velvet gift box into her hands. "Tucker..." she whispers, not even knowing what's inside yet.

"Just open it."

She finally does and sucks in a breath when she takes in the contents. "Tucker, it's so perfect."

Inside is a sterling silver necklace with three charms on it. The largest is clearly an adult bird with a small red ruby placed in the eye position. The other two charms are identical baby birds, one with a small blue sapphire eye and one with a green topaz.

"You're like the mama bird, raising these crazy babies, so I thought I'd get you something to always remind you of how important you are to them. And to all of us."

Lacy gently grabs my chin with her fingers and pulls me in for a sweet kiss. "Thank you. I love it so much."

"You're welcome."

"And I'm glad you didn't go over the top with presents for me. This one is just perfect."

I laugh because she has no idea. "You think that's it?" Reaching under the couch again, I pull out keys to her brand new car.

"You bought me a car?" she bellows while I continue to laugh. I knew she'd have that reaction. I was actually kind of hoping for it. "My car is just fine."

"Your car is a piece of shit and you know it. So I got you a red version of mine."

She stares at me in disbelief. "You got me a Porsche."

I cover my heart with my hand, feigning offense. "I got you a Cayenne."

Lacy shakes her head but doesn't throw the keys at me which I've been half expecting. She's probably realizing it doesn't matter how much she says not to spend so much money on them. I'm going to spoil them for as long as I can.

"But that's not all!"

I jump up from the couch, ignoring Lacy's grumble of "You've got to be kidding me" as I check my hiding spot in the storage closet. I pull out the five identical boxes no one found.

"There are rules with these boxes, guys." I pretend Lacy isn't looking at me skeptically and hand my mom a box. "Don't open your gift until I say 'go', got it?"

"Oh god. Now I'm afraid." Lacy takes her present when I hand it to her and holds it in front of her like it's a live bomb.

"Nothing to be afraid of, my sweet."

Ellie takes hers without a problem, even though I'm still trying to reassure her friend.

"This is going to be fun, I promise." Holding the last two

boxes out to the kids I look them in the eyes. "Don't open this present yet. Got it?"

They both nod in understanding, but I can see the anticipation in their eyes. I better make this fast.

Handing them their gifts, I settle myself back on the couch so I have the best view of the coming madness.

"Are you ready?" I ask, almost as excited as everyone else.

Little heads nod and yell, "Yeah!"

Big heads just groan and grumble about what an impulsive shopper I am.

"On your mark, get set, go!"

The kids tear at the boxes like they're in a race to get it open first. They're beaten by Ellie who pulls out her shirt before they've even gotten through the tape.

She reads the front, then drops it onto her lap. "No way."

I waggle my eyebrows and wait for everyone to reveal their matching clothes. The shirts themselves are not that exciting—they're the standard Disney shirts with an outline of Mickey Mouse and their individual names added.

"It's Mickey Mouse, Mommy!" Kody yells and launches his shirt at his mother. She catches it one-handed.

"Does this mean what I think it does?" Mom asks and I nod.

"Season passes for everyone!" I yell and throw my arms in the air in victory. I doubt the kids understand what's happening here, but they start jumping up and down anyway, getting in on the excitement.

"Even for me?" Mom asks.

"Your box comes with the information on how to redeem your travel vouchers. You've got four round trip tickets so you can come visit us several times this year." I glance over at Lacy who is smiling, and not a maniacal smile that makes me wonder if she's going to punch me in the junk. It's a real, genuine smile.

"Is this okay with you, Lacy?" Mom asks. "This is your home, too. I don't want to be the overbearing Grammy who wears out her welcome."

Lacy tears her eyes from mine to address my mother. "We talked about it and that gift is from both of us. Well," she waves her hand in the air. "Not the money part. That's all him."

"How far is Disney from here?" Ellie asks as she pulls the shirts over the kids heads and down over their pajamas. "Like an hour and a half?"

"Should be a little less than that. And they open in a couple hours." I clap my hands together and rub. "Anyone want to spend an impromptu day at Disney World?"

Amid the hoots and hollers, I glance over at the woman I love again and raise an eyebrow in question.

She raises her eyebrow back and says the words I was hoping to hear.

"I'll drive."

CHAPTER THIRTY-ONE

LACY

"This is so fun," Muriel yells in my ear.

"What?" I yell back. Amidst the cheers, air horns, and ruckus the kids are making, I can barely hear her.

"I said," she yells louder, "This is really fun. Thanks for inviting me."

"Thanks for coming with us."

"I wouldn't miss it!"

Apparently, that was the general consensus with everyone because there are six of us sitting together. We had to take two cars to get to the game tonight.

Tucker was able to get us tickets right up next to the glass and it's been quite an experience, especially for the kids. Someone, and I'm pretty sure it was Ellie, showed them how to bang on the glass whenever the players skate by and that's been their favorite thing to do since the game began.

Until now.

Tucker slams into the glass right in front of Sutton and there's a scuffle for the puck. At least, that's what I assume is happening when he and whoever has him pressed up against the wall shove each other back and forth, Tucker's face hits the glass several times, leaving sweat marks. I might find it gross if I wasn't too busy watching my daughter's face as she takes in the violence of it all.

The smile she was sporting disappears, replaced by a grimace, followed by horror as she watches. The pink Mickey Mouse ears she hasn't taken off since our impromptu visit to Disney World on Christmas morning is holding her hair back, so not even rogue strands of hair are blocking her view.

"Daddy!" she screams and looks over to me for help, as if there's anything I can do.

I guess these seats were great in theory but they may be a little too close to the action. I'll remember that next time.

I assume the puck is finally passed off when the players all race to the other side of the rink, but Sutton's worry remains. Squatting down next to her, I pull her close and try to reassure her.

"Daddy's okay. They were fighting over the puck."

"They're not supposed to fight." She buries her little face in my neck and I pick her up so we can shift into her empty seat. "It's not nice to fight."

"It's nice to take turns," Kody says and I can't help but smile. Their three-year-old logic hasn't quite figured out that the rules don't apply when it comes to sports.

"They're not fighting," I try to reassure them. I'm not having much luck considering Sutton is still snuggling into me, avoiding watching the game. "See? Look." I point out to the ice just as they go slamming into another wall. "Okay maybe don't look. But they're playing a game. It gets a little rough out there. They're fine, though. Daddy didn't get hurt. He has lots of pads on."

Holly sits down in the vacant seat next to us and pulls Kody on her lap. "What's got my grandbabies so upset?"

She gives me a knowing smirk and I appreciate that she's come to help me calm them down a bit. Ellie, on the other hand, is deep in conversation with Muriel and merely waves at me when

I point to her child and all the drama. I'm glad she trusts me with her child, but I have a sneaking suspicion she just doesn't feel like touching this one.

Sutton pops up into the sitting position to give Grammy the lowdown.

"They're fighting with Daddy!" She sounds appalled. "They're being mean to my daddy and they're not taking turns." Kody nods in agreement, a stoic expression on his face.

"I can see why that's frightening," Holly says with a deep concern I know she doesn't actually feel. "They do a lot of fighting in hockey."

"They hurt my daddy." If Sutton was standing, she would have stomped her foot on the floor.

"Your daddy isn't hurt. See?" Holly points onto the ice. Sutton finally chances a glance at the game just as Tucker goes sliding into another wall.

Seriously? It's like he's timing this shit on purpose at this point.

"Oh!" Holly exclaims. "He hit another wall. But look how he just skates away."

Sutton's brows crinkle the slightest bit. "Daddy's not hurt?"

"No. Your daddy is very strong."

"Like a superhero!" Kody yells, making Holly laugh at the comparison.

"Exactly. He's like a hockey superhero. They run into walls and fall down. And look at that goalie at the end. See him with all his gear on?" The kids nod. "Look at how many times the puck hits him and it doesn't hurt. He just keeps fighting them off."

"He's an Avenger," Kody whispers, reverence suddenly in his voice.

I was skeptical when Tucker introduced the kids to the Marvel movies, only because they're his favorite and they're still so young, but clearly there was a benefit I wasn't expecting. Namely, smoothing the rough edges of hockey violence. Fingers crossed Tucker doesn't lose a tooth or the kids will never get over it.

Holly hugs Kody, who is too busy watching the game from a different perspective to notice her squeeze. His eyes are wide as saucers, and I can practically hear the gears turning as he tries to figure out what other superpowers the guys on the ice have.

"They are. They're hockey Avengers," Holly agrees.

"Wow," Kody breathes.

The buzzer sounds signaling the end of the second period. As the guys slowly leave the ice to do whatever it is they do during this down time, Tucker veers off into our direction.

Skating straight up the glass, he taps it with the top of his stick. "I'm okay," he mouths at the kids who jump off our laps and head straight toward him. "I'm okay," he says again while they jump up and down, Kody yelling, "You're an Avenger, Not-Daddy!"

Other fans crowd in, banging on the glass as well, so I crouch right behind the kids, making sure they don't get lost in the chaos.

"I love you, Daddy." Sutton presses her face to the glass and puckers up. Tucker smiles and presses his own lips to the barrier, giving her a kiss.

If it wasn't so damn sweet, I'd be grossed out by their mouths being on that glass. Seriously. How many germs just hang out there from people banging on it and players slamming into it? Yuck.

Tucker glances up at me and mouths, "They okay?" His voice sounds muffled over all the other noise, but I understand.

I nod and smile, saying, "They're fine now," knowing he has to read my lips to understand me.

He nods once and winks, mouthing, "Love you," before booking it to catch up to his team.

I bite back a smile, my heart swelling with the fact that he loves me. Me. Lacy. He doesn't love who he hopes I'll become. He doesn't love who he wants me to change to be. He loves me exactly as I am, even with my reactionary ways. It's a heady feeling and not one that I'm used to.

"Better put those googly eyes away. The television cameras are still on you," Ellie says behind me.

Sure. *Now* she decides to join us, once the crisis is over.

"I do not have googly eyes," I half-heartedly argue. "I'm just pleasantly surprised that the man plays a mean game of hockey but is also still very aware of what's going on with his children and checks on them as soon as he can. It's impressive, is all."

"I'll agree with you on that last point, but that's not why you're smiling."

"I'm not smiling!"

I'm totally smiling.

"You're in looooove." She nudges my shoulder with hers.

"Maybe." I stop fighting and let the emotion show on my face. "Okay fine. I'm in love with Tucker. I love him. Are you happy now?"

Ellie puts her arm around me and lays her head on my shoulder. "I am. You deserve to have found him. Not just for Sutton's sake, but for yours. You guys complement each other in so many ways. It's like it was meant to be."

"You just say that because he's rich and you're living in his fancy pool house," I joke, starting to feel a little uncomfortable with the depth of this conversation. Ellie won't let it go, though.

"No, I say it because it's true. You're my best friend and the person I trust most in the world for a reason. All I've ever wanted was for you to be happy." She pauses and purses her lips. "And it helps that I live in his fancy pool house."

"Do you guys want anything from concessions?" Muriel asks, thankfully interrupting our conversation. "I need a restroom break but I can get some stuff on the way back."

"I want cotton candy!" Of course Sutton pays attention long enough to hear the word "concessions".

"I want French fries," Kody jumps in.

"And chicken!" Sutton adds loudly.

"And hamburgers!" Kody adds because he won't be outdone.

Muriel's brows furrow and it's clear she wasn't anticipating a mini-riot over concession food.

Ellie holds up her hands to stop the kids from naming off more food they'll never eat. "Okay, okay. How about we go with Aunt Muriel to the potty and then we'll see how hungry we are on our way back?"

That seems to appease the kids. Temporarily anyway.

"I warned you they were a handful," I say to my sister who blows out a breath.

"I think I underestimated how energetic they are when they're together."

"Even though you've seen them at my house?"

"I thought it was a fluke or something. You know Mom and Dad never let us have any fun." She looks at Sutton. "I mean, obviously you had it anyway."

I snort a laugh. "And somehow that got me a hot, rich boyfriend. Go figure."

I tell them I don't want anything, knowing I'll end up eating Sutton's leftovers anyway, and the entourage heads toward the stairs. I take advantage of this moment without children to breathe in the cool air and just be.

Sitting next to me, Holly stretches out her legs and rubs one of her knees.

I furrow my brow in concern. "Are you okay?"

"What?" She glances down, noticing her actions that she must be doing absent-mindedly. "Oh that. It's just an old injury that aches a bit in the cold. Nothing to worry about. It happens to the best of us."

"I'm really glad you're here, Holly," I say honestly. "I was scared before you got here, but now that we've gotten to know each other and I see how much you love Tucker and the kids, I just really appreciate you claiming us as your own."

She clasps my hand in hers. "You are my own. No matter what. The best gift of my life was my boys, until my grandbabies came along."

I quirk my lips to the side in amusement. "Is that because they're still too young to mouth off to you?"

"That's definitely part of it, I'm sure. But you grew our family in a way I wasn't expecting and it's made me just so happy. In fact, I wanted to run something by you."

She turns in her seat to face me.

"I haven't mentioned it to Tucker yet, because I wanted to discuss it with you first." That has me sitting at attention. "What do you think of me moving down here. Not into your home, but maybe to Tampa so I could be closer to you guys and the kids?"

I find myself leaning in, intrigued by the idea. I love having Holly around. She's quickly becoming like the mother I've never had.

A small pang of longing hits me at the thought of missing my own mother, but I push it away. That's not my doing. It's hers. There's nothing I can do now, except wait and hope she comes to her senses.

But Holly...she's here. She wants to be part of our lives and I want that more than I realized until this moment.

"But what about your other kids? You don't want to be closer to them?"

She waves me off. "I'm sure someday they'll find themselves good women and start their own families, but they haven't yet. I don't want to miss out on any more with these two than I already have. Plus, I like the warmth of Florida. My knee doesn't ache nearly as much."

"What about your house?"

"I'll sell it." She says it so nonchalantly, like it's easy to let go of the home where she raised her kids. Then again, I never looked back after we moved out of the apartment, so maybe it *is* that easy. "I'd rather have something smaller like a condo or duplex anyway. A small garden home where someone else does the yard work would be lovely. I wonder if Tucker's realtor can help me find something."

"I know its technically a media room, but you're welcome to stay with us until you find exactly what you're looking for. Or I can bunk up with Sutton and you can use my room. That probably works better, actually"

"Thank you, honey. We'll figure something out." She pats my hand. "I'll have to go back to Minnesota to pack up and sell my house, but this just feels like home to me now."

"You know Tucker can be traded at any minute," I remind her. "We'd go with him, of course, but hockey is really fickle that way."

She doesn't look concerned at all. "And if that happens, I'll turn my house into an AirBnB and find something new wherever you guys go. We'll consider it an adventure."

A couple weeks ago, I never would have dreamed Sutton's new grandma would even like us, let alone want to uproot her entire life to be closer to us. But here we are—adding onto the family Ellie and I accidentally built—in ways I never imagined. It's a little scary, but mostly exciting. I can't wait to see how it all shakes out, and yet, I'm perfectly content to just enjoy the ride for a while. There's just one small problem.

"Holly."

"Hmm," she breathes as the start of the final period is announced.

"You realize Tucker is going to give you a whole lot of shit for moving here, since that means you have to stop harassing him about moving there."

She turns to me, an amused gleam in her eye. "I wouldn't have it any other way."

Her and me both.

CHAPTER THIRTY-TWO

TUCKER

We won our New Year's game, which means poker night is tonight.

I tried to be considerate and discussed it with Lacy and my mom first. Since the media room is currently our guest bedroom, and it's a little too chilly to host it on the back patio, that leaves the living room area.

Since it's a holiday, Lacy didn't mind having it at our place. In fact, we turned it into a New Year's Eve party of sorts, with the whole team invited, including their significant others.

I made sure to lay down ground rules in the locker room: keep the booze away from the kids, keep the women off their laps—Maks complained about that one, of course—keep things somewhat kid-friendly.

Almost everyone found those rules reasonable, so the party made its way here, where we currently have a full house, just the way I like it.

As the host of a bigger party than normal, I opted not to play poker tonight, letting our newest recruit, Tristan Phoenix, play for me instead. I've got too much going on and he needs some bonding time off the ice.

Kody is sitting on Nick's lap, telling everyone what cards he has, much to the delight of the other players. Sutton is dancing to whatever New Year's Eve program we have going on the television. And my mother is in the kitchen, cooking.

"Mom, you don't have to keep making snacks. These are grown men. They can do it themselves."

"Let me have my fun, dear." She places a hot baking sheet of what I think are taquitos on the stove and tosses the hot pad to the side. "It feels like all those years ago when I was trying to feed you and your brothers. It makes me happy."

I kiss the top of her head. "I don't think I ever thanked you for everything you did after dad left."

She bristles and I know it's still a sensitive topic for her. Old wounds heal, but that doesn't mean they ever go away completely. You just learn how to play them off quicker. "That's what a good mother does."

"It is. But I know now how much effort it was. I mean, there are three adults raising those two," I point at my kids, "And I can't keep up. I don't know how you did it alone with five boys."

She pats my cheek. "Once I learned how to run a frat house, I just used your egos against you."

"Wait... wait, what?"

She laughs. "Oh Tucker, do you really think you were the best window cleaner in the whole house? That you truly did what no one else could do?"

I narrow my eyes as I think back to how much she would praise me for a job well done, saying I was her perfect little window cleaner. It made doing the job not just worth it, but I looked forward to giving her that gift every week. Now the depth of her deception hits me.

"You played me!" She giggles. "You made me think I made those windows more sparkly than anyone else so you wouldn't have to do it yourself."

"Consider yourself lucky. Your brother still thinks he's the best toilet cleaner in the world."

I shake my head and walk away from the evil genius while she laughs. I can't believe I fell for that. Also, I better remember that for future use. Fingers crossed Sutton is as much of a sucker as I am.

I approach Lacy and Ellie and interrupt what seems to be an intense conversation, as Ellie gives the rundown on all my teammates.

"So Patrick is married and unavailable, Maks is..." He guzzles the last of his beer, crushes the can on his forehead and belches loudly, "... Maks is a no-go unless you like that neanderthal sort of thing. Nick seems nice. Look at how he is with Kody."

"You would chew Nick up and spit him out," Lacy says. "He's too nice. What about Anthony?"

Ellie cocks her head to the side. "Don't you think he's a little young?"

"Maybe. But that makes him trainable."

This conversation is getting a little bit *ew* for me. "Please tell me I'm not listening to you guys rank my teammates in order of date-ability."

"Of course not," Lacy scoffs. "We don't do ranks. Just a yes or no system is fine."

They giggle and I grimace. "I can't believe you would look at us like we're pieces of meat."

"Really," Lacy deadpans.

I can't keep up the ruse. "No I totally believe it. Also Becker's a cool guy and is magic with his stick. No idea if it's an indicator of his sexual prowess but since I'm also good with my stick and magic in bed, I can only assume."

"Ohmygod, you're so gross," Lacy laughs, shoving me. Of course I don't go anywhere because of that strength that helps with my prowess.

I sling my arm over her shoulder and pull her close. "I may be gross, but you love me."

She looks up at me and shrugs sheepishly. "Yeah, I kind of do."

Ellie shakes her head as I give my love a quick peck on the lips. "You guys are starting to cross the line from cute to gross."

"You said you loved seeing us together," Lacy argues.

"I said I loved *knowing* you were together," Ellie counters. "That was before I walked in on you practically banging up against the wall, and on the kitchen counter, and on the couch..."

She's not wrong. Ever since Christmas Eve, I've had a hard time keeping my hands off Lacy. And I'm not sure I care who sees.

"First of all..." Lacy's finger goes up and I know things are about to get salty. "That time with the wall... you were supposed to be at the children's museum because you wanted time with the kids, remember?"

"You vastly overestimate how long anything, museum or otherwise, will hold their attention."

Lacy ignores Ellie's weak argument. "Second of all, you've never caught us on the couch, or the kitchen counter so don't exaggerate."

Ellie bats her eyelashes at her best friend. "Just because you didn't know I saw you, doesn't mean it didn't happen."

Lacy's jaw drops. "Ellie!"

"What? You looked like you were having fun. At least one of us should be getting laid, so I just walked away." Ellie gestures to the poker table where her son is still running the show. "Which is what I'm about to do, so I can get my kiddo off poor Nick's lap."

"You're going to hit on him, aren't you?" I ask.

Without missing a beat, Ellie says, "Why would I hit on my own son?" and saunters toward the poker table while I laugh.

"That's it," Lacy says. "No more hanky panky in the common areas. Too many people live here."

I grunt with displeasure. "I will make out with you anywhere I want in my house. If they don't like it, they can move."

Making my point, I turn her to me and pull her to me, kissing her fiercely. Lacy giggles against my lips but doesn't pull away. "Oh is that right, huh?"

"Yup. My house, my rules."

"Don't you mean *our* house?"

"Still my rules."

Lacy shakes her head but we're quickly distracted by the television, when someone turns it up, yelling, "It's time!"

On cue, everyone starts counting down. Not well. No one can seem to agree on what number we're on until we get near the end.

"Three, two, one... Happy New Year!"

Our guests begin blowing party horns and popping miniature confetti poppers. But I have no interest in that kind of celebration.

Instead, I press my lips to Lacy's again and take full advantage of our first New Year's kiss. I'm not sure how long I kiss her for. Could be minutes. Could be hours. All I know is this is right where I'm supposed to be and nothing will keep me away from her again. Even the catcalls don't deter me.

Lacy is mine and I am hers and I've never been happier.

What a way to start a new year.

EPILOGUE

LACY

Six months later

"I'm home!" I shout, dropping my shoes on the floor by the front door. I know I'm trying to be professional, but heels have never been my thing. I remember why now.

"We're in here!"

I smile at the sound of Tucker's voice. It's been nice having him home consistently for a couple months while they're in the off season. I'm able to drop the kids at daycare in the morning, and he picks them up after he's done with practice or whatever endorsement meetings he has. That's assuming Ellie doesn't get to them first.

It's a little weird having three parents living with two kids, but we've fallen into an easy routine over the last several months and it works for us.

Bypassing the living room, I find my two boys sitting at the kitchen table. I kiss Kody on the top of the head, and then do the same to Tucker.

"What are you guys up to?"

"Working on this damn Lego kit," Tucker grumbles, not even

looking up to greet me. "Why is it so hard to put a Minecraft character together?"

I pick up the box that clearly notes "Ages 10+" and shake my head.

"For starters, this kit is about six years too old for Kody."

"Are you sure?" I hold the box out in front of him so he can see the printing. "Dammit. How does that always happen?"

"Because you don't look at the box, my love. And because you got a kit that is what, ninety-eight percent black Legos? What is this? And how do you expect and almost four-year-old to follow along?"

"It's Wither Storm, Lacy," Tucker says incredulously. "It's a no-brainer."

I glance at Kody's creation which looks more like a heap of nothing I can decipher than a Minecraft villain. "Clearly."

Tucker tosses the small bricks aside with a huff. Leaning back in his chair, he finally looks up at me, eyes softening. "Hi, baby." He purses his lips so I bend down and cup his cheek, giving him a better kiss. "How was class?"

"It was great actually." I head toward the fridge and pull out a juice box. For me, not Kody. "I can't believe I'm this close to being done already. I know I have a bit to go, but it seems like it's going fast."

"That's because you found something you love doing."

"I really did, huh?"

After quite a bit of debate, I finally decided to become a paralegal. I haven't regretted the decision once. Since I was only three semesters away from my bachelor's degree in legal studies when I had to drop out, I decided to finish up my degree and get my paralegal certification at the same time. It's three years faster than going to law school. Plus, it keeps me in the industry I'm interested in without having to work a horrendous number of hours like a beginning attorney would. It'll give me the chance to have the best of both worlds—a job I love, and a reasonable amount of time with my family. That's all I've ever wanted.

Plus, I can always go to law school once the kids are off on their own. No one ever said a career change in my forties is out of the question. Hell, Tucker will have to change careers around that time, too. Why can't I?

"I still have to finish up that project tonight for my economics class. You don't mind if my study group comes here, do you?"

"Of course not." Tucker pushes away from the table and grabs his own juice box. All the beer has been relegated to the patio fridge to make room for the juice we're suddenly all addicted to. Who knew apple juice was this good? "And once again, Lacy, you don't have to ask me."

"I appreciate that, but I'm trying to be considerate."

"I know. You always are." He leans in for a kiss, but what I see when he smiles has me pushing him away instead.

"What the hell happened to your face?"

Tucker puts on the full wattage of his smile, knowing he's grossing me out. "Got an accidental elbow to the face today at practice. Do I look rugged and manly?"

He rubs his scruff in my neck, grossing me out and making me gag.

"Ew! Get your toothless face away from me!" I squeal, trying to push Tucker off me, but he's having way too much fun with this. "Stop kissing me! Ew! Kody, where is your mother? I need backup!"

"At work." The little traitor doesn't even look up from the black blob he's making.

I feel Tucker chuckle against my neck and it makes me shiver with all the disgustingness. "It's only one little missing tooth, babe. I already put in a call to my dentist. They're getting me in tomorrow."

"Ugh. I hope so. You can sleep on the couch tonight so I don't have to look at it."

"You know I can fit my tongue right through that hole, don't you?" He nuzzles into me and I relax into his embrace. "Even better," he whispers in my ear. "That gap is the perfect place to fit your clit while I suck on it, making you come."

I know he's trying to be sexy, but it's not working.

"That might be the most Podunk hillbilly thing you've ever said to me."

"But did it turn you on?"

"Not even a little." I shove him off me and grimace as I inspect his toothless grin. "They'll fix it tomorrow?"

"Hopefully. I already had dental molds made just in case something like this happened. I told him which tooth it was so they should be making the fake one right now."

"A fake tooth." I shake my head. "This is what I get for falling in love with a hockey player. I'm gonna go get changed real quick. Where's Sutton?"

Tucker points outside and I lean around him to see out the window. She's in the pool with Muriel.

"Oh good! How are the swimming lessons coming?"

"That depends on what you mean by good."

I groan. "Oh geez. What's she doing?"

"Last I looked, she had Muriel convinced she needed piggyback rides across the pool instead of learning to doggy paddle."

"Sounds about right. I'll be right back." I lean over to kiss Tucker on the lips before thinking better of it and going for his cheek instead. He takes it in stride and swats me on the ass, mumbling something about doing it doggy-style tonight so I don't have to look at him.

I love that man. He makes me laugh every day and takes everything in stride. His *go with the flow* demeanor has done a lot to calm my own anxiety.

I head into our room and the giant master closet my clothes are now stored in. A couple of months after our declarations of love for each other, Tucker and I decided to take the plunge and officially move in together. It sounds strange to say it that way since we already lived in the same house, but it felt different living in the same bedroom. It made the solidity of our relationship seem more real. More permanent. And I haven't regretted it for one second.

Not only do I know this relationship is it for me, come hell or high water, I like having a real guest room for Holly to stay in. She won't use it for much longer. She's already found a condo on the beach she loves and will be moving in next month. That leaves an empty guest room I'm still hoping will someday be filled with my own mother.

I still haven't heard from her, but I know Muriel keeps her updated on how I'm doing. My sister says she can tell my mom is on the verge of standing up to my dad. I'm not sure I believe it, but I'm still holding out hope that one day we can have a relationship again. I miss her, but the rift isn't my doing. It's all about her and her insecurities. Until she can overcome them, all I can do is wait and be prepared to work through our shit when she finally gets here.

Clad in sweatpants and my favorite oversized Florida Glaze shirt, I pad back down to the kitchen to start making dinner. I round the corner just as a shivering Sutton is coming in the back door.

"Mommy!" she says and tries her hardest to race over to me, but the towel is too tight around her little body so it looks more like a penguin waddle.

I rub her little back as she leans into my legs, the closest thing she'll get to giving me a hug when she's wrapped up this tight.

"Hey baby girl. Did you have fun with Aunt Muriel?"

"I was swimming!"

"I think it was riding more than swimming," I say with a laugh.

"We'll get there," Muriel states, adjusting her own towel around her waist. "You wanna go practice Kody?"

He doesn't even look up from his Legos. "Nope. I don't like swimming."

I cock an eyebrow at Muriel. "I think he means he doesn't like swimming without the vest."

She smiles, completely unfazed. "We'll get there, too. It just means I get to spend more time with my niece and nephew."

"So swim lessons is just a scam to hang out with them?"

"Of course," she jests. "Why else do you think I want to come over to your place so much. For you? I love you sis, but you're not nearly that cute."

"So that means you're coming over for me?" Tucker flashes us a missing tooth grin and we both grimace.

"He's going to flaunt that as much as he can until he gets it fixed, isn't he?" Muriel asks.

"If you ignore him, maybe he'll stop."

He mouths, "*Doggy-style*" my direction and I roll my eyes. Muriel's used to his antics by now, so she doesn't even address it.

"Unlikely. But I need to help this little one get dressed anyway so I'm out. Come on, Sutton." Muriel holds out her hand so Sutton can waddle up next to her, her little teeth chattering from the cool air on her wet body as they head down to her room and the promise of dry clothing.

Confident that my sister has everything taken care of, I head back to the kitchen. "What are the plans for dinner? Or are we going to get take out?"

"I actually have steaks marinating in the fridge." Tucker pulls a sack of potatoes out of the pantry and begins peeling them.

"Steaks? You sure you can chew well enough for that Lloyd Christmas?" I grab the potatoes as he's done peeling them and wash them off, preparing to dice.

Tucker gasps. "Did you just refer to me as a character from Dumb and Dumber?"

"It's the gap. All you need is a weird haircut and you'd look just like him."

"I'm offended."

"No you're not. You love that movie."

"Okay, I'm not. But I don't plan to rip the meat apart like a caveman. I have a knife to cut it first, ya know."

"Mmhmm. I don't trust you not to make a show of it just so we all have to suffer through your weird smile."

"Normally I would, but today we're celebrating."

That's news to me. "Celebrating?"

"Yep. My—"

He's cut off by the front door opening and Ellie's shout of "We're home!"

We? Who is we?

I find out quickly enough when both Ellie and Holly come into the room.

"Holly!" I exclaim and quickly dry my hands.

Kody has the same idea when he yells "Grammy!" and takes off running. He beats me to her so I have to wait for my hug.

"What are you doing here?" I finally get to ask.

"The house in Minnesota finally sold so I thought I'd come down early. Start shopping for some furniture for the new house. Tucker didn't tell you?"

I look over at him, pleased with his surprise. He just shrugs and says, "Celebrating that she's here early."

"He didn't, but I like this way better. I don't think I would have been able to concentrate in class if I'd known you were on the way."

She pats my cheek in a motherly fashion. "You're so sweet. This is why I like you the best."

"Hey!" Tucker calls out, but he doesn't dispute it. He knows to give her a break. She raised five boys for goodness' sake. A pseudo-daughter is probably a relief.

"Grammy!" Another little voice calls out and I know I've lost Holly's attention for now. I don't mind. I love that the kids have such a loving and doting grandmother. They deserve it.

We all do.

I get back to my potato washing, listening the happy sounds around me. I've got my best friend, my sister, the woman who has stepped in as my mom, happy kids, and the best, if not orneriest boyfriend. I have everything I could ever want. The thought has me freezing in my tracks, fighting tears in my eyes.

Washing and drying his hands now that the peeling is done, Tucker comes up behind me, putting his arms around my waist. "You okay?"

The fact that he doesn't just notice my mood changes, but he cares about them makes me feel so incredibly loved. I lean back in his embrace, enjoying the warmth and safety of his arms.

"Yeah. Just thinking about how blessed I am. To have all this family here and even just having food on the table. Sometimes it feels a little overwhelming." Turning my head, I look up at him. "I have you to thank for all this."

"No. You have *you* to thank for this. No one in this room loves you because of me. They love you because of *you*. The wonderful, generous, strong woman you are. What you're seeing is the results of all your hard work. You've created a family and a home. You should be proud of that."

I look back at the scene in our kitchen and realize he's right. I created this family. It didn't happen the conventional way and it was certainly not easy, but here we are. In a house filled with laugher and love and complete acceptance, even of our flaws.

We're finally home.

SECOND EPILOGUE

PRESTYN

Dropping my keys in the bowl next to the front door, I sigh at my own bad luck.

I really thought I found a good one this time. I should have known better.

Online dating is its own special circle of hell. No one likes doing it, but in a world where electronics takes the place of the real world every day, there's not much choice if you don't want to be single forever.

Flopsie and Mopsie, my beloved chinchillas hop over tentatively to greet me. At least they love me more than anything.

Scooping them into my arms, I nuzzle into their fur. "Hi there. Did you have fun without me? I see you busted out of your cage again."

I wander through my small apartment, looking for any damage they may have caused while I was gone. The nice thing about having two of them is they can be left alone during my long work hours, and as long as they have food and water, they're happy. Sometimes they make a mess when they find a way to run free, but the lack of destruction reminds me that my night out was shorter than I had hoped it would be.

Sitting gently, so I don't disrupt my two little loves, I settle on the couch and stroke them. Their tiny squeaks of contentment fill the quiet air. Wish I could say I'm as happy as they are. But I'm not. I'm lonely. Sure, I've got friends and a demanding job, but that's not the kind of relationship I desire. I'm not even sure what kind of relationship I want, but it's something. Maybe I need a fuck buddy. Or a gay best friend.

I shake my head at myself. What I need is a full body massage and a new boss, but clearly I'm not getting that tonight either.

Sure there are a couple guys in my office, but they're older and married. And I meet people every day at the hotel, but they usually come with a significant other.

Online dating seemed like the best way to go, which was confirmed when I met Gary. Or so I thought.

It didn't matter that he was just an average white collar guy with average looks. He seemed nice. It's why I jumped on his invitation to have dinner tonight and bought a new dress for the occasion.

And then he didn't show.

I waited for over an hour, the server getting more and more impatient the longer I nursed my martini, until I finally gave up. I'm sure the twenty dollar tip I left on the table doesn't make up for what he would have made off two meals and drinks, but it's the largest bill I had.

Still, it seems so out of character for Gary not to have at least told me something had come up. Maybe I should message him.

Yeah. Just to make sure he's okay. If he ghosted me, I'll know pretty quick, but I'd feel terrible if he was in an accident on the way to dinner and I didn't at least check on him.

I fish my phone out of the large handbag I had dropped next to the couch, Flopsie and Mopsie hopping down and taking off toward the bedroom where I have some of their toys scattered about. Searching and finding Gary's contact information, I send a quick message.

Sorry to have missed you at dinner. Hope everything is okay. Let me know if you'd like to reschedule for a later date.

There. Done. Not too desperate, gives him an out, and shows I care all at the same time. Covering all my bases.

Not wanting to sit around waiting for a reply, I head to my small bathroom to get ready for bed. It's still early enough I can catch up on the new fantasy novel I downloaded yesterday. I'm not a huge reader, but I've made it my New Year's Resolution to change that. Gotta stop rotting my brain with reality TV and all that mess. I've never read a time traveling book before, but the addition of vampires and werewolves makes it seem like it could be an exciting adventure, so I'm willing to give it a try.

Soon enough, I'm settled in my bed, my girls back in their cage, happily snuggling up to each other.

Our heroine has just begun tracing the portal with her finger when my phone rings, making me jump.

Picking it up, I see it's Gary calling. My heart beats even faster than it already was. He's never called before. We've only recently upgraded to texting after chatting through the website for several weeks. This is exciting. And a little nerve wracking.

I stare at his name on my phone for a little too long before shaking myself out of my stupor and swiping to answer.

"Hello?"

"Hi, is this Prestyn?"

It's a woman's voice. That's not what I was expecting. Maybe it's someone from the hospital? Or his sister?

"This is she."

The woman on the other end sighs deeply. "I was afraid of that."

"I'm... what?"

"I was hoping you were some old man who liked to catfish people for kicks."

Now I'm really confused.

"I'm sorry... who is this?"

"My name is Delaney. I'm Gary's wife."

Things are about to get heated. *Open Fire* is coming Summer 2022! Get it now, right here!

ABOUT THE AUTHOR

My name is ME Carter and I have no idea how I ended writing books. I'm more of a story teller (the more exaggerated the better) and I happen to know people who helped me get those stories on paper.

I love reading (read over 100 books last year), hate working out (but I do it anyway because my trainer makes me), love food (but hate what it does to my butt) and love traveling to non-touristy places most people never see.

I live in Texas with my four kids, Mary, Elizabeth, Carter and Bug, who was just a twinkle in my eye when I came up with my pen name. Yeah, I'll probably have to pay for his therapy someday for being left out.

To keep up with all the happenings, sign up for my newsletter!
www.authormecarter.com/newsletter
Instagram: @authormecarter
Facebook: Mary Elizabeth Carter (M.E. Carter)

www.ingramcontent.com/pod-product-compliance
Lightning Source LLC
Chambersburg PA
CBHW071239190726
48292CB00007B/2359